D1566485

e-male
a novel

palari
Publishing

Library of Congress Cataloging-in-Publication Data

Pomfret, Scott.
  E-male : a novel / by Scott Pomfret and Scott Whittier
      p. cm.
  ISBN 978-1-928662-16-7 (trade pbk.)
  1. Gay men--Fiction. I. Whittier, Scott. II. Title.
  PS3616.O58E19 2009
  813'.6--dc22

                                        2008054863

Palari Books is a division of:
Palari Publishing LLP
PO Box 9288
Richmond, VA 23227
www.palaribooks.com

CHAPTER 1

punkid: Hi there. E-male seems to think we're compatible.
burbboy: What do you think?
punkid: It's kinda weird having a computer match us up.
burbboy: Agreed. But u r hot. ;-)
punkid: In agreement again. ur hot 2.
burbboy: Maybe we should see if e-male is right. In real life.
punkid: Agreed. Again.

The glowing type of the computer screen still hung before Kory's eyes the morning after he had shut down his computer. It was as if the online dating site's chat rooms and member profiles had permanently burned his corneas during those late-night viewings. Or maybe it was the four hours of sleep he'd gotten before showing up at the Whine 'n' Dine to work.

The diner was abuzz with customers and conversation. But

Kory Miles couldn't take part in the chatter. It wasn't his exhaustion. It was the secret he had to hide from his coworkers and clientele. Actually, it was two secrets.

"I met the greatest guy on that E-male site last night," Jeff said as he topped off cups of coffee and glasses of Merlot for men at the counter. He flipped his new blue bangs dramatically out of his eyes and away from his pierced eyebrow for dramatic emphasis.

"Really?" one of the customers cooed, taking a sip. "I'm totally addicted to that site."

"I don't know what we'd do without it," another added. "I mean, where are you supposed to meet men... here?"

They looked around and laughed and clinked glasses together to congratulate their wit. They spun on the Whine 'n' Dine's red vinyl barstools and fed quarters into the jukebox under the mounted deer's head they had named Bam Bam.

The Whine 'n' Dine was the hot-but-not-stuck-up spot in the neighborhood. Kory, Jeff and the other waiters served meat loaf and tuna tartare, shirred eggs Benedict and corn-beef hash, chili-cheese fries and champagne. Their customers were hairdressers and actors, businessmen and bike messengers. The Whine 'n' Dine was a slice of the city's gay culture as thick and rich as the diner's chocolate cherry devil's-food cheesecake.

Kory loved the friendly melting pot of customers and the bitchy banter in the kitchen. He loved the kitschy decor and the way customers ordered vintage port with their banana splits. The only thing he didn't love was when talk turned to the one subject he couldn't speak openly about: E-male.

"Hey, Kory," Jeff hollered across the restaurant, "when are you going to get on E-male and get some action?"

"How do you know I'm not getting plenty?" Kory asked. "Just look at these dark circles around my eyes. Maybe I've been up all night."

"Sure," Jeff said. "The only one who sees less action than you around here is Bam Bam."

He jerked a thumb toward the stuffed deer's head, and all the customers laughed. At the mention of his name, they lifted their glasses and toasted Bam Bam with their traditional, "Sorry about your mother, Bambi."

The regulars at the counter were used to Kory and Jeff's banter. They were waiting for Kory to make a clever retort about Jeff's eyebrow piercing or his freshly dyed electric-blue forelock. But Kory was in no mood to ridicule Jeff's attempts at punkdom today. He knew if he left them alone, the others would soon abandon their teasing to continue prattling on about Jeff's new E-male connection.

And Kory certainly wasn't interested in discussing that. Instead, he focused his attention on clearing greasy dishes from an empty booth. Ignoring the gossipy scene, he wiped his hands on his jeans and brushed the hair from his eyes. The sandy bangs fell across his forehead like limp straw. They dangled, unstyleable, in his field of vision. No matter how many hair-dressers he knew, Kory would forever have a boyish bowl cut. No matter what the season, his eyes always glowed like autumn sunlight. And no matter how close he got to 32, he was still the baby-faced lanky guy who got carded every time.

But Kory wasn't the innocent boy he appeared to be. These men in the Whine 'n' Dine didn't know as much as they thought they did about their favorite friendly waiter. And Kory didn't want them to find out. So he pretended not to listen to them gush about romantic possibility and compatibility and online dating. It wasn't that those things didn't hold interest for him. He just couldn't risk giving anything away. Besides, he didn't need to hear about E-male's ingenious matching system again. He'd invented it.

The E-male web site had started as a hobby. It was little more than an experiment to determine whether Kory's computer skills had survived the dot-com bomb any better than his useless technology degree. Nearly a decade after graduating from tech college, he was an expert only in the science of waiting tables and observing gay social life. He was curious how his programming abilities had held up in light of all the new tools, tricks and templates available online.

He was proving to himself that a site could be built without all the annoying features of online straight personals or sleazy gay chat rooms. He heard about the deficiencies of those other sites every day at the Whine 'n' Dine. Straight personals were like trying to get laid in high school. Gay chat rooms were like trying not to get laid in a bathhouse.

Straight dating sites may let you select a man-for-man preference, but then they threw you into a sea of desperate hetero singles. It was theoretically possible to find a date in there somewhere, but it was also theoretically possible to find your future husband in sophomore biology.

The gay sites were almost worse. They could hardly be classified as "dating" sites at all. They were more like interactive pornography—so interactive that the naked pic you were looking at could show up at your door in ten minutes. That service could be useful in a pinch, but when you asked a guy what his hobbies were, he'd likely send a list of sexual positions and fetish acronyms. Not exactly the "walks on the beach" you may be looking for.

There had to be something in between. But there wasn't. Kory had looked. And as most every customer in the Whine 'n' Dine endlessly complained, there was no online option that provided a sense of community or a way of weeding through the wackos.

What they all really needed was an online equivalent to the Whine 'n' Dine. Gay men needed a fun, social place to meet on the web and chat. But instead of food, the online menu would serve up hobbies, habits and potential husbands. And instead of attitude, gossip and bitchery, the anonymous interaction would offer men a nonthreatening way to express interest without having to announce it awkwardly in the middle of a bustling diner. All they needed was a friendly waiter to serve it up, help navigate the menu and place the perfect order.

E-male was that place. The concept was simple. It was one big, ongoing social event like a party in a giant mansion. Guests could enter different rooms based on interests or location (which did not include orgies or dungeons). Kory simply didn't give them the opportunity to detail those preferences up-front. It wasn't that kind of a party.

E-male was designed as a personality-driven site. People met others with similar interests and attitudes. They introduced themselves, sent messages, and chatted in groups or in pairs. When two men clicked, they could exchange pictures and personal details, or they could wait to do it in person. In fact it was even better than a party because it was completely anonymous, up until whatever point a man decided to reveal himself. And Kory was the anonymous host.

When he'd first started, Kory hadn't even known whether anyone would look at his web page. He couldn't have predicted that word of his simple solution would spread so quickly across those other sites—the ones that left everyone single and searching. And he certainly didn't know that E-male would take off like a rocket and suck up all his free time so that he was the only gay man in town without a free night for a date.

But Kory loved his new role. It was certainly much more satisfying than serving someone a perfect slice of cheesecake. He was helping connect men from all over. It reminded him that there were millions of gay men out there beyond his tiny world. He was bringing them together from miles and states away. He was making true love a reality for gay men in a way that never would have been geographically possible without E-male. The power was slightly dizzying, but it gave Kory a tickle of excitement in his chest that felt a little like falling in love.

That was the good part, the part that kept Kory playing this secret double life. However, it resulted directly in the part that drove him absolutely crazy—the part that made his secrecy a necessity. Quite simply, he knew everything about everyone. As host to this endless party, he had keys to every room. He knew every guest. He could see the pictures and profiles and romantic pairings—all the little secrets that E-male customers kept hidden from the "public" areas of the site.

It was like being psychic. Kory forgot who he knew and who

he "knew" through E-male. Out at bars he would call someone by name before he'd even been introduced. He knew practically every gay man in the greater metropolitan area and had to pretend he didn't. He knew about new boyfriends before best friends were told. He knew everyone's turn-ons and playing positions way before those first awkward moments in the dark. And more than anything else, Kory knew that this would all come crashing down if he was ever "outed."

If everyone at the Whine 'n' Dine discovered that it was Kory who was behind E-male, they would never trust him or use the site again. They'd think he was some kind of cyber stalker or high-tech peeping Tom. If the greater gay world beyond found out that E-male was run merely by some scrawny waiter at a gay diner instead of an enormous but trustworthy corporate entity, people would pull their personal information from the site faster than the click of a mouse. Kory would be friendless, unemployed, poor, and of course he'd still be single.

So as E-male connected everyone else, it was isolating Kory. Things were getting too close for comfort, and he was getting farther away from everyone else. Kory himself never had a date. He was constantly afraid of saying the wrong thing to the wrong person. And he simply had way too much information about everyone on E-male. Everywhere he turned his biggest secret and biggest success was staring him straight in the face.

People would come into the Whine 'n' Dine and say, "Guess what?" And Kory could have told them. He had already witnessed the new boyfriend or most recent dating exploit on E-male. Kory had no desire to rehash the details. And he couldn't let any of them slip.

Every customer, all his friends and day-to-day associates, almost every man Kory met—they didn't know the truth about the real Kory. But he knew way too much about them. Secrecy and information-overload were torture enough. But it was downright creepy when he discovered he was orchestrating his good friend's love life.

Kory saw Jeff approaching him from across the diner. The dinner crowd had settled into a low-key weeknight drinking crowd. Jeff's blue bangs bobbed as he walked, and he gave them a playful toss. He was obviously proud of his new punk attempt.

Kory knew that a bottle of blue hair dye didn't make his buddy a punk. The eyebrow ring and clunky boots didn't get Jeff much closer to the genuine article either. But Kory also knew that the guy on E-male last night seemed convinced and very interested. Because Kory knew that punkid was Jeff's online identity. And Kory already knew about the date he had arranged with burbboy.

"So, you're quiet tonight," Jeff said.

The lights were lowered. The jukebox alternately played jazz and pop remixes. The two waiters perched themselves on the barstools closest to the kitchen where they could survey the room and keep an eye on their lingering customers.

"I guess I'm just tired," Kory answered.

"Please," Jeff shot back and shook his electrified forelock at Kory. "I was the one up half the night typing away on that damn E-male."

Jeff had found the segue he needed to keep talking about his favorite subject of the night. Not again, Kory thought.

"But I tell you," Jeff continued, plowing straight into the conversation he'd wanted to have all along, "I met the absolutely most amazing man."

"Really?" Kory tried to sound casual. The truth was he'd been plenty interested as he sat up all night watching Jeff flirt and flatter the guy online. Since Kory already knew about Jeff's new cyber-beau, he was not looking forward to pretending he didn't. But he realized that not having the conversation would seem even more suspicious. Being cold and aloof was not like Kory at all. Of course he was thrilled for his friend. Of course he wanted Jeff to find love and happiness and all that good shit. He just didn't want to lie and pretend to make it happen. Unfortunately that was exactly what he was going to have to do. "What's so amazing about him?"

"You wouldn't believe a man like that even exists around

here," Jeff said. "I mean we have the same taste in music and food and movies. You should have seen his pics. He is gorgeous. And he loves punks."

"Then maybe he should go find one." Kory laughed.

"What are you talking about?" Jeff protested. "This is totally punk." He pointed alternately between his blue hair, eyebrow ring and general ensemble, as if to put the whole punk package on display.

"Alterna at best," Kory insisted. "It's not exactly counterculture."

"Well, the retro-seventies-waif thing is a little overdone, don't you think?" Jeff asked accusingly. "I mean you could at least put some highlights in that dirty-blonde mop."

"Ouch!" Kory said. "I guess I just don't have as much time for hair care as you do."

"Well, fortunately for you, the skinny and cute thing still works." Jeff said, sneering dramatically. Then he ruffled his own hair. "Some of us just prefer a little more flair."

"Even if your hair flair is a bit more skunk than punk."

"Bitch! I think we'll let Mr. E-male be the judge of that one."

"Ugh! Back to that again?"

"You're the one who keeps trying to get me off track," Jeff pointed out. "Don't think I didn't notice."

"OK, OK, tell me all about it. Please, I'm dying to hear." Kory yawned for emphasis.

"Fine. I will."

Kory smirked. He did love seeing Jeff all riled up and excited. He couldn't remember the last time his friend had a date with any potential. And Kory loved to see his creation work its magic. Witnessing it right here in the flesh with someone he actually cared about was even more exciting than watching it unfold on screen. Keeping the entire thing a secret was the only bittersweet part.

"He's sporty and rugged," Jeff said. "And kind of outdoorsy."

"Does he bathe?"

"If he doesn't, I will personally give him a bath. 'Sporty, rugged and outdoorsy' are all polite ways of saying he's got a rockin' bod."

"And this triathlete needs a punk for what reason?" Kory asked. "To go camping with?"

"I'm already pitching a tent for him," Jeff said lewdly and winked.

"Dis-gusting!"

"Seriously, I have no problem with camping," Jeff said, "in a nice little bed-and-breakfast somewhere, perhaps."

"Exactly my point."

"I'm kidding," Jeff insisted. "I'll try anything once. Twice if he begs for it... on his knees."

"OK, enough!" Kory covered his ears. "God, I hope you do get laid. I am tired of hearing about it. I hope Mr. Sporty-and-Rugged loves punks as much as you say."

"I'm just repeating what he said," Jeff reminded him. "Besides, I'm sure he likes a little contrast. Stylish with studly. Hip with totally hot. We would make such an adorable couple!"

Jeff was practically bouncing up and down on his barstool. His blue bangs fluttered, and Kory had to admit they were cute if you were into that kind of thing. This burbboy from E-male certainly seemed to be into it. And Kory silently agreed with Jeff. Last night he had the exact same thought—burbboy and punkid would be an adorable couple.

"Seriously, Kory," Jeff said, "you just do not find men like that around here."

"Well, maybe you should go to the suburbs more often."

"I'm planning on it. We have a date Friday."

"Do they even have coffee shops out there?" Kory asked.

Kory grinned. He knew this guy was a great match for Jeff, and he smiled at the thought of a blue-haired club kid mowing the lawn behind a white picket fence. He looked around at the tinkling glasses and motley characters in the restaurant and wondered if they'd all be better off if they escaped their little world in the corner of the city. That is what E-male was doing. It was letting them escape without ever leaving. It was connecting people like Jeff and burbboy who would never have met otherwise.

"What did you just say?" Jeff asked suspiciously.

"Huh?" Kory snapped back to the conversation. He hadn't noticed the moments of silence that had just inserted themselves in Jeff's rant. He hadn't noticed the way Jeff's eyes had narrowed to study Kory's face as he daydreamed.

"You asked if there was a coffee shop," Jeff reminded him, "in the suburbs."

"Yeah. So is there?"

"I never said we were going for coffee," Jeff pointed out. "And I certainly didn't say anything about the 'burbs."

"So?" Kory tried to sound clueless.

"So, that's exactly what we planned," Jeff said. "How did you know that?"

☆ ☆ ☆ ☆

The burden of Kory's knowledge was compounded by his second secret. Because Kory wasn't just the inventor of E-male. He was E-male.

His site's popularity wasn't simply due to its ingenious design and functionality. It had very little to do with the cool blue and green color scheme or the cute little icons that represented likes and dislikes. E-male had a matchmaking function that was impeccable. When it found a potential Mr. and Mr. Right, they both got "E-maled" and introduced. The successful track record was quite impressive.

Other, bigger dating sites had matching programs. They were probably so advanced and complicated that Kory couldn't have even understood the programming behind them. Their statistics and algorithms served up lists of potential dates with precise percentages of how well-matched they were. However, they weren't nearly as accurate as the E-male matchmaker. Because E-male didn't rely on some convoluted set of formulas and computer coding. It was Kory's own intuition.

E-male may have been anonymous and confidential between members. But as the secret creator, Kory had full access to everyone else's secrets. He wasn't just monitoring the content, reviewing pictures and profiles for forbidden material. He was using that information to match men up. When he found compatible profiles—whether the men had seen each other's info or not, whether they had expressed slight interest or none at all—he made the match.

He knew all these men because he read every little detail about them. He watched their private chat sessions. He saw who they checked out and who checked them out in return. He couldn't help it. The information was right there at his fingertips and he was simply putting it to good use, or so he hoped.

He desperately wanted E-male to succeed. And he truly wanted to help all those men out there find the perfect match. As their gracious cyber-host at this online party, Kory felt that he was simply passing through rooms full of people, listening in on different conversation, and introducing men to one another along the way. They just didn't know he was there.

It was probably illegal in addition to being immoral. But he reasoned that using his omniscience for matchmaking good made up for his voyeuristic evil.

He was just too good at it to stop. If others thought they were addicted to E-male, they had no idea. Kory was absolutely strung out on it. He couldn't pull himself away from matching his members. He knew the ins and outs. He watched those men and he understood them. He knew what they wanted, what matched them, what suited their likes and dislikes.

It was like filling an order before a customer even saw the menu. Kory understood the current tastes, the scrumptious bits, the satisfying courses that satisfied the deepest hungers. However, he himself had never been fulfilled.

Kory had the curse of cupid. He was such a natural matchmaker that he was blind to his own desires. All the time he spent bent over his glowing computer screen secretly manning E-male, he never once matched himself with anyone else. It didn't even cross his mind.

Self-fulfillment wasn't why he invented E-male. It was for the challenge of solving a technological problem. It was for all those others he listened to complaining every day at the Whine 'n' Dine. If he discovered a great guy on E-male, he already had another great guy in mind for him. Kory never thought of himself. In fact, he didn't even have a profile on E-male.

Kory's true love was E-male. As soon as he'd cleared the technological hurdle of designing the site, he found that matching—not mating—was what truly captivated him. Besides, the most effective way of meeting a man was not available to him. It was him. And somehow his matchmaking talents didn't turn themselves inward.

It wasn't that he was a celibate eunuch toiling away for all gay mankind. Of course he'd dated. Of course he'd had sex. He had plenty of experience under his very fashionable belt.

But somehow he felt uncomfortable in his own skin, let alone in his very stylish outer layer. One on one, he treated men like bad tippers. I see it in your eyes, he thought. You're going to walk out of here and leave me with nothing.

And so he found his romance in secret. In the dark. On a computer screen. Blinking in the night. In other people's love lives. Those, at least, he could control. Like he was writing the menu himself.

And when he wasn't parked in front of his computer, Kory's dark-blonde bangs fell in front of his eyes like the perfect shield. Sexy and coy and detached from the rest of the world—his very own screen between the extroverted gay world he lived in every day and the reluctance he felt in his own heart.

Outwardly, he had two full-time jobs. And on the inside he was working overtime to keep E-male a secret. But the problem was that he was much better at keeping other men's secrets than his own.

This slip with Jeff was just one more example. Kory was too tired, too fried, too stressed to even keep his mouth shut. It was like when someone says, "Do not think of a pink elephant." What else can you possibly think of? E-male was all Kory's obsession. And it was only exacerbated by everyone else's obsession with the site. When it kept coming up in every conversation, it was difficult to keep the truth from bubbling to the surface.

The guilt and anxiety kept Kory on his toes. Was he doing the right thing? Would someone find out? No matter how much he loved E-male, he knew that the ulcer it was causing and the situation it was creating would be the end of him.

E-male's sudden success had him between a rock and a hard place. If he stopped matching men, E-male would no longer be successful and neither would the resulting relationships. If he kept doing what he was doing, he would also keep digging himself deeper and driving himself crazier.

Kory had no doubt he would be punished for all his secrets sooner or later. He only wanted to help people. But when he found himself staring into his friend's suspicious glare, he realized that no one, not even those close to him, would believe that. It would be one more lie on top of the many other lies he had told them all along.

"Does Mr. Suburban know you're a paranoid freak?" Kory asked Jeff.

Jeff was no Sherlock Holmes. Hell, he couldn't even manage a good Angela Landsbury circa Murder, She Wrote. But he squinted and examined Kory like the prime suspect. If only he knew how close he was to revealing both of Kory's secrets. If only he could see the sudden flush of panic that was creeping up Kory's neck in the dim light.

"What are you talking about?" Jeff asked.

"Seriously, if we don't know him, he must be from the 'burbs," Kory said. "You kept saying there were no men like that around here. So he mustn't be. And what else do gay men do on the first date but have coffee? Well, that they'll admit to."

"Are you saying that you think I'm going beyond first base on the first date?"

"Is coffee the new first base?" Kory asked. "I'm sure you will go way beyond that. I'm predicting a grand slam."

"Bitch!"

"Whore!"

Jeff's eyes widened a bit. He flipped his blue locks back dramatically. But Kory was glad that they seemed to have passed the crucial moment of revelation and ventured back into the familiar territory of bitchery.

"Oh my God, did I mention he has a dog?" Jeff practically squealed. "I absolutely love dogs."

Jeff prattled on and on, but Kory couldn't focus on a single word. Not that he needed to. Kory already knew every detail of the impending relationship. He'd read each word of it right along with Jeff last night. He was the one who had matched Jeff up with burbboy in the first place. It was almost as if he could predict exactly how it would all turn out—what movie they saw, what sex they had, what pattern of China would be on their civil-union registry. But Kory only thought about now how close he had come to being discovered.

Sitting there in the Whine 'n' Dine with Jeff was when the danger of E-male really hit home. E-male's members were all around him. He was surrounded by secrets—his and everyone else's. He couldn't keep this charade up for much longer. People were suspicious. And they would find out. Then Kory would be run out of town on a rail. All these men would lose their best portal for meeting husband material. But Kory would lose everything.

☆　☆　☆　☆

Kory's paranoia was at an all-time high when he returned home after his shift. He kept running his fingers nervously through his blonde bangs, raking them away from his eyes furiously. So when he powered up his computer, he almost didn't believe what he saw. He held his hair from his face and squinted at the screen as if it were a mad man's hallucination.

It was ironic that as creator of E-male Kory rarely ever received any true e-mail. The administrator's inbox was his only legitimate connection to his site's members. It was a small link at the bottom of the page that made people think they were sending a message to a tech help desk located continents away. And he only occasionally had inquiries about how the site worked, advertising opportunities, or praise for finally creating an online oasis for gay men. He never expected what was waiting for him that night.

Business Offer for E-male, inc.

Leading gay travel agency proposes a partnership with E-male. We hereby offer a temporary consultancy position to provide dating services to match both our in-house employees and traveling customers with potential dates. Possible long-term merger based on initial results of trial period.

Kory wondered if he had finally met his financial match. Could this possibly be real? Could he actually make money from this experiment? And most importantly, could he really merge or sell his fledgling company and leave all these secrets behind him?

CHAPTER 2

> *b4sunset*: I love to travel.
> *DOMinick*: i've been known to get around too
> *b4sunset*: It's cheesy, but long walks on the beach
> really are my favorite.
> *DOMinick*: as long as i'm leading u on a collar.
> *b4sunset*: Yes, sir! perfect!

From the outside, Djorvzac Travel didn't look like much. It was in one of those nondescript gray buildings that squatted in the middle of an immense parking lot in the middle of nowhere. It was located just over two hours from the hubbub of city life

Cheap property and isolation tend to make for ugly business parks instead of national parks. The soulless concrete building was surrounded by dumpy straight salesmen in cheap suits driving boxy sedans. It was three solid stories of bad design and narrow windows with parking lots in all direction. Here and there was a sunburned marigold planted between fire hydrants and parking spaces.

Despite its unimpressive appearance and location, and despite its unpronounceable name, Djorvzac Travel was one of the top agencies for the gay and fabulous vacationer. People didn't know or care where the phones rang when they dialed the travel hotline. They were thinking of palm trees or powdery slopes, circuit parties or cruisey cruise ship. They weren't thinking of ugly buildings in far-suburban hell. And they certainly weren't thinking about the kind of man who would isolate himself and his company there.

"What's wrong now?" Zac Djorvzac looked up from his desk at the two employees standing on the verge of his windowless office. It was Monday afternoon, and the last thing Zac needed during the busy start to the work week was yet another employee conflict.

"Mike stole clients right out from under my nose!" Danny screeched.

"That's a total lie," Mike snapped back. "Danny sabotaged my booking by giving the reservations to college kids who can't even afford it."

"How many times have I told you, 'No drama'?" Zac tapped a pencil angrily against his notepad. He was in the middle of putting together new packages for next year's spring break, the phones were ringing off the hook for the upcoming holidays, and two of his best employees were having a cat fight instead of closing sales.

Zac hated employing gay men. He didn't actually admit this to anyone else, but it was obvious enough that he didn't have to. Despite the fact that he was gay, despite the fact that his entire company thrived on the gay community, Zac could not stand the fighting, the bitching, the gossip, the attitude—all this drama!

"I know," Danny said to his boss, "'No Dancing. No Dating. No Drama.'"

He recited the Djorvzac pledge perfectly, but it didn't keep him from standing there and breaking the rules. The two wiry men could have been brothers or boyfriends the way they looked and they way they fought. Typical gay men, Zac thought. Blonde highlights and black-framed glassed. Skinny guys with enough attitude to bump them up into another weight class.

No matter how much he would have liked to, Zac knew that he couldn't avoid hiring gay men. They made better sales to other gay men. Only gay men could plan the trips and activities and give all the local tips and secret locations that made customers call Djorvzac Travel first. But Zac couldn't stand all the associated baggage that came with a gay company. So to minimize the complications, he had instituted the "No Dancing. No Dating. No Drama." rule at Djorvzac Travel.

No Dancing. That meant they were a business, not a nightclub. They were businessmen, not buddies, not "girlfriends." There was no cocktail hour on Friday afternoons. There were no get-togethers after work. No birthday parties or social events of any kind.

No Dating. That was the most important rule. An entire floor of gay men sitting feet apart in open cubicles could not endure the temptation and disastrous repercussions of inter-of-fice relationships and inevitable break-ups. The dating rule also extended outside the office. If you had a boyfriend, Zac didn't want to hear about it. And he didn't want him coming by the office to pick you up. And he surely didn't want him coming in for an interview.

No Drama. This was what it all boiled down to. Do your job and leave the attitude at the door. No gossip. No fighting. No gay bullshit. And of all his rules, this was the one Zac could not enforce completely no matter how much of a hard-ass he was. He could overwork gay men till they had no social lives and no relation-ships, but he couldn't take the drama out of the drama queens.

Zac closed his green eyes for a moment to regain his composure. He ran his fingers through his jet-black hair and settled his hands deliberately in front on him. He made a conscious effort to unclench his square jaw so his words could be heard clearly from across the room.

"Stop your hysterics and tell me what happened." His deep voice boomed in the tiny office. "Just the facts."

"This nice—and rich may I add—middle-aged couple had been planning a ski trip with me for weeks," Danny said. "We'd figured out every detail. And when they were ready to book it, Mike took the call and the commission, without forwarding them to me."

"And what did you do?!" Mike burst out. "There were no reservations on hold, nothing for Danny to lay claim to. They'd just been talking to him. But as soon as he heard me making their flight reservations, he called up the resort in Colorado that they had their hearts set on and he blocked the last room."

"I had another client," Danny retorted. "It was the first place that came to mind."

Zac's broad shoulders tensed as he listened to the two men argue. The sound of screeching gay voices was like nails on a chalkboard. It was all Zac could do to keep from reaching out and knocking their heads together.

"So what you're telling me," Zac growled at Danny and Mike, "is that you've blocked a definite sale with a bunch of kids who will cancel before paying. You've lost two sales with your bickering. Because of your drama."

"It wasn't my fault!"

"He did it!"

The two shrieked at one another simultaneously. It was obvious they knew they'd broken the rules. But they couldn't resolve the situation without involving the boss. Zac was going to find out about it sooner or later. He always did.

In all the confusion, Zac didn't even notice the stranger at the door, lingering behind his employees. Danny and Mike paused when they saw the unexpected guest. There was no receptionist to welcome him. There was no need for one. This was a call center, not a walk-in agency. This was strictly business. And a warm "reception" was not what Zac was about.

"Excuse me, are you Zac Dee-vor-zak?" Kory mispronounced the name just like everyone else.

Kory was probably the first visitor Djorvzac Travel ever had. But that wasn't what stopped the argument dead in its tracks. Kory was also the first cute young man who had ever come around looking for Zac Djorvzac. As far as any of his employees knew, Zac was as celibate and single as he was ruthless and angry.

They all knew exactly how he felt about frivolous gay culture and its ridiculous dating scene. That's why he started this company. That's why he was so successful. If gay men wanted to squander away all their money to party and chase every piece of ass around the world, he was more than happy to take advantage of them. But he wasn't part of it. He didn't travel. He didn't party. He didn't date. It was "No Dancing. No Dating. No Drama" in his own life, too.

"And who are you?" Zac asked. He didn't have time for more complications.

"I'm Kory Miles," he said as he stepped into the room. "I'm here for the partnership we agreed to."

For once, Mike and Danny were absolutely speechless. What was this cute little city boy doing here in his low-slung hipster jeans and his tight wool sweater? What brought someone like that into the wilds of suburbia? And what kind of "partnership" did he have in mind with Zac Djorvzac?

"Partnership?" Zac asked with such disgust that it could have been a dirty word.

"Yes, I'm from the dating web site."

It was a drastic decision. Kory knew that. But he really didn't have any other choice.

This wasn't exactly the solution he had imagined for E-male. The real problem was that he couldn't imagine any answer that would get him out of the sticky situation he'd created. So he had to take the chance, no matter how crazy it seemed.

By the time Zac's e-mails had outlined the proposed business partnership, Kory's time at the Whine 'n' Dine was obviously coming to an end. He had gotten so paranoid that he barely spoke to his coworkers or customers. He dropped dishes and stared at his own shoes. Everyone thought he was slipping into a moody depression or some trendy new drug addiction. And they were jealous of both.

Over the past week, he'd been asked repeatedly why he was

the only guy in the restaurant who wasn't regularly going on E-male dates. He'd offered two new customers a drink on the house for their first date before they'd even spoken to him. And after three apple martinis at a nightclub, he'd scoffed at the idea of the stranger Jeff was pointing out across the room by saying, "Oh God, you know I don't dance, especially not with a football fan."

It was becoming increasingly obvious that Kory was either an antisocial psychic or there was something fishy about this waiter. People were catching on. Kory could feel them staring, scrutinizing him. He heard gossipy whispers every time he turned his back.

So when Kory found out that Djorvzac Travel was based 150 miles from the impending disasters in the city, this odd partnerships seemed like a smart move. At the very least, it would be a nice break from his mounting paranoia.

Anyway, he couldn't be a waiter forever, he reasoned. Well, actually he could. But he couldn't be a waiter and a secret webmaster all his life. He needed to find some breathing room and figure out where his future was headed. And there was plenty of open space in suburbia. The parking was free. And Kory had found an apartment for half his city rent.

Besides, Zac wasn't offering to buy E-male outright. Kory wasn't giving up a thing. A six-month consultant position was simply a very lucrative offer. If this man thought a dating web site was going to help his employees and business, Kory wasn't going to argue.

All Kory had to do was spice up these drab employees' love lives. Send them on a few dates. Boost morale. Connect them to the outside dating world in a way selling travel packages over the phone never could. Plus, he could help them match up a couple of single vacationers to split the cost of a double-occu-pancy room somewhere. Send some lonely old men to Palm Springs together for a weekend or something. Kory and E-male could do that in less than six months. And he could use the downtime to figure the rest of this mess out. Then he could return to the city guilt-free with money to spare.

So Kory had sublet his apartment and taken an official leave from the Whine 'n Dine. Everyone thought he was going back to school for a technical upgrade. The mere mention of such a daunting and boring life decision was enough to squelch any further conversation. They'd baked a cake and thrown a good-bye party for him. Half of them speculated Kory was probably going off to rehab.

So after driving endless hours past leafless trees on highways without service stations, passing towns and rivers as unpronounceable as Zac's last name, and suffering from a complete lack of civilization and static-free radio stations—Kory was in a sub-suburb, a rural business park one-hundred-fifty miles from everything he knew. He stood there in a drab gray office inside a drab gray building with three men staring at him.

"Dating web site!" Zac shouted.

Kory looked around the office at the expressions of absolute puzzlement surrounding him. What was this place? And what was going on? He'd never seen such a sorry group of gay men. They couldn't manage to decorate the colorless walls, let alone find boyfriends. No wonder they needed him. But why did everyone seem so surprised?

"Mr. Dee-jor-rak," Kory slaughtered his name again, "you're the one who wrote me."

"It's just Zac," he roared, wincing at the mangled sound of his last name, "and I most certainly did not write a dating service."

"Listen, Mr... Zac," Kory stated firmly, "you and I have an agreement. A six-month deal. That's what your letters said."

He handed the printed contract to the big man behind the desk. Kory could see the tensed balls of muscle in the wide shoulders under Zac's white dress shirt. He could read the dark lines drawn on Zac's forehead beneath his neatly parted black hair. His chiseled features were as tense as if they were truly set in stone. Only his eyes moved. And Kory watched those bright green orbs flit back and forth beneath knitted brows, scanning the typed pages Kory had handed over.

Despite his booming dominance, this man couldn't have been that much older than Kory himself. And if it hadn't been for his scowl and his short fuse, he could have been quite attractive. At the very least, he and Kory were both successful, young gay businessmen. And Kory expected a hint of professionalism from this meeting, even if he had to demand it. He was not about to cave and cower like one of this man's employees.

"And Mr. Dee-jor-vor-zer-ack, we have a professional agreement," he insisted, purposefully adding a few stumbling syllables to the name.

"Not with me, you don't," Zac said, handing the contract back. "I didn't write a single word of that."

Kory snatched the sheet of paper from Zac's hand in disbelief. As he did, he noticed how soft the long white fingers were, how clean the square blunt nails looked. This entitled bastard had never done a day of hard work in his life. Kory got burns and scrapes and grease-blackened cuticles at the Whine 'n' Dine. Hell, he practically got calluses typing into the wee hours on E-male.

What did this guy know about agreements or ethics or what it took to build a successful company? Any employer who would subject an office full of gay men to rows of cubicles and fluorescent lights and telephone headsets that ruined their hair was obviously a heartless and untrustworthy monster.

Kory should have known this was a mistake. But it was too late to turn back now. And he wasn't about to give in this easily. He couldn't. There was nowhere left to turn now that he'd left everything behind and accepted this man's offer. So whether or not Zac was actually the one who sent that contract printed on very official-looking Djorvzac Travel stationery, Kory intended to make him stand by it.

"Well, I'm not so sure my lawyer would see it that way," Kory bluffed. "These are clearly from your company and signed with your name."

The only lawyer Kory knew handled real estate closings exclusively and had a fondness for banana pancakes. Kory wasn't so sure he'd be much help with an online contract dispute.

Regardless, his empty threat had the desired effect. Zac Djorvzac's eyes clouded angrily like flawed emeralds, and his two employees issued a sudden chorus of horrified gasps. The reaction from the peanut gallery only reminded Kory that they were not alone in the office. He was prepared to challenge this man, but not before they had some professional privacy.

"Would you like to resolve the matter with your employees first?" Kory asked. He had no desire to share the stage with these two. If he was going to have to fight with this man, he wanted a clear battlefield. "Then we can get down to business."

"If you two can't resolve your dispute, you'll both lose commissions," Zac proclaimed, waving them away dismissively. He didn't have the energy to squabble over two reservations when he had to contend with big-city attitude wrapped in this slim little package in front of him.

"What?"

"Wait a minute!"

Danny and Mike's attention snapped back to their own dispute, despite the enthralling scene that was unfolding before them. Their "drama" may have paled in comparison to a hot little number with shaggy hair and a firm body fearlessly confronting their intimidating boss, but they weren't about to drop their case and their commissions.

"What's the problem?" Kory asked impatiently. "It didn't sound like such a big deal to me." He had heard half of the story as he'd walked in on the stormy scene. Not many people could have ignored the high-pitched shrieks. The matter seemed simple enough from the outside. He was endlessly amazed by the inability of gay men to cooperate and compromise.

"Fine, if you know so much about running a business, then you solve it," Zac said smugly. "Otherwise, I don't want to hear about it again."

Kory turned and took a seat across the desk from Zac. He took his time. He smoothed his snug sweater over his lean chest muscles and tight, narrow waist. Here he didn't have to play waiter. He didn't have to pretend that he was anything other than what he was—an ingenious entrepreneur who had created a company that could be just as successful as Djorvzac Travel. And he could prove it.

He looked up at the expectant, fidgeting men in the doorway and over at the self-righteous set jaw of their boss. Zac's face had the healthy shine of a meticulously fresh shave. Kory turned his boyish face to the two men at the door. He wiped his golden bangs from his eyes.

"So where did you leave this issue with your clients?" he asked.

"Well, Danny blocked the resort where these men thought they were staying with a party of poverty-stricken college boys, all in one suite! I had to take the only other thing available," Mike whined. "I've reserved a giant ski house with six bedrooms and three separate floors for two 40-year-old men. They will not be happy. I'm just waiting for them to cancel the entire trip."

"And are your college boys ever going to be able to afford that resort or fit in one room?" Kory asked Danny. "Are they going to follow through with this reservation?"

"They're 25 and there are only four of them," Danny defended himself. "And how am I supposed to know? I can't discriminate like that. Besides, that resort is ridiculously overpriced anyway."

"So what's the problem?" Kory asked annoyed.

"The problem," Zac interrupted, "is that everyone is paying more than they should for the wrong lodging. We're not delivering what we promised. And we'll end up losing all these reservations."

"Ridiculous," Kory dismissed his reasoning. "You're providing an even greater service than you promised."

"We are?" Danny and Mike asked in unison.

"Of course," Kory insisted. "No one should be paying for that pricey resort. You said so yourself. You found a better place for all six of them—a huge house with separate levels for each couple. It's like a private resort where they can have their own suite of rooms. And they can have an even better time by turning the house into one big party if they all get along. It's more fun than the 40-year-olds ever expected. And more space than the young guys had at the resort. Split six ways, it's cheaper for everyone, and you guarantee you make both sales. You can probably even bundle their airfare and ski tickets for a further discount. You just need a little smart matchmaking."

"Huh." Danny looked stunned.

"That just might work," Mike added.

"There's only one way to find out," Kory said. "Go call them."

The two quarreling parties looked at each other, shrugged and smiled. But before they turned to leave and finalize the deal with their respective clients, they looked back at their fuming boss.

"He's a keeper, Zac," Mike said.

"Yeah," Danny chimed in, "you sure know how to pick a boyfriend."

"What?" Kory erupted, managing to beat Zac to the punch. The boss sat there with his mouth half open, ready to bark at his employees. But Kory was on his feet at lightning speed, as defiant and full of self-righteous attitude as any gay man could be. "I am not a mail-order bride! I'm not here to be anyone's boyfriend. I own the E-male dating web site. I'm here to find boyfriends for all of you."

"Really?" Danny and Mike's eyes widened, reflecting the greenish glow of fluorescent bulbs and the utter beige-ness of the godforsaken decor.

"Out!" Zac roared at the two travel agents. "And close the door behind you."

After his employees had left the room with smirks on their faces and curiosity in their lingering glances, Zac could finally get to the bottom of this. He would deal with them later. But he certainly couldn't deal with Kory Miles and his tight little city attitude while there was a drooling audience gaping at him.

With the door closed, the office seemed even smaller, cramped, too close for comfort. When Zac Djorvzac stood up behind his desk, he knew his broad frame engulfed the entire room. And that's exactly how he intended to control this entire situation. This skinny young thing might think he could throw his attitude around, but he was no match for the presence of a real businessman.

"Would you like to explain what is going on here, Mr. Miles?" Zac asked as if he didn't have a moment to waste on Kory.

But Kory wasn't about to be rushed. He had stood his ground so far and he wasn't going to budge now. Zac watched this little man stand there as if he were planted, looking him straight in the eye, gold eyes on green, glinting like a treasure.

"Mr. Djorvzac, I've traveled a long way on the good faith agreement set forth in these letters." Kory shook the papers for emphasis. "You contacted my business. I expect you to honor your word, professionally if not morally."

"Are you claiming that I answered some personal ad on your dating site?" Zac asked in disbelief. "And you're basing a business decision on it?" He stepped from behind his desk to confront this stranger. They were mere feet apart. Zac could feel the tension in the tiny space humming like static electricity. It strengthened with each inch he advanced toward this infuriating person.

"It was not a personal ad." Kory insisted. "As I have said, I am not here to date you. Or anyone. I am here as a business owner with a business agreement, to enroll your employees into E-male." He leaned forward, challenging the short distance between the two. They were face to face now. Zac really wasn't that much taller, but his breadth made him loom large.

"My employees?!" It was the closest Zac could come to a laugh. But there was nothing funny about it. The very last thing he wanted was for his employees to date, to find boyfriends and distractions, to fall into the disarray that people called love.

"Yes, your employees. It seems they could really use it." Kory turned to peer out through the thin strip of glass beside the door.

"My employees have everything they need... professionally," Zac stated flatly. He knew Kory was looking judgmentally at the rows and rows of dingy cubicles, the worn carpeting, the bad lighting and the few dozen men slumped over computer screens and telephones. Zac felt a slight twinge of doubt as Kory turned his face away from their confrontation. But what did Zac care? This was not a fashion show. This was a functional business. His employees didn't need flashy offices or tight designer jeans to be successful. And they certainly did not need boyfriends.

"It's all right here in these records of correspondence." Kory tossed a neatly organized packet onto Zac's desk, printouts of the e-mails he had exchanged over the past week with whoever was pretending to be the owner of Djorvzac Travel.

Zac stepped behind his desk to scoop up the papers. He scrutinized them as if this were the first time he had ever seen them. As if he really hadn't written them. And in fact, he hadn't. Zac Djorvzac had never seen these e-mails and agreements and contracts. If this city boy thought he could march in here and produce random computer printouts and forged documents, he had another thing coming. A cute smile and a tight ass weren't enough to win over the real owner of Djorvzac Travel. Zac had learned that lesson many years ago.

"Add some spice to lives? A little excitement? Some much needed romance?" Zac scoffed at the claims typed on the pages before him. He looked almost nauseous under his skepticism as he located the offensive words sprinkled throughout the correspondence. "Mr. Miles, I most certainly do not use phrases like that."

Kory approached Zac slowly and deliberately. There was not a shred of fear in his steady gaze. He stepped boldly into the narrow space behind Zac's desk as if he were invading enemy territory. Zac saw the determination in those gold-flecked eyes. He saw the set serious expression on that boyish face.

"Well, someone used those phrases," Kory said angrily. "In fact, Mr. Djorvzac, most normal people use phrases like that."

Zac clearly detected the challenge in Kory's voice as the smaller man stood tall before him. However, Zac didn't know how he was expected to respond. How was he supposed to answer this man's desperation and determination? How was he supposed to react when a handsome, young, insistent man walked into his office and challenged everything he had built his business on? Whatever had ignited this fire in Kory was not Zac's fault. And no matter how strongly he could feel the heat of its flame as they stood face to face leaning into one another aggressively, it was not Zac's responsibility to extinguish it.

"I've never even heard of your E-male dating site until this very moment," Zac said. "And for the last time, I did not write these letters."

"Then who did?" Kory asked the obvious question, almost hopelessly.

"I don't know," Zac stated plainly. "But perhaps in the future you will confirm business deals with something more official than forged e-mails. Not everything can be resolved over the Internet, Mr. Miles. This is not a nightclub. This is an extremely busy office—a real business. No one here needs a boyfriend. No one needs this kind of distraction."

Zac stepped forward and crossed his arms. This discussion was over as far as he was concerned. He meant for the advance to shove Kory out of the office, but the angry young man would not be moved. Instead, Zac's step only meant he was now pressing his elbows against Kory's thin frame. He could feel that intolerable heat of youthful confidence against him, but Zac refused to budge.

"Distraction?" Kory yelled. It was as if that one word had sent him into an absolute rampage. He shook his head so that pale, limp bangs fell to cover his scowl. He put his hands on his narrow hips. "E-male is a business, too. A very successful one. One that obviously takes official agreements more seriously and more professionally than you. How is that a distraction?"

Kory looked defiantly up into Zac's face. He leaned over the barrier of those crossed arms as if he were challenging the boundaries of their two worlds. Zac could feel that tight chest against his forearms. He could smell the warmth of skin and the faint lingering aroma of Kory's morning's coffee. He could feel the pulse and passion and life of this man coursing through that body as it pressed against him.

"This is how it's a distraction."

And with that, Zac uncrossed his arms. He wrapped one firmly around Kory's waist. He used the other to grab the man by the back of the neck. And then he kissed him, hard and insistently, his stubble scrapping those soft lips. He held Kory tight for several moments without breathing, just lips on lips, as if time were not truly passing.

When Zac released him, they both took deep gasping breaths. They stared straight ahead unblinking. Zac couldn't believe it. It could not have happened. He could not have allowed himself to act like that, after all this time, after he'd worked so hard. Desire, passion and spontaneity were simply not part of his day-to-day vocabulary. He was a businessman, not an animal, not some basic creature that responded to tempting stimuli.

"I'm... sorry," Zac managed. "I was just trying to make a point."

"Oh, I felt your point all right," Kory said. He let his golden eyes dip briefly beneath the waistband of Zac's pants. "And now maybe I should make mine."

When Kory rushed toward him, Zac was still stunned. He wasn't sure he could have resisted this aggressive young thing if he wanted to. And he had no idea whether Kory intended to fight or fuck him. Kory never gave him the chance to decide.

Kory's fingers were at the buttons of Zac's shirt and pants simultaneously. He pulled them free indiscriminately. Two tan buttons popped from the starched white dress shirt. He had those pressed khakis pulled around Zac's thick thighs with only a moment's hesitation to tug them roughly over the bulge of his erection.

Zac had never been so flustered by a kiss. He had never kissed someone so forcefully. As he was pushed back onto the floor in the narrow space behind his desk, he told himself that his own misbehavior was what had caused this delirium. This confusion is what allowed him to be overpowered so completely by a thin, young, beautiful man. It wasn't because he wanted it. It wasn't because he needed it. It certainly was not because this kind of crazy out-of-character moment was the only way he could break through his strong business façade to realize the passion within.

Suddenly, Zac was on his back half-naked, looking up as Kory peeled off his own pants and crawled on top. They were tucked behind Zac's desk, shielded from even the limited view through the door-side window. This tiny pocket of floor was theirs for this one moment. And no matter how his mind tried to reason it away, Zac felt that this small secret space was abuzz with indescribable electricity. It was revenge or hatred or something too strong for either of them to question.

Against his will, Zac thrilled at the sight of Kory forcefully climbing atop him. Kory held him down. One pale hand pressed between Zac's thick furry pecs. The other reached behind to grasp Zac's painfully erect penis and guide it into place. Kory produced a condom, seemingly from out of nowhere, and as he slid it onto Zac's awaiting shaft, he slowly sat upon it.

Within seconds they were fused together. They moved as if neither of them had a choice. Kory's arms stretched to brace against the solid foundation of Zac's chest. His hips moved with the pulse of their bodies. And Zac looked up, watching as if he were a mere spectator as this man rode him. He saw the sharp points of Kory's pale hips as they bucked. He saw the way Kory's golden eyes half-closed as he turned his head upward. He saw Kory's own erection pointing up over the thin sweater that still clung to that toned torso.

But Zac was not a spectator. He felt every subtle shift of their bodies. He lay there unmoving, but the throbbing hardness buried deep inside Kory could not be ignored. Every shift of the hips, every breath, every slow agonizing descent—Zac felt himself inside the warm depths of Kory. And as his disbelief melted away, he couldn't help from reaching forward to hold Kory's hips. Zac grasped that tight thin waist and pulled Kory toward him, onto him.

They thrust together as if they were fighting. Kory's arms shoved against Zac's chest. Zac's fingers dug into Kory's hipbones. And as they slammed against one another, their eyes locked for one still moment.

When Kory broke their gaze, he threw his head back. He came in desperate, grunting spurts, covering Zac's hairy muscled torso. For a moment, he looked back in shocked embarrassment with Zac still inside him. Then he felt the torrent of Zac within him and heard his gasping pleasure. They both finally exhaled.

CHAPTER 3

EmaleAdmin: Jeff, we need to talk
punkid: Who's this? How do you know my name?
EmaleAdmin: It's Kory. Could I get you to drive 2 hrs?
punkid: nthng to do w/ tech college is it?
EmaleAdmin: No
punkid: uv got A LOT more question to answer.

"I can't show my face in the city," Kory told Jeff.

"Oh my god!" Jeff shrieked as he stepped over the threshold into Kory's temporary apartment. "Why in hell's name are you showing me this?"

They were standing in the middle of one of the most hideous living rooms either of them had ever seen. The place Kory had rented over the internet had come unfortunately furnished. There were pink silk flowers and sprayed-on brass finishes. It had gray painted walls and gray wall-to-wall carpet. It even had a gray couch.

"Is that corduroy?" Jeff asked in horror.

"It's a sofa," Kory said.

"Hardly."

"Jeff, I did not ask you here to help me redecorate."

"That's unfortunate," Jeff said. "Do we actually have to get serious now?"

"I'm afraid so."

"Well, I didn't drive an hour beyond Jon's house just to be subjected to suburban décor."

"Jon?"

"The hot, outdoorsy, rugged dog owner, remember?" Jeff asked. "I thought you knew everything, Big Brother."

And then there was a pause. Kory didn't know what to say, how to respond. He couldn't broach the subject he had called Jeff here to address. Jeff was his best friend, and if Kory couldn't tell him, there was little hope that he would ever be able to lift this burden from his back.

"Big Brother?" was all Kory could come up with. "I thought I was a year younger."

"Once you're in your 30s, it's all the same." Jeff smiled. "But seriously. I'm not used to friends finding me on E-male. Or asking me to drive into the sticks to visit them. This is all very creepy, to be honest. What's going on?"

"I think I've gotten myself into a really bad situation," Kory said as he plopped down onto that deplorable gray corduroy couch. "And I think the only way out is to start telling the truth."

"God. I hope it's a really bad addiction for you to settle for something like this," Jeff said as he reluctantly perched himself on the edge of the couch. "You must be really high."

"What are you talking about?"

"Well, since the rumors are obviously true, I at least hope the rehab facility out here is worth it." The look of sincerity on Jeff's face was an odd fit with the blue hair and punkish charm. "But I still don't understand how you hacked into my E-male account while all strung out on drugs. Don't worry, I know you must have been out of control."

"Jeff, I don't do drugs."

"Booze, then? Could a gay boy possibly be so drunk that he'd stumble into this apartment?" Jeff asked with his pierced eyebrow raised. "I didn't even know that was possible. This looks like the work of some crazy alphabet drug—E, K, GHB, LMNOP?"

"Jeff, it's E..."

"I knew it!"

"E-male!" Kory just blurted it out.

"You're addicted to E-male?" Jeff asked, clearly confused. "Honey, that's completely understandable, but I really don't see how that requires professional detox."

"Jeff, I am not addicted to E-male. I invented E-male."

For once, Jeff had no witty response. The look of concern slid from his face, leaving pure shock that made his reaction to the room's furnishings look almost pleasant by comparison. Jeff listened intently and silently as Kory explained E-male's origin and rapid growth.

Kory tried to gloss over the details. There was no need to get too specific with Jeff. He probably didn't want to hear about technological gadgetry or functionality. The important thing was that Kory was telling someone. The entire situation had just gotten so crazy and out-of-control that Kory couldn't handle it. And it was critically important that Jeff realize that Kory's intentions were good. Because if Jeff couldn't understand, Kory had very little hope of returning to the city and his previous life without the guilt and suspicion of E-male absolutely ruining him.

"You little bitch!" Jeff shrieked. "I can't believe you."

"I'm so sorry, Jeff," Kory insisted. "Honestly, I wanted to tell you. I wanted to tell the truth. But it all happened too fast. No one would have trusted me or E-male ever again."

"I can't believe you didn't give me a free E-male membership!"

"You're not really mad?" Kory asked in shock.

"Mad? Kory, without E-male, I never would have met Jon. It's the best thing that's happened around here. Well, maybe not around here," Jeff said. "How the hell did you end up here anyway?"

Kory looked away quickly. He pretended to be interested suddenly in a dusty plastic rose in a tacky bud vase.

"Don't tell me there are more shocking details to come," Jeff said, but the curiosity in his voice betrayed his surprise. "I don't know if I can take any more."

"Well, I was going to work out here," Kory admitted.

"What, do soccer moms and little old ladies tip better than city folk?" Jeff joked.

"No, I was going to... help out this gay travel agency."

"Help out? Gay travel?" Jeff asked incredulously. "What the hell does that mean? Weren't we just talking about your other mystery job? You don't know a damn thing about travel. This is as far as you've been from the city since I've know you."

"You know," Kory began awkwardly, "match single travelers up. Introduce the employees to other guys they might get along with. Or maybe even date."

"Like a matchmaker?" Jeff asked skeptically. "Like E-male."

"Kinda."

It was the best he could do. He was tiptoeing as carefully as possible around the bomb of that truth. Now that Zac Djorvzac had destroyed the entire plan, Kory didn't want to delve into that portion of the disaster. The problem that needed to be addressed was that he was no longer poised to get rid of E-male cleanly and quietly and make a boatload of money.

If he wasn't going to be working at Djorvzac Travel, he was going to have to find a way to get back to the city and the Whine 'n' Dine without any more screw-ups. He couldn't stand to create yet another lie about why his "return to school" had been canceled. It would just be one more lie piled on top of the others—a pile that was getting so high it was about to collapse and crush Kory under the weight of his own dishonesty.

For no logical reason, he hoped that Jeff would be able to help him come clean and rebuild his life. In a way, it really was a kind of detox. Kory wanted to purge the poison of deceit from his conscience for a fresh start.

"Why couldn't those travel guys just sign up for E-male like the rest of us?" Jeff asked. "That's the beauty of the internet, right? Why did you have to come all the way out here?"

"I just needed to get away," Kory said, somewhat honestly.

"I get that," Jeff said. "But it sounds like you should have called a travel agency instead of going to work for one. Sign 'em up, take their money, then head to the tropics or something. Why in the world would you need to be here? Let E-male work its magic while you get some rest and relaxation."

"It doesn't work that way," Kory said quietly.

"What are you talking about? E-male works perfectly. You did a great job designing it," Jeff praised. "Just look what it did for me and Jon. I've seen it work myself."

"That's not really E-male working," Kory admitted. "Well, not exactly."

"What do you mean? What exactly is happening, Kory?" Jeff asked. He stared past his blue bangs straight into Kory's gold eyes. Now even Jeff's curiosity was wearing thin. There was no way he was going to put up with Kory's vague bullshit forever. He was his best friend. He had traveled well beyond his new suburban boyfriend's town and well beyond his city-boy comfort zone. Kory had skirted every issue that had come up this evening. And now he couldn't expect to get away with one more thing. "Look, you're the one who wanted to talk. So talk. I'm just listening."

Kory fell back into the stale corduroy cushions. He closed his eyes and held his blonde hair back from his forehead in frustration. He gripped his skull tightly as if he could squeeze some brilliant answer from his brain. Jeff was right. The truth was the only possible answer. That is why Kory had begged him to come all the way out here. This was his last chance—if it was even a chance at all. Kory didn't know whether Jeff could help him, but Kory couldn't stop his confession halfway through. He owed Jeff the complete truth even if it cost him their friendship.

"I am E-male."

By the time Kory had finished entering his guilty plea as E-male's secret matchmaker, Jeff was also slumped back into the couch. That deplorable piece of furniture he had been so loath to touch was now the only thing supporting his shell-shocked body. He hadn't yet spoken. So far, Kory hadn't given him the opportunity.

Once Kory had finally started to speak, it was obvious he'd been waiting all this time to spill his true secret. The answers flowed out of him in a stream, like bytes of data blipping across a computer screen late at night. He hadn't even known it, but he'd wanted to explain to Jeff, to confess, to share his joys and success, his fears and mistakes, with someone important to him.

As Kory spoke faster and faster, he felt a flush come to his face. Not a blush of embarrassment, but an excited heat-like passion. He explained the true roles of compatibility and anonymity on E-male. He explained matching and chatting and his tricks for pairing men. He explained his view of the World Wide Web as an updated version of destiny and his own role in making it happen. Thousands of paths crossing electronically that would never have intersected offline—men who would have walked right by one another if it hadn't been for E-male, if it hadn't been for Kory.

When he'd finished his tale, he was practically breathless. His golden eyes glinted like candlelight, flashing wildly in the monochromatic gray of this cold room. And the silence that remained seemed charged with his words and ideas, buzzing with his passion for things he had confessed.

"So you know about the chocolate syrup thing?" Jeff finally said. Kory didn't answer, but the blush that bloomed like roses on his round cheeks said more than enough. "And every other embarrassing, private detail of my sex life?"

"Only the ones you mentioned online," Kory answered meekly.

Now it was Jeff's turn to blush. Suddenly he grabbed a dusty gray pillow from the couch and started smacking Kory with it more aggressively than playfully. "And it was you who matched me and Jon up in the first place?"

"I knew you'd be perfect together. I just knew," Kory said guiltily, cowering beneath his arms to shield himself from the pillow's repeated blows. "He's a chocolate lover!"

Jeff ceased the beating and threw aside the pillow. The two friends burst into laughter and fell exhausted and overwhelmed beside one another on the couch. They couldn't help it. Things had gotten far too serious, and they still hadn't found a way out of it all.

"So do you absolutely hate me?" Kory asked. He looked timidly over at Jeff as their laughter subsided. He didn't know if he was going to lose his friend or get another pillow-whooping, or both.

"Almost," Jeff answered. "If you didn't sound so desperate and pitiful and completely, geekily in love with the whole thing, I think I might. But you did match me up with Jon after all."

"Well, thanks," Kory said. "I know it's not right. It's just the way it worked out. And I'm really good at it."

"In a deceitful, tech-geek kind of way, it's sort of romantic," Jeff conceded. "If I could ignore the scary, futuristic, arranged matchmaking, I could almost think of you as a modern-day cupid."

"A chubby kid in diapers?" Kory asked, feigning insult.

"That's as good as it gets," Jeff said, "don't push your luck."

Kory was a natural matchmaker. He liked the feeling, whatever it was. It was like sharing hundreds of first dates and first kisses and fluttering stomachs full of butterflies. It may have been vicarious and voyeuristic, but Jeff was right—it was kind of romantic. However, even Cupid was a manipulative little flying imp with an occasionally bad attitude and a sick sense of humor.

"You're helping people find friendship and love," Jeff continued. "That's a hell of a lot better than serving them plates of cholesterol."

"I'd never really thought of it that way," Kory admitted. "But I really think I might need to go back to my less romantic profession, Jeff. I can't keep living like this. I can't keep living with these lies."

"You can't go back now." Jeff stated it so quickly and so vehemently that they were both shocked into momentary silence. Kory had so desperately hoped that his friend's understanding and advice would help him see things clearly and help him return to some kind of normalcy. But Jeff's sudden insistence that Kory remain in exile only confirmed his worst fears. "Honestly, Kory, all romance aside, this whole thing is really creepy. The creep-factor is way higher than the You've-Got-Mail

Meg-Ryan factor. And no one even saw that movie. Trust me, you cannot tell anyone else about this. I barely understand it. The guys at the diner would rip you limb from limb."

"I could just give it up," Kory said quietly. "I could end E-male." His voice rasped and his eyes swelled with tears. Until this very moment he had never realized how much it all really meant to him—why he couldn't simply let it go. He was in love with E-male.

"No you can't, Kory," Jeff said. "Just look at you. It's like your puppy died. And besides, it's too late for that. You've gone too far. If E-male disappears and you reappear from 'tech college' what are people going to think? Even if they don't figure it out, it's still creepy. And you haven't solved anything—their love lives, your work life, hell, your life in general."

"So I'm stuck either way," Kory said hopelessly. "Either I ruin E-male or I ruin myself. What am I going to do, Jeff? I really hoped you'd understand."

"I do. But only a little," Jeff said. "I'd do anything to help, but I don't know how. I think you already know what you have to do. Otherwise you wouldn't be in this godforsaken rat hole. So this travel company is really your only option? This Dork-zic guy?"

"Djorvzac," Kory corrected him absently. To his own surprise, he had somehow figured out how to pronounce that last name correctly—even though he had promised himself he would never speak it again. Simply saying the name reminded him of his other problem. The weight of it came crashing down on him like a ton of bricks. He was trying so hard to focus on his original mistakes, the ones he hoped he and Jeff could fix, that he had pushed thoughts of Zac Djorvzac almost completely from his mind. Almost.

Kory had glossed over the specific details of his failed deal with Djorvzac Travel. He'd mentioned how matchmaking could help travelers and travel agents. He'd thrown out a few vague examples. And he'd briefly touched upon the solution he'd created for Mike and Danny's ski-trip dilemma. What he hadn't mentioned was that the entire deal was a sham, that he'd been turned down and turned away. And he certainly never mentioned the surreal scene that had unfolded so inexplicably behind Zac's desk.

"Well, it makes a little more sense now," Jeff concluded. "Now that I know the truth, this whole travel thing doesn't seem so crazy. You're getting away from it all. You're finding a more honest use for E-male and figuring out how to make it work."

"That was the theory," Kory said.

"You don't sound so thrilled about it," Jeff observed. "It sounds like the perfect solution. You're using evil for good, taking all those lies and manipulation and turning them into something positive. You're bringing a little love to the heartless world of corporate America."

Kory was well aware of Jeff's disdain for anything businesslike. He hated overweight straight men in cheap suits. He would rather join the circus than work in an office. Jeff truly believed the only honorable jobs were those that truly served his urban gay community: waiters, bartenders, hairdressers, actors, singers, drag queens and entertainers of all kinds. Retail sales-people were barely tolerated out of sheer necessity. Jeff thought these gay stereotypes existed for a very good reason, and he wanted to keep it that way. To Jeff, corporate boredom was the "Heterosexual Agenda."

This was why Jeff disliked the suburbs so much. That is where the corporate zombies went after they left their over-lit cubicles and under-lit pubs. Kory also knew that Jeff's diehard beliefs were being challenged by his recent experiences with burbboy Jon. Kory worried that his own business confessions and retreat beyond city limits would push Jeff over his un-urban tolerance level.

"Taking two giant profit machines and turning them into happiness." Jeff sounded suddenly excited. "The travel industry meets the Internet, and their love child is romance."

Kory hated to burst his bubble. It was as if Jeff had regained a bit of hope for E-male as a tidy solution to corporate drudgery and Kory's own conundrum. Kory only wished it were that easy, that he could simply turn his lies into something good.

"Well, not exactly," Kory said, breaking the spell.

"What do you mean?" Jeff whined. It was if Kory had shattered Jeff's dreams instead of Zac destroying Kory's.

"I already tested that theory, I'm afraid," Kory explained. "Turns out, the owner of the travel company doesn't want to work with me."

Kory tried to explain generally, nicely. He tried not to let anger rise into his throat as he remembered his discussion with Zac Djorvzac—as he remembered much more than their discussion.

"Well, that doesn't seem fair," Jeff insisted, pouting and crossing his skinny arms. "It doesn't make any sense. Why would anyone make up a fake business deal like that? Maybe you should talk to him again."

"I don't think that would do much good," Kory admitted. "He wasn't the nicest guy and...well, I might have told him so... and... I just don't think we would have the best working relationship."

"Why not?" Jeff looked at Kory suspiciously. His furrowed forehead put his eyebrow piercing at a freakish angle. But Kory couldn't avoid those accusing eyes. "It's exactly what you need. A merger would fulfill all your needs."

"I don't think a merger would fulfill anything," Kory snapped much too quickly. When he heard the urgency in his own response, his gold eyes flew wide open and a hot flush leapt to his cheeks.

"You did not!" Jeff screamed. "You had sex with him!"

"What are you talking about? Are you crazy? Have you listened to a thing I've said? We are not working together. He was a complete bastard to me. We had a fight right there in his office."

"And then you hate-fucked him!" Jeff accused as if he were simply completing the list of facts Kory had begun.

"Hate-fuck" was an unpleasant but popular term at the Whine 'n' Dine. It was supposedly a crazy, impassioned bout of sex that you engaged in with someone you hated with such intensity that fucking his brains out was the only way to express it. Kory never quite bought that fabricated definition. He hadn't until yesterday.

"Look, Kory," Jeff said, "you may be able to lie to me about E-male and matchmaking and whatever techy, cyber, double life you've been leading, but you cannot lie to me about sex! Look at your face! Trust me, I haven't seen you look like that in a long time! You got laid! And I want to hear all about it! I loves me a good hate-fuck."

"Well, now you know why it will never work," Kory said, admitting defeat for the moment, but hopefully winning the ultimate argument about the Djorvzac Travel "merger."

"Tell me everything!" Jeff bounced his legs up onto the couch and wrapped his arms around his knees.

Kory couldn't begin to explain the situation, even if he had wanted to share the intimate details with his friend. And the details were surprisingly intimate for a "hate-fuck." Kory had never taken such sexual control in his life. He didn't know what had come over him. There was just something about Zac Djorvzac that drove him absolutely mad. Kory was infuriated, humiliated, and so turned on he was seeing red behind his eyelids.

Zac's kiss had pushed Kory over the edge—the edge of anger and arousal. He was not about to let that man have the upper hand for another second. If Zac thought he could treat Kory like that—yell at him, cheat him, belittle his company and then kiss him—he had another thing coming. But what that thing was had shocked them both beyond words and explanation.

Kory had just grabbed Zac. He had allowed his body to do what it insisted on doing. He had allowed their instant magnetism to pull them together like gravity. Kory had barely managed to push their tangled limbs into the hidden spot behind Zac's desk. He had reached into his pocket as a natural response to the conditioning he preached on E-male to carry a "just-in-case" condom at all times. But beyond that, the entire fall onto the floor and into this mistake had been sheer momentum.

It had been like a reflex. An instinct. Like the flood of an orgasm after passing the point of no return. Kory had reached his saturation point on every emotional level possible—fury and frustration, hopelessness and horniness. But neither man had been ready for the explosion.

After E-male and Djorvzac Travel had "merged" more violently and passionately than any forged contract could have promised, they were left with the aftermath. It was beyond any normal postcoital awkwardness. It was absolute shock, disgust and regret. They had dressed quickly and silently. It helped that they were never fully disrobed. That was the only fortunate part of the situation. Kory grabbed his stack of papers from Zac's desk and turned to leave without looking back. He'd been prepared to complete his short walk of shame to the office door with as much dignity as possible. But then Zac had spoken.

"I'm sorry you came all this way..."

Kory had turned and taken one long final look at Zac Djorvzac. "You're sorry all right," he said. And then he had slammed the door between their two worlds forever.

Even the limited, cleaned-up rendition of events that Kory admitted to his friend had Jeff bouncing up and down on the couch as if he'd just heard the best bedtime story ever. Kory was just exhausted and confused. He was so ashamed of his stupid business and personal decisions that he couldn't even allow himself to be amused by Jeff's delight.

"Well, now it's decided," Jeff proclaimed. "You have to give it one more shot."

"You must be kidding, Jeff," Kory said firmly. "Have you heard a thing I said? He's an ass. He didn't sign that contract. We hate-fucked each other. And then we insulted each other again right before getting as far apart as fast as possible."

"You were the one who walked away," Jeff pointed out. "Maybe he wanted you to stay."

"I'm sure he misses me terribly," Kory said sarcastically.

"Look, even if he didn't write those letters, he should give you a chance," Jeff made his case. "You helped his employees, helped his company. You made him money before even working with him. That should make Mr. Big Business happy. Money is all those businesspeople care about anyway. He owes you."

Kory didn't want to get into another discussion about the evils of the corporate world. But maybe Jeff had a point. If Kory's travel plans had actually worked out for Mike and Danny's clients, he just might be able to prove Zac Djorvzac wrong. And that was the only thing Kory would like better than never seeing that man again.

"Maybe," Kory conceded. "Maybe if he thought it was for his customers. For profit, not romance. I don't know... but just maybe."

"Not to mention the other 'favor' you did for him." Jeff winked. "Kory, you're in complete control here. You just don't know it because you're a bottom."

Jeff was the one who didn't know the half of it. Kory wasn't about to tell him exactly how much control he had taken there on that office floor. Maybe it was time for Kory to take control in the rest of his life too.

"Besides, Kory," Jeff continued, "you may be in control of this situation or not, but you really don't have any other options."

Kory wasn't so sure. As soon as he allowed himself to start thinking about what he and E-male could do, Mike and Danny's predicament seemed like child's play. Kory's matchmaking mind started connecting potential people and places and possibilities as if he were back in his old apartment late at night watching people fall in love on his glowing computer screen. But this time he was matching up pieces of a plan to prove Zac Djorvzac wrong once and for all.

"Well, now that we know what you have to do, can I give you some real help?" Jeff seemed satisfied with the sudden look of resolve on Kory's face. So he started to gather up the trinkets and knickknacks that littered the bland apartment without adding a single hint of whimsy or charm. "This gruesome chore is more proof than anything else that I would do anything to help you—"

"Well, if you really want to help," Kory interrupted, reaching to take the dusty decorations from Jeff's arms, "there's no need to redecorate. I don't plan on staying here long."

"But I thought we decided you were going to give Zac another go," Jeff winked lasciviously, "so to speak."

"'Go' is precisely what I have in mind." Kory's eyes widened and the corners of his mouth lifted for the first time that day. He finally looked sure of what he was going to do. "So if you're going to help, go pack your bags."

CHAPTER 4

EmaleAdmin: What's the hottest gay travel destination right now?
Circuitboy69: U kiddin? Beach Ball is comin up!
Partee: Yeah man. hottest party of the year.
EmaleAdmin: Where is it?
Globetrottr: Seriously?? Baytown Beach. Where else?
Circuitboy69: "Gaytown" is more like it.
Globetrottr: Totally! Boys Boys Boys!!!
Partee: Party all nite long!
EmaleAdmin: You want to go?

Zac had barely slept in days. He was fairly sure he hadn't gotten a single wink the night before. He tried to tell himself that it was the upcoming holiday-travel season or the spring break packages he wanted ready before New Year's. But the truth was holiday travel had been pretty much booked by now. And Zac had finalized spring break plans during his first sleepless night—months before they were needed.

It was hard for him to admit that it was the thought of Kory Miles that was tormenting him. In fact, it was more than the thought. It was the memory, the image, the feeling of Kory that kept creeping up from his subconscious. And each time he remembered a scent or sensation, his fury doubled until he was a ball of anxious anger.

He stomped around the agency in a rampage, with rings under his stormy green eyes, snapping at employees. All he'd heard during his workdays was the buzz of gossip about Kory Miles and E-male. His repeated reprimands only seemed to fuel the whispers.

Zac told himself he was concerned about the effect this disruption was having on his company and his employees' morale. That was the real concern that kept him awake. That and thoughts of Kory Miles with his slender waist and tight-wound attitude to match, not to mention that hot ass.

Zac had purposefully built this company as far away from the city beat as possible. He'd left all that behind years ago for many, many reasons. He didn't need this cyber-matchmaker virtually connecting his men to the sins of the city and the larger gay culture. Just one city boy had walked into the place, and suddenly it was in an uproar.

So when Zac saw Kory walking straight up the center aisle of cubicles toward him, for a moment he thought it must just be another tenacious hallucination—a flashback to that regrettable day and those regrettable events. But when the entire floor of Djorvzac Travel fell silent, when men on lunch break froze with sandwiches halfway to their mouths, when heads popped up from cubes like moles and Zac could hear echoes of "Please hold" throughout the office—he knew this wasn't a dream. It was his nightmare.

Kory paused when Zac made eye contact from the other end of the room. Kory seemed to stand there a moment for effect. He was completely on display. He was dressed absolutely inappropriately in a snug pair of dark blue jeans and a fitted baseball shirt that molded to his boyish contours. After he let everyone get a good look at him, he walked—well actually, he sauntered—

right up to Zac Djorvzac.

"Mr. Miles, did you forget something?" Zac growled as Kory approached.

"Yes, I forgot how absolutely charming you can be."

Ripples of laughter passed through the office. All the employees were peeking out from around their cubicles to spy on the impromptu meeting. Zac set his jaw firmly, bracing himself and controlling his anger.

The news about Kory had been spreading like wildfire all week. And here he was again, that disruption, swishing his hips and causing another scene in the middle of Zac's business. Dating service! That's the last thing Zac needed here.

Faces peered out of the break room. Zac could see Mike and Danny beaming at Kory from their desks. Danny even waved. But looming over the top of the maze of cubicles, Zac Djorvzac simply stood with his arms crossed. His intended to stop all this right here and now.

"Mr. Miles, I have made it perfectly clear that there will be no business dealings between our companies," Zac boomed loudly enough for all his employees to hear. If they wanted to eavesdrop, he was going to make his message crystal-clear.

"Mr. Djorvzac," Kory said, "I have another business proposition for you."

"I don't believe any proposition you could make would interest me in the slightest," Zac replied. There was total silence. None of his employees dared laugh. But Zac had to concentrate suddenly to make sure his anger retained control over that embarrassing slip of the tongue. Especially when he realized Kory had pronounced his last name correctly for the first time.

Kory didn't bat an eye. He simply smiled his youthful grin and let his golden eyes linger on Zac calmly.

Kory knows he's a good looking man, Zac thought. And he obviously wanted Zac know it, too. Zac was certain that it was for no other reason than to make him uncomfortable and tip the scales in Kory's general direction. Zac knew he probably looked flustered and tired and totally worn-out. He wasn't sure why he should care that he didn't look his best here in front of this young man, but he didn't want to appear at any kind of a disadvantage with his entire company watching.

When it became apparent that Kory was just going to stand there before everyone with his tight little outfit and penetrating stare, Zac said "Mr. Miles, there is absolutely no one here interested in a dating service."

There was a contradictory murmur from the crowd, but the mumbles were low enough that Zac could not identify the voices for later punishment.

"How about your customers?" Kory suggested.

"What?" Zac was caught off-guard. His dark brows knit together, adding several more confused and angry furrows to his forehead.

"If you don't want your employees paired up, I can match your customers just as easily," Kory continued. "Singles' trips. Travel groups. Gay men from all across the country could find friends and potential boyfriends with common interests."

Ears perked across the agency. Interested "hmms" and "huhs" bubbled through the air.

"Clients don't call us for dates, Mr. Miles." Zac insisted. "This is a travel agency. And those travel concepts of yours already exist. People go to singles' weekends. They join travel groups, activities and tours."

"And what do they find?" Kory asked before Zac could go on. "Nothing. No one compatible. Nothing new and exciting. And why?"

"Because it's a bad idea to start with?" Zac jumped in with his own question before Kory could make another good point. "So why are you wasting your time on a flawed travel model? People go on vacation to escape, to leave everything and everyone behind. They might think they want to meet people, but they don't. They want to be by themselves."

"Not if I can introduce them to someone better," Kory stated confidently. "What they're really missing is a matchmaker, someone to make the perfect group, the perfect vacation and a whole lot of money. What they're missing is my E-male."

"Travel has nothing to do with a dating service," Zac insisted. "It would never work."

"It worked for your employees the other day," Kory pointed out.

Zac paused and narrowed his green eyes, as if he were trying to remember the details or burn a hole through Kory with his hateful glare. That smug little twink, he thought. Life isn't that simple. It takes hard work. Not everyone can cruise through the years with a sexy little grin, floppy blonde bangs and a cute ass. Just because Kory had some crackpot solution to Mike and Danny's screw-up didn't mean it would ever work again.

"That's true, Zac." The sound of Danny's voice snapped Zac back to reality. "The customers were thrilled when they heard about the ski house. It's better than any of them planned. They're all getting in touch with the other housemates to plan everything."

"Would you all get back to work," Zac roared. "No one needs this distraction!"

However, his employees seemed more distracted by their boss' sudden outburst than by the sight of Kory Miles and the promise of his forbidden E-male.

"Oh, right," Kory seemed to remember offhandedly, "The 'distraction argument.' I remember that point well." Kory looked Zac up and down before continuing. He acted as if he were the one in control here, as if he were the boss. "Zac, you seem to be the only one who's upset about the whole thing. Maybe you could use a 'distraction' every now and then."

"Fine," Zac said, but there was no agreement in his voice. "See if they want to split their commissions with you. See if they really believe their performance is so poor that they need to bring in a consultant to take all the credit—a consultant who runs a dating web site, by the way, not one with a shred of travel experience. If my employees really need your help, I think we all have a lot more to be concerned about than who's wearing the tightest jeans."

"Thanks for noticing," Kory said. But Zac just turned, walked into his office and slammed the door. As Kory watched Zac's wide back retreat from him so defiantly, he didn't truly feel any of the bravado that he'd been spouting. Kory had been trying to "take control," "be aggressive" and whatever other advice Jeff had given him that sounded suspiciously like a high-school cheerleader chant.

Suddenly, Kory felt stranded among the cubes and unknown faces. Zac had established him as the enemy and then left him to fend for himself. The troops looked restless, and all Kory could manage for defense was a tight forced smile.

"Come on, Kory," Mike said with a genuine grin, "let me show you around."

"And the rest of you can join us," Danny added as he rose to join to duo, "if you're not too afraid."

They dragged Kory into another windowless room. It was a white-on-white break area with plastic chairs and a large folding table. It wasn't any better than the other spaces Kory had seen at Djorvzac Travel. But somehow it felt safer. This was obviously employees' territory. Kory could almost sense that Zac rarely stepped into this room. It smelled reassuringly of stale coffee and junk food, reminding Kory briefly of the diner.

As other employees slowly and silently joined them, Kory felt a little more relaxed. These poor guys looked just as horrified as he felt. Despite their fear, curiosity about Kory's E-male travel plans had drawn them in—although it could well have been just curiosity about Kory. It was quite possible they simply wanted to see, up-close, the man who had gotten their implacable boss' panties in a bunch. But as they gingerly pulled chairs around the table, Kory felt the first real sense of welcome since he'd stepped into Djorvzac Travel.

"So I've been waiting for you to come in here and turn this place upside down again," Mike said, patting Kory's shoulder. "What took you so long?"

"I wanted the perfect plan," Kory said. "Business proposition, I mean."

"You should have just dropped a house on him," Danny added, and the entire break room exploded into laughter.

Zac's two affable hosts adjusted their fashionable glasses as the tension eased around the break room. Mike and Danny could have been slinging hash right alongside Kory at the Whine 'n' Dine with very little makeover work. Kory would have toned down Danny's highlights. He would have rethought Mike's checked button-down shirt. But then again he had never been able to exert control over Jeff's blue patch or his black cowboy boots. When he thought about it, the Wine 'n' Dine wasn't exactly a model of gay perfection.

Mike and Danny introduced him to the men around the table. There was Steve, Rick, Chris, Andy and on and on—all the expected gay names and types. Some were plain, but they were all plainly gay men in their own individual ways.

Everyone seemed to have all his teeth. Eyes were properly aligned. There were no Jim-Bobs or Bubbas. These men just had the warmth of hometown shyness instead of the sharp edge of city boldness. Another person might have seen the difference as quietly friendly versus loudly obnoxious—it was a matter of perspective.

And Kory had more perspective than most. E-male had given him a glimpse into suburban lives and lusts. He knew these guys wanted many of the same things his city friends did. That's why he was here. That's why he thought this just might work. But for the life of him, Kory could not understand exactly why they all wanted to live here. Or work for Zac Djorvzac. For some inexplicable reason, they did.

"It's nice to finally meet you all," he said. "I guess you're probably wondering why I keep showing up here, huh?"

There was no response. From the blank, slightly expectant stares, Kory wasn't sure if they were interested at all. They were probably terrified by Zac's words and, of course, Zac himself. Kory admitted, at least to himself, that Zac's argument for not disrupting "business as usual" was pretty persuasive. Why rock the boat when it's chugging along at full speed? Everyone was making money and doing just fine. Why did they need Kory? These men were probably just here for the finale of Kory's freak show.

"Go on," Mike urged. "We've already told them how you helped us."

"Sure." Kory smiled. He tried to refocus his thoughts, to gather his wits that had been scattered during his encounter with Zac. "The thing is, what I did for Mike and Danny was solve a problem. Luckily, it worked. What your boss doesn't understand is that I can create solutions without there being a problem to begin with."

Faces were still blank. This wasn't going to be easy. Had Zac brainwashed them so thoroughly that they couldn't think beyond his box of rules, procedures and standard travel packages?

"For example," Kory continued, "what if Mike and Danny hadn't had all those unhappy clients? What if they had started with the big empty ski house or a block of rooms in some fabulous resort? Negotiate a great deal with the destination. Then find the perfect group to fill it. You get a huge discount, multiple sales and giant profits. Why sell one ski trip when you could sell 20?"

"Because one person might call asking for a ski trip," someone, maybe a Greg or a Gary, said from the end of the table, "but 20 people aren't going to call in a row. Especially not 20 who all want the same ski trip. That's too much of a coincidence."

"Like love," Kory said. "Like two people crossing paths who are completely compatible, as if they were made for each other. It's rare, but it happens. And my E-male makes it happen. Every day."

Suddenly there was a spark of interest around the table. Kory had to smile as he saw ears and eyes perk up in the bright white room. The promise of love did that to people. That's what Kory enjoyed about playing cupid. But he knew that Zac would never allow that. He had to convince these men that he could make their clients fall in love with travel.

"E-male finds people so they don't have to find each other," Kory said. "And I can help you create vacations that really are made just for them. It's too hard for people to do themselves, just like they can't force themselves to fall in love. People try to organize travel groups and get discounts, but they just end up fighting with friends or getting stiffed by strangers who don't fit in and never send their checks. Destinations try to offer group travel, activities, singles weekends. But Zac's right. They don't work. Because no one knows what he's walking into. And there's no one to make sure the right people show up.

"That's where I come in. I have... I mean E-male has an incredible track record of matching men, creating couples, introducing people to one another." Kory paused to let his expertise sink it. He looked slowly around the table before making the final leap from love to travel. "We can introduce them to vacations just as easily. If I could match up your profile, your wish list and your personality with your perfect dream vacation and then tell you that there will be 50 other gay men with the same dream on that same vacation—plus you get a group discount—wouldn't you go?"

"In theory, it sounds great," said Steve or Stuart. "But from my experience, it really doesn't work out in real life. That's not how people shop for vacations. They call us. We don't go looking for them."

"We might put together packages like we do for spring break," said another man whose name Kory couldn't even guess at. "But it's just airfare and hotel options. It's not customized per person. That's just too much work."

"That's what Zac was saying," pointed out another. "We have plenty of business. We don't need to go to that much trouble."

"That's why I will," Kory said. "Because I doubt Zac could have too much business. So he should be happy when I prove him wrong. Look, I know the only way to prove my theory is to make it real. That's why I've done this."

With that proclamation, Kory spread his pile of pamphlets and papers out in a fan on the table before him. He gave the stack a little shove toward the men and waited for them to take the bait. There was a long moment of silent hesitation, and then they pounced. They passed brochures back and forth. They scrutinized the spreadsheets and pages of financial information. They weighed the specific details of the excursions, activities and accommodations Kory had pieced together.

"This is amazing," Andy said.

"Prices like these for that many people?" Chris asked. "During high season at the last minute?"

"That's the power of buying in bulk," Danny said.

"It's surprising the space and pricing hotels and airlines

come up with," Mike agreed, "when you promise them over three dozen bookings at once."

"This is unbelievable," Rick said.

"Thank you." Kory nodded and smiled politely, but inside he was jumping up and down. How could Zac turn Kory down when all his employees thought it was a great idea?

"And Zac will absolutely hate it," Steve concluded.

"What?" Kory was jolted from his reverie.

"Did you see the profit margin?" Mike asked.

"He's right, Mike," Chris piped in. "This has 'Dancing, Dating and Drama' written all over it."

"What are you talking about?" Kory asked confused. "Aren't those all good things?"

The men in the room laughed, and all their heads simultaneously turned to stare at the plain black-and-white sign on the far wall. There were three word printed there in bold, each with an all-caps "NO" in front of it: "NO Dancing. NO Dating. NO Drama."

The men bumbled and stuttered a bit as they talked over one another and tried to explain the logic of Zac's rules to Kory. They talked about the complications that could arise from unprofessional social interaction. How bringing relationships to work could affect morale and productivity. They made a valiant attempt at denouncing drama of any kind. But Kory wasn't buying it.

"Is this a cult? Or the Middle Ages?" Kory asked in disbelief. "And what happens if you break the three commandments? Do you get sent to the gallows? Why in the world do you guys work here?"

Zac's employees bristled at Kory's last question. Suddenly they all looked uncomfortable, as if they were being put on the spot to defend an abusive spouse.

"It really is great company, Kory," Steve said. "And Zac isn't so bad really. He's a great boss and a brilliant businessman."

"You can make decent money doing this," Andy said. "And the travel discounts are unbelievable. I went to Hawaii for $50 last winter."

"And you came back?" Kory asked.

"Kory, this is where we live," Mike explained. "We all love to travel. That's why we do this. But this is home."

"I have an entire house, a yard, a driveway—you don't get that in a city," Chris pointed out. "We've been all over the world and we still like living out here."

"That's the biggest reason for working here," Danny said. "How many gay companies are there out here? With gay bosses and gay perks and a real chance to be something other than someone's stereotyped receptionist or hairdresser or waiter?"

"When you think about it, three silly rules aren't really so bad," Rick said quietly. "Maybe they even protect us a little."

Kory was speechless. Was this what it was like in 90% of the towns around the country? Kory understood that not every gay man was a city boy. But suddenly he wondered if moving to the hip and accepting cities was a little like running away. What about the vast majority of gay men who stayed where they started, where they wanted to stay, where they had to stand their ground in their own hometowns and fight for who they were?

Somehow Kory had always assumed men like this were stuck. He figured family or finances or some psychological disorder must have shackled them to these hetero prisons. Was Zac Djorvzac really creating an outpost, a gay presence on the frontier of society? Kory had a hard time giving him that much credit. Kory wondered if Zac himself wasn't running away in his own way, hunkering down behind his desk, within his business and beneath his layers of rules. But if Zac was running away, what was he running from?

"But don't you think Zac would bend the rules," Kory suggested, "for a trip and a profit like this?

All these ridiculous rules and restriction only made it less likely that Zac would ever consider Kory's plan. Kory knew that. But it made Kory want to make his plan a reality more than ever. He wouldn't just be proving Zac wrong about E-male. He would prove him wrong about his entire ridiculous approach to running a gay company and his even more ridiculous attempt at being a gay man. These tortured employees could be his best allies.

"A trip like this is certainly not his usual thing," Greg said.

"But it sounds like a blast," Andy added. "Where did you find all these travelers?"

"E-male," Kory said. "And of course, all of you are invited."

"A circuit party!? With my employees!?" Zac was furious. He couldn't believe this man was still here in his company. He was slightly relieved to see that Kory had left the office door open this time, but nothing could alleviate the rage he felt as he looked down at the elaborate travel plans Kory had created.

"And you, too, Mr. Djorvzac," Kory pointed out. "It wouldn't be any use if you weren't there to see it for yourself."

"Baytown Beach of all places!" Zac shouted loud enough for his men out on the floor to hear him. "I hate Baytown Beach!"

"Well, I didn't really customize the trip for you," Kory said. "Sorry if it's not your cup of tea. However, you will see there are many paying customers who are absolutely thrilled to have an inclusive Beach Ball vacation."

Zac looked at the reservations and accommodations. Kory had matched groups from across the world and paired up lodging, activities and transportation. It was a complex web of travel matchmaking.

"How did you do this?" he asked less frantically.

"With E-male," Kory answered as if it were the stupidest question in the world. "And with a little help from my friends."

Zac sensed sabotage, mutiny and corporate espionage all at once. If his employees were in on this, he was done for. If Kory Miles had gotten to them with his charm and wit and flirty little glances, Zac didn't know what he could do to get them back on track and operating by Djorvzac standards.

"I've been told this might bend your triple-D bra rules or whatever," Kory said innocently. "But since they won't technically be in the office, your employees agreed that this was an invaluable firsthand learning experience."

"I'm not sure a drug-soaked circuit party is the kind of training my employees need," Zac said bitterly.

"I'm not suggesting they do anything unprofessional," Kory insisted. "But they need to understand how trips like this could function. They need to see in person how successful they can be. And you do, too."

"How in the world do you think this is going to be beneficial to my company?" Zac demanded.

"I think you'll find your answer on the bottom line."

Zac didn't like the way Kory emphasized "bottom" whatsoever. But when he looked at the amounts tallied in the financial report, he was blown away. Basically every one of his employees was going free, and everyone else was happily paying for the premium experience. When the incredible group discounts, favors and itineraries were figured in, the profit margin was incredible.

"And if this doesn't work as you've predicted on paper, Mr. Miles?" Zac asked skeptically. "As I predict it won't?"

"Then you can try and forget you ever met me."

CHAPTER 5

> *newbie*: What can you wear to a circuit party?
> *DoneThat*: what can't you wear??? leather, rubber, lace, feathers...
> *newbie*: I am not packing a boa for airport security to find in my bag.
> *DoneThat*: well i'm just packing sunblock. thank god for clothing optional resorts!!!
> *newbie*: See you there!

Kory was hyperventilating. However, he was trying his damnedest not to let Zac see. Somehow, although members of this E-male/Djorvzac adventure filled half the airplane, Kory had been seated directly beside Zac. Mike and Danny had also managed to upgrade the "bosses" to first class, so that they sat alone in two cushy seats side by side, all alone. However, Kory was in no state to ponder travel and seating arrangements. He turned his head toward the window and tried to take deep breaths without looking at the ground far below. He was fogging up the tiny plastic pane.

"So I gather you don't like flying," Zac said calmly. His composure just sounded smug to Kory.

"So far, no," Kory answered without looking back at Zac.

"You've never been on an airplane before?" Zac asked. His composed tone was replaced by shock, which only annoyed Kory more.

"Why would I need to?" Kory snapped. He turned his head back a bit too quickly toward Zac. His head swam with vertigo, and when his eyes refocused he was much too close to Zac's chiseled face. "I live in the city. I went to school in the city. I work in the city. I don't need to escape."

"Well, I bet your beloved city seems a little smaller now."

"It just looks that way from up here," Kory said, pulling back from Zac's green-eyed gaze and forcing himself to look out at the tiny, retreating city between the clouds.

Even if he had to get on a plane and fly a thousand miles, Kory was not going to let Zac destroy his plan. Despite unprofessional confrontations, name-calling and hate-fucking, Kory still had a business to run.

"Didn't you ever want to get away?" Zac asked. He looked at the back of Kory's sandy-blonde head and willed him to turn back to face him. Zac had never seen Kory so flustered, not even in those few awkward moments that had followed the tryst on Zac's office floor. Zac almost felt bad, pity, something tender. But at the same time, he was relieved to see a moment of weakness in this city boy's bitchy exterior. It made Zac regret this trip a bit less. It made the thought of the coming days a little more tolerable.

Zac knew he had to follow through with this trip. He couldn't let stubbornness outweigh a smart business decision, no matter how loudly that obstinate voice in his head shouted and warned him. No matter how he feared what Baytown might hold for them.

The trip sounded too good to be true. And it probably was. But Zac knew he had to prove that to his employees, Kory and himself. Zac's logical arguments weren't convincing once everyone had seen Kory's magical internet itinerary. Zac couldn't ignore the tempting fruit Kory had dangled in front of him and his entire company. He had to prove it was rotten at its core. Unless underneath its shiny skin—against all odds—there really was something sweeter.

Kory turned back slowly from the window. "Well, I got to take a nice trip all the way out to Djorvzac Travel," he said. "Other than that I didn't have the need, the time or the money."

Zac steeled his expression and his thoughts. So much for Kory's vulnerability. "I thought you were a wildly successful businessman, or so you keep reminding me. I didn't realize your funds were so limited that they'd restrict you from travel."

"They're not." Kory's golden eyes flared. "But my 'wildly successful business' has taken up my every free moment for the past year."

"I wasn't aware that your 'wild success' was so newfound," Zac commented. "No wonder you know so many waiters."

Zac let himself enjoy the flicker of weakness in Kory's eyes. He only felt slightly guilty for taking advantage of Kory's first flight to chip away at that city cockiness and businessman bluster. When Zac had seen the flood of waifish waiters at the airport terminal, there had been little question that Kory's more modest past was not ancient history. All those city boys chatted about the diner and treated him like one of them, not some web guru hiding behind the curtain. But Zac knew better than most people that everyone has a past.

Now all those waiters were back in coach class mixed in with Zac's suburban employees. Zac winced at the thought of all these mismatched vacationers. They took up half of the large airplane's interior. And this wasn't even the entire group Kory had planned. There were other men on other flights coming from all over the country; a handful were even crossing oceans and international borders. However, this flight alone included most of Djorvzac Travel's agents and a good portion of the Whine 'n' Dine's wait staff.

Oddly enough, Zac's most enthusiastic employees had

volunteered to stay in the 'burbs and hold down the fort. After helping Kory book flights, accommodations and negotiate prices for the group he'd assembled—Mike and Danny insisted on staying behind. They claimed that they didn't need any convincing of Kory's value. And leaving the agency in their capable hands was the only way Zac was ever going to allow most of his staff to take off for Baytown Beach.

Despite the obvious excitement that bubbled throughout this plane full of gay travelers, Zac himself was dreading it. Of all places. But he couldn't make a decisive judgment if he didn't see for himself. Zac wishfully reasoned that Baytown had probably changed over the years. Hopefully the people had too.

"If you'd done your research," Kory snapped suddenly, "you would have known E-male was a young company. You also would have known that fast success in the internet world is the only way to succeed."

Kory couldn't believe this man's pompous ignorance. Zac had been lecturing Kory about business from the moment they met. But he didn't have the sense to learn a thing about the business that had his entire company on a plane to a gay resort? Kory couldn't believe it. Just like he couldn't believe that Zac had nothing to do with the business offer that had started this whole mess. If Zac hadn't made that agreement, who had? And why would he agree to get on a plane and test Kory's theory? There was something Zac wasn't telling him.

Kory stared at Zac's solid expressionless face. He let his challenge hang there between them, but Zac didn't betray a single thought. His face was completely composed, just those cold green eyes and the steely shadow of stubble.

"Forgive my inexperience with the internet world," Zac said. "I deal with the real world. The only computer research I do is for travel. I don't use a computer outside of work. Frankly, if you're not working, the internet is really just a portal for pornography and random hook-ups."

"You sound like an 80-year-old Republican campaigning against the 'gay agenda.'" Kory was exasperated. He knew his frustration was clearly displayed on his mouth, in his eyes, and written across the lines of his forehead. And he didn't care. He had his suspicions that his outward displays and eruptions had their subterranean effects on the stone bedrock of Zac Djorvzac.

"Well, if there were a 'gay agenda,' I'm fairly certain I would be against it," Zac replied. "It sounds like a bad porn movie...or a dating web site."

"Touché," Kory said. The jab was so quick and unexpected— almost funny, almost human. Kory couldn't manage to remain insulted. The bitchy remark actually brought Kory out of his state of anger a bit. Perhaps Zac Djorvzac was a little normal after all. Kory thought he saw a glint in those emerald eyes. "Look at you. You're smiling without smiling."

"That's always been my best feature," Zac said without lifting the corners of his mouth a single millimeter. "By the way, you stopped hyperventilating."

The landing was worse than the takeoff for Kory. No matter how Zac had tricked him out of his previous panic, there was no distracting Kory from this rapid plummet. It was like the horrifying plunge of a roller coaster after the dull dread of its ascent— unavoidable and even worse than expected. But Kory kept his face blank and stared straight ahead, because he knew Zac was watching him. He only hoped that Zac didn't notice the white-knuckled grip he had on the armrests.

As soon as Kory stepped from the plane, he was even more overwhelmed. He had expected to fall down to kiss the solid ground. But Baytown literally took his breath away. The heat was like hyperventilating all over again. Kory had never experienced anything like it.

It's not as if he'd never left the city before. He'd been on trips in cars, buses and trains. He'd just never been 30,000 feet above the planet. And he had never emerged from any mode of transportation to be smacked in the face with 100-degree heat and views of palm-tree jungles encroaching on all manmade structures.

Everyone else appeared to be having a grand old time. The

happy travelers poured into shuttles, piled their luggage in taxis and headed gleefully toward the destination Kory had planned for them. But what truly disoriented Kory more than anything—more than the heat or the flight or the landscape—was Zac Djorvzac.

This was supposed to be Kory's ultimate plan. He was going to prove himself right and prove Zac to be the uptight, controlling jerk he really was. Instead Zac sat casually poised on the bench seat of the airport shuttle bus. His left ankle was propped loosely on his opposite knee. One arm stretched out across the seat back as if there were an invisible boyfriend sitting next to him. His linen shirt fluttered in the humid breeze, and a patch of chest hair poked from the undone top button.

Kory thought he'd be throwing Zac out of his element by forcing him to leave the suburbs and that god-awful business park. It was all part of the plan. Now Zac looked almost relaxed. It was as if his brow had smoothed and he had gotten instantly one shade tanner when he stepped off the plane. And when he caught Kory staring, he almost smiled. What the hell was going on here?

"You don't look like you're having fun yet," Zac called out from across the shuttle. "Don't tell me you've never been on a bus before either?"

"Funny," Kory said flatly. "My ears just haven't popped yet, thank you very much."

"Hey, Kory!" Jeff screamed from the back of the bus. "This is totally tropical!"

The entire shuttle bus roared with applause and cheers. Kory tried to look smug in light of the early praise. Despite sitting there sweating literally and figuratively, Kory tried to take pride in the fact that the group thought his trip was working out so far. However, he also knew they weren't technically even off airport property yet.

Kory looked back at the motley troupe. Jeff was stretched across burbboy Jon's lap in a black tank top and a dog collar. But his all-American boyfriend and the buttoned-up travel boys in their plaid shirts and khaki shorts didn't seem to mind. They even joined Jeff in a round of "Ninety-nine Bottles of Beer on the Wall" when he insisted.

At least it wasn't "The Wheels on the Bus," Kory thought. He noticed Zac wasn't singing along. Maybe he wasn't quite that relaxed. Kory tried to stop noticing what Zac Djorvzac was doing or not doing. Kory just stared out the window at the palm trees whizzing by and tried to focus on not getting carsick.

Cabana Boy was not a boy or a cabana. It was an enormous luxury resort that spilled onto a private beach and used its ridiculous name to ensure that only half-naked gay men booked rooms there. The many thatch-roofed buildings were connected to the main lodge with cobbled pathways, tropical gardens and gurgling fountains. The entire back of the resort opened to the outdoors and a panoramic ocean view. Seamlessly, the lobby turned into a patio, which turned into a polished dance floor, which turned into an ornately tiled poolside just step from the beach. And in two weeks, the entire property would turn into the enormous Beach Ball circuit party.

But for now, from the front, Cabana Boy looked like an intimate village of quaint cottages, lush gardens and a central main lodge hidden in some magical mountainside jungle. From the back, it was one huge entertainment complex, with tiki bars and disco balls and a hi-tech lighting and sound system in the DJ booth.

Business in front, party in the back. Isn't that what they say about mullet haircuts? Kory thought to himself as he lugged his bag to his little hut on the edge of the property.

Under that thatched roof, however, there was nothing hut-like about it. It was all mahogany and marble. A ridiculously large pedestal bed was perched under a whirring ceiling fan with blades shaped like banana leaves. There was a whirlpool tub in the bathroom and fresh flowers, fruit and champagne laid out on the ornate side table.

Kory had to hand it to Mike and Danny. They had really done their part for him. Not only had they made Kory's vision of this trip a reality with all the details of reservations and rates, they had also made sure he had the absolute best. While everyone else was happy to pay for coach-class airfare and the more modest accommodations in the main lodge, Kory was traveling in five-star luxury.

He stepped out his back door into a private garden nook surrounded by flowering vines growing over a stone wall. Finally he was able to take a deep breath. This really was relaxing. And the weather here was tempered by the jungle shade and the ocean breeze. Kory sat in the cushioned chaise and thought that this all might actually work out. In fact, he might even be able to enjoy himself.

"Pretty nice accommodations," Zac remarked from over the chest-high wall.

Kory jumped straight out of his seat. He must have looked like one of those cartoon characters leaping vertically in fright. "What are you doing here?"

"This is my cabin," Zac answered, leaning over the wall to evaluate. "Looks like we have abutting patios. Almost identical, but yours has a better view."

"I wouldn't say that looking into my back window was such a bad view."

"My point," Zac stammered and leaned back from the wall, "was that with rooms like these and an entire city of gay men beyond the gates, I'm not sure anyone needs the 'benefits' of group travel. Kind of makes you want to sit back and relax all by yourself."

"Which is what I was trying to do myself before you decided to be so friendly," Kory retorted. "I suppose if someone had an incredibly antisocial disorder, he could take this trip just for the price break. But there are more 'benefits' than that. See for yourself."

Kory reached into his pocket and produced a slip of paper about the size of a Chinese cookie's fortune. Kory had handed these out to the other travelers as the exited the shuttle and left additional copies at the front desk for latecomers. He had purposely left Zac out. But he was asking for it now.

"Is this your phone number?" Zac asked as he took the slip from Kory.

"Almost as good. It's the E-male vacation passcode."

Kory had no intention of leaving this trip's success up to chance and the whims of gay party boys. E-male had made him accustomed to much more control than that. He knew how to program success. Everyone on the trip received this unique passcode, which allowed them entrance into the exclusive E-male vacation section of the site. They could chat, flirt, exchange tips, make plans and share their vacation experiences. More importantly, Kory could orchestrate the entire thing and monitor the trip's success.

"The miracle of wireless internet access means people never have to unplug their online lives back home," Kory pointed out. "Don't tell me a workaholic like you left your computer at the office."

Kory left Zac standing there holding the slip of paper and went inside to get started. He shoved aside the champagne welcome basket, powered up his computer and entered E-male through his own secret administrative backdoor. The entire world of E-male opened up on his screen, and Kory felt suddenly at ease. The other men were already logging on. The vacation section of the site had two dozen members online.

trvlr44: Let's hit the beach.
beachboy: string bikini, here I come.
freEasy: bikini? Hell, I'm going to the
nude section of the beach.
beachboy: NUDE??! Where is that?
freEasy: All the way south beyond the palm grove.
beachboy: Count me in!
clthswhore: Well, I hitting the shops in town. some of
us still wear clothes!
vaca4me: Lol. I'll join you.
clthswhore: yeah, clothes can come off later.
lushlife: Anyone for drinks?
Sporty1: Parasailing?
delish: Lunch?
trvlr44: This is great! So many choices.

so many men.
vaca4me: This is the way to travel!
delish: Thank god for Kory!
freEasy: I'll second that.
Sporty1: me too...

Kory hadn't touched a single key on his computer. He hadn't had to do a thing. This was working. It was really, really working. He only hoped that Zac was sitting in front of his computer right now watching his own employees and everyone else praise Kory's hard work. But Kory figured Zac was probably still struggling with the passcode on the login page.

Kory's work was far from over. He closed his computer and headed out to explore the rest of Baytown Beach. He walked through the gardens, past the towering bamboo gates at Cabana Boy's entrance and suddenly found himself smack dab in the middle of a bustling and glittering gay strip.

Baytown Beach was a like gay Las Vegas. But instead of casinos, the main drag was lined with funky bars, leather stores, couture boutiques and sex shops. It pulsed with lights and lust, as if the entire town was its own nightclub despite the high burning sun. Baytown made the city Kory lived in look like it suffered from a severe outbreak of heterosexuality. Everywhere he looked there were the kind of gay men he thought only lived in porn movies and Tom of Finland drawings.

Tan muscles, short shorts, mesh tank tops and even sarongs—pumped-up homosexuality and exposed skin were the norm. Kory felt like a vampire stranded in paradise and suffering from third-degree sunburn. He was all black jeans and funky belt buckle. His tee shirt seemed much too vintage amid the glam and glitter. He felt absurd in his urban-hipster gear that was off by several degrees latitude.

As he tried to blend in or disappear, Kory took note of the trendiest restaurants, clubs and hotspots to recommend to the E-male travel group. His pale legs were sweating furiously under his dark denim as he walked down the street. He desperately needed to change, but the last thing he wanted to do was expose his thin white arms and legs. It looked like he'd need a tanning bed and a steroid habit to fit in around here.

Kory may have planned the perfect trip for all these men, but he hadn't really taken himself into consideration. As usual, he was matchmaking with little regard for what would match him, and now cupid was sweating his ass off.

At the corner, Kory ran into a crowd that he couldn't simply skirt with his head down. There was a small plaza paved in coral and stone. There were benches and pedestals, and every surface was covered in shirtless, glistening men. Dance music emanated from somewhere, lending a throbbing soundtrack to the entire scene. And everyone was dancing—if that's what one would call it.

The men stood on benches, low walls and platforms that must have been built with this odd activity in mind. They were not in pairs. Each man stood alone, gyrating toward the crowd, lifting his hands above his head, bending and moving as if the entire bouncing audience were his dance partner. Kory felt as if he were simultaneously receiving a dozen lap dances.

At the center of it all, monopolizing the largest center stage and most of the attention was a single dancer. His jet-black Caesar cut was pasted to his scalp with gel. His aquamarine eyes had to be contact lenses. And his lean muscles looked stretched and sinewy.

He was a middle-aged man who worked out too much and ate too little. His tan bordered on leathery, and his eyebrows were too perfectly symmetrical. His severe bone structure was emphasized by what could only be very expensive plastic surgery. Every feature was just a bit too tight, buffed and glowing. However, somehow he pulled off handsome charisma as if none of this took any effort at all.

He seemed to regard all the other men there as his backup dancers. Boys half his age flocked around him and copied his dance moves. He ignored muscled go-go dancers as if he were looking right through them, and more importantly, they appeared deeply hurt by it. Everyone seemed to want his attention. They struggled to place themselves in the spotlight of his fake blue eyes.

When that electric gaze picked Kory out of the crowd, he felt like an escaped convict caught in a searchlight. It was the final confirmation that he truly stuck out of the crowd here like a black-clad and very pale sore thumb. But when the featured dancer jumped from center stage and walked toward Kory, he knew he was in more trouble than any prisoner. The crowd parted like a blasphemous miracle as the man approached Kory. Each step was in time to the music's pulse.

"I'm Trevor," he said. He struck a pose instead of extending his hand for introductions. "I haven't seen you around here before. And I've seen everything."

"Kory," was all Kory could say.

"Well, I like the look, Kory," Trevor said. "But you're going to need something a little less punk-rock to dance at Beach Ball. And I expect you to save a dance for me."

"I don't dance," Kory said. He wasn't much for conversation under the circumstances. It seemed Trevor had moved the main show from the stage to right in front of Kory. The men around them continued to bounce to the beat, but Kory could tell all ears were on him. And unlike Trevor, Kory did not like being the center of attention.

"I bet I could teach you some moves," Trevor said suggestively. He started to shimmy and sway, returning to the pull of center stage. "I'll see you around, Kory. You won't be able to miss me."

As Trevor returned to the stage and all eyes followed, Kory slipped from the crowd as quickly and quietly as he could. Punk-rock! Kory thought. He knew he was a little too urban to fit in, but he was definitely not "punk-rock." Imagining just how hilarious Jeff would find this whole scene, Kory ducked into the nearest clothing store.

CHAPTER 6

beachboy: You were right man. no bathing suit required!

freEasy: it was fun. i knew waiters were good at taking orders.

beachboy: We know how to serve. lol.

freEasy: and travel agents know how to get around!

trvlr44: Hey, boys, get a private room. we all saw it on the beach today.

lushlife: and we have piña coladas to plan

beachboy: Cheers, fellas!

freEasy: See you there.

clthswhore: This time with clothes on I hope!

Zac was not necessarily thrilled with E-male so far. Since logging on earlier that day, he had watched members in the vacation chat room introduce themselves, arrange excursions and make dates. These were all things that would presumably spell success for the entire trip. But that's not what annoyed Zac.

The thing that was driving him absolutely crazy about this blinking computer screen was that he could not pull himself away from it. He had not typed a single keystroke. However, he had read every single word. He had watched every single member enter and leave.

Zac was desperately trying to figure out who was who online and in real life. Which one of his employees knew the ins and outs of Baytown's leather scene a bit too well? Was that member proposing morning cocktails and massages someone who worked for Zac, or one of those waiters, or another traveler he'd never met? And more than anything else, Zac wondered if Kory Miles was hiding behind one of these suggestive screen names.

Zac had seen the praise the online members had heaped on Kory right after entering the passcode. If he hadn't just watched Kory walk into his cabin, if he thought Kory had had time to or-chestrate it or the ability to type quickly and simultaneously on several computers—Zac would have thought that the entire scene had been fabricated. But even after he had watched Kory leave his cabin and strut down the pathway in his tight little black jeans, the praise had continued.

Zac had felt a slight twinge of regret at being proven wrong so unanimously, right there on screen for everyone to see. But he still wasn't convinced that this formula would work every time. All this demonstrated was that his employees could be turned into vacation-crazed party boys. And that was the exact opposite of what Zac wanted.

He made money from party boys. He didn't employ them. He hadn't built his company on the "No Dancing. No Dating. No Drama." rules to throw it all away for a couple weeks min-gling with waiters and club kids.

Glued to that site for hours, Zac realized that there was a lot more at stake than who was right and who was wrong. E-male wasn't just a dating web site. It wasn't just a tool for orches-trating vacations or organizing an afternoon snorkeling trip. It was an addictive, mysterious portal that had transported Zac and his entire company to a very dangerous place—mentally and physically.

His employees were letting loose. They were using secret identities and online anonymity to break every rule in Zac's book. What's more, they were using the virtual world of E-male to change their real world. They weren't just chatting aimlessly. They were actually showing up at nude beaches. They were flirting and mingling and hosting blender parties in their rooms. These were not the men Zac had hired. And he seriously worried that they would be very different men when they returned to the cubicles of Djorvzac Travel.

Zac's own mental state wasn't much better. He wasn't dabbling in the mind-altering drug of E-male. But he also hadn't left his cabin since talking to Kory. It wasn't just the disturbing distraction of the chat room. It was everything outside this deluxe room, too. His first breath of humid tropical air had reminded him how much he loved this weather, how much he had loved this place. But panic had immediately followed that moment of familiarity and relaxation. Because no matter how soft the breeze, how glorious the sun or how lulling the sound of the surf—Zac knew deep inside that this place was not good for him.

It had been over ten years. And Zac had grown much more than a decade in that time. He was not the same confused young man who had gotten on a plane and never looked back. But here he was again. And he refused to let this place win. He would not take a single step backward.

Zac slammed his laptop shut and walked straight out the cabin door. E-male may be turning his employees into children. The entire town may be overrun with immature testosterone-fueled "boiz." But Baytown was not going to get the best of Zac Djorvzac this time. He was going to face it like the man he had become.

The long, slow sunset over the ocean had already started by the time Zac emerged from his solitude and joined the others on Cabana Boy's huge outdoor patio. Rainbows of paper lanterns swayed in the breeze and candles flickered around the pool. The soft light seeped across the beach toward the oranges and blues of the setting sun.

Zac arrived to tipsy cheers from his employees—not exactly the reception he received each morning at the agency. He smiled and waved and settled into the end of one of the many picnic tables that had been placed along the edge of the beach. He had known about the luau the resort was throwing to welcome the group. It was one of the many perks Kory had prepackaged, and Zac had heard plenty about it in the chat room all afternoon. He was just surprised that grown men who had traveled from far and wide could get so excited about free pork. But he was even more surprised to look around and see the group assembled there. There must have been 40 men all gathered to kick off this crazy trip. And whether Zac liked it or not, he was along for the ride.

Everyone applauded and whistled as the staff carried out enormous platters of beautifully arranged fruits and vegetables and a roasted pig on a spit. Of course it helped that the servers were tan young musclemen wearing only grass skirts. As all eyes followed the parade of flesh—barbecued and exposed—across the torch-lit beach, Zac's attention was drawn back toward the resort. Beyond the bars and disco balls, entering along one side of the long pool, was the last member of the party to arrive.

Zac almost didn't recognize Kory. Gone were the Euro jeans and drab colors. Bright yellow shorts with low square-cut pockets reached the bottom edge of his downy knees. A slim baby-blue tank top clung to his taut torso, and an open white shirt billowed around him as he walked.

When their eyes met, Kory shoved his hands in his pockets self-consciously, halting the fluttering of his shirt around him. Zac noticed the nervous move and did his smiling-without-smiling thing. The brighter colors suited Kory. The shorts made his sandy bangs look lighter, as if he'd spent the day in the sun instead of the downtown shops. The scoop neck of the tank emphasized his lean build. Zac could see the ridge of muscle that bisected Kory's chest. And there was something about the light that made his eyes even more golden as he approached the table.

"Someone's been shopping," Zac remarked.

"It's just one of the many exciting activities you can learn about on the exclusive E-male vacation site," Kory said in his pseudo-friendly salesman voice as he took a seat across the picnic table from Zac.

"So I saw," Zac said, trying not to stare at that crescent of bare skin between Kory's tank top and collarbones. "Although, shopping was not exactly the most exciting 'activity' being discussed on there."

"Well, I suppose for those of us who came with our own safari wardrobe there were more titillating things to chat about."

"It's linen," Zac said, which was true, but not a very good comeback. He did feel a little odd in the thin gauzy material and flowing pant legs. He knew there was nothing wrong with an off-white button-up shirt and tan pants. Linen was a completely casual yet appropriate option for this weather. Zac now regretted his moments of admiration for Kory's new look. If only he could see what I used to wear around here, Zac thought.

The rest of the group took plates of food from the scantily clad servers and chatted with their newfound travel companions as the sun dipped into the ocean. The half-dozen picnic tables were a grand smorgasbord of indulgence of all kinds. Food, drink and conversation passed from one guest to another. Excitement floated in the air around them. This truly seemed like a communal kickoff to the next two weeks.

"Seriously," Zac said, passing platters along the table, "this is nice. Aside from the raucous behavior and lapses in moral judgment being displayed in that chat room of yours, I'd say you're off to a fairly successful start."

"Well, thank you," Kory sad looking genuinely appreciative for the first time since Zac had met him. Of course, it's not as if Zac had gone out of his way to make things work out. "But I couldn't have done this without your agency. That's the point. It's a partnership, or it's supposed to be."

"Well, I guess we're on this safari together then," Zac said.

"OK, honestly you don't look like you're on safari," Kory said. "Not unless you put on one of those little helmets."

Before either of them could laugh, the tables erupted yet again in cheers as the hula-boy servers started shaking their hips and carrying out trays of mai tais and scorpion bowls. Their balancing act was admirable, but Zac could detect a distinct expression of displeasure on Kory's face.

"Could I see a wine list?" Kory asked one of the waiters, whose swiveling hips were shaking dried grass in his face.

"You really are out of your element, aren't you?" Zac couldn't help pointing out the obvious. Kory's cute little outfit didn't change the fact that he was city boy through and through. He must have really believed in this experiment to put himself through all this.

"That has nothing to do with it," Kory insisted as the hula dancer presented a wine list printed on something that looked like a palm frond. "Just look at all this fruity food, barbecue sauce and tropical whatchamacallits. If you think I'm dumping more sweet syrupy flavors on top of it with those cocktails, you've got another thing coming. I think I'll have the dry Riesling."

"Make that two. Heck, make it a bottle," Zac said to the hula waiter. "So you know about wine, Mr. Miles?"

"As you so gracefully noted," Kory answered, "it wasn't so long ago that I was a waiter. Besides, matching food and wine isn't that different than matching men. Finding complementary tastes and creating the perfect combination. It's a talent I have."

"So I'm learning."

The wine arrived and Zac watched Kory do the swirl, sniff and sip routine. It was a cute affectation, but there might have been something to it all. Because Kory was right. The wine was the perfect balance. Acidity and sweetness danced on Zac's tongue, mingling with the flavors of the food and somehow making them fuller.

They ate and drank as conversation bubbled along the tables and night settled in. The sun sank completely beneath the waves. Other guests and Baytown travelers started filling the seats at the tiki bars and mingling along the pool. There was a tranquil energy here that almost contradicted itself. Baytown was at once a laid-back tropical destination and an incomparable party town. It was as if at any moment you could break into dance or fall asleep in a hammock. Like the Riesling, it seemed to be the perfect balance.

It could have just been the wine, but Zac felt himself relax. Perhaps he simply let himself relax. The weather was perfect. The scene was beautiful. And so far nothing disastrous had happened. Maybe Zac had outgrown the stage where Baytown could consume him. Maybe there was nothing to worry about here. It was possible that he could get through these two weeks without losing his employees, his composure or his mind. Everyone has a past, Zac reminded himself, that doesn't mean it has to come back to haunt me.

"Well, look who came back from the dead!"

Zac looked up to see that very past approaching. From over Kory's shoulder, Zac could see the one and only Trevor—no last name required. Zac couldn't believe it. Although this exact encounter was what he had been dreading since agreeing to return to Baytown Beach, it seemed impossible. How could Trevor still be here? How could he appear out of the blue to make a grand entrance back into Zac's life? It was like watching the ghost of his past floating toward him. But Trevor was much too real and much too ominous to be a simple specter.

He was a bit worse for the wear, but he still had that cocky saunter, and he still commanded the attention of every set of eyes present. The entire group at dinner turned to see him in his skinny-strapped tank as he arrived at Zac and Kory's end of the picnic table and leaned forward, placing his hands deliberately on the table so his triceps were on maximum display.

"Trevor," Zac said cordially, as if he were greeting an old business associate. However, the business Trevor and Zac had gotten up to was the least professional and least successful venture of his life. And he'd certainly never made any money from it. In fact, that phase his life had nearly bankrupted him, or killed him.

"My man, Z!" Trevor screeched. "I thought you'd been kidnapped. Or maybe you just ran away."

"I abducted myself," Zac answered ambiguously. "It was

against my will, but absolutely necessary. I see you're still here."

"I woke up and you were gone," Trevor said loudly and suggestively. "I've just been waiting for you to get back."

"You should have held your breath."

"You two know each other?" Kory asked in disbelief. People pretended to go on with their dinners; however, each and every eye was not-so-subtly fixed on the unfolding conversation at the far end of the table. Now that Kory was involved, this was an official main-stage event—just where Trevor wanted to be.

"Me and Z go way back," Trevor cooed.

"Unfortunately," Zac butted in before Trevor could say too much. "How do you two know one another?"

"We just ran into each other today," Kory said. "We do not 'go way back.'" He looked skeptically at Zac, past Trevor's flexed tan arms. It was obvious that any moment of mutual comfort or camaraderie he and Zac might have shared had been instantly destroyed.

"Yes, little Kory was admiring my dancing, and I was admiring his rock-and-roll fashion sense," Trevor said. "Looks like you took my advice. I like the makeover, sweetheart. Very Pretty Woman. Did daddy let you use his charge card?"

"Kory and I are business partners," Zac insisted. Again, it was best to cut Trevor off before he took things too far. Zac knew all too well what happened when Trevor started to hog the spotlight.

"Is that what they're calling it now?" Trevor said, fixing his electric-blue eyes on Kory predatorily.

"More like a technological consultant," Kory tried to clarify.

"Ooo," Trevor squealed. "Sounds very formal...and dirty. Maybe I should get a consultant if they all look as pretty as you. I always thought they were old men in cheap suits or frigid bitches in bad pumps. What are you two consulting on, honey?"

"I own E-male," Kory said a little defensively, "the dating web site."

"I've actually heard of it," Trevor said. "This just keeps getting better, doesn't it, Z? A dating-web-site, technological-consultant business partner. You always did like a mouthful."

"That's enough, Trevor," Zac said firmly. "We're not kids

anymore. And this is not a game."

"Oh how you forget," Trevor snapped, leaning in even closer without lowering his voice at all. "This is all a game. You just lost. But now you're back for another round. So, Kory, if you want to be with a winner—someone who never quit—maybe you and I can talk business. I've always wanted to get into the internet. Now it's looking like an even more attractive investment. Let me know if you ever want to consult."

"Trevor, what are you doing here?" Zac insisted.

"You've been away far too long, Z. Did you forget that it's almost Beach Ball? And did you forget who the belle of the Beach Ball is?"

"No, Trevor," Zac corrected. "I meant, what are you doing at Cabana Boy two weeks before it starts?"

"You're asking me that?" Trevor snapped. He stood straight up as if making some kingly proclamation for all to hear. "I am Baytown. I might not stay in this rathole, but I can go wherever I like. You're the one who doesn't belong here anymore, Mr. Travel Agent. Yes, I know what you do out there in the middle of nowhere. Making other people's travel plans while you just sit there and rot. Making their dreams come true and forgetting you ever had any. You and your little consultant here seem to have more in common than you know. You're perfect for each other.

"Just don't think you can burst back into my dream life after all these years. 'Cause I've made it all come true, without any help from you. I don't need some old man trying to relive his past. I wouldn't want to have to prove it to you all over again. That would just be too much fun. Like the good old days."

"There were no good old days." Zac said bitterly. He took a sip of wine, but it suddenly seemed sour.

"I thought you quit drinking?" Trevor remarked cattily.

"I just quit doing body shots," Zac said, pushing the wineglass away from him.

"That's too bad," Trevor said. "It was your specialty."

"Things change, Trevor," Zac said, looking at this overly preserved remnant of his past with disgust. Trevor was like a poisonous flower that had been pressed between the pages of a book. "Well, most things do. If you'll excuse me, I saw more than enough of the Trevor show ten years ago. I don't need an encore."

Zac got up from the table and walked away without looking back. That's exactly what he thought he had done to Baytown a decade earlier. He never should have allowed himself to revisit ancient history. He be damned if he let it repeat itself. Zac would have to fix this mess later. Everyone had already heard too much. Too many questions had been raised. Too much damage had been done. So he left Trevor there before the table to do what he would. Zac knew taking away Trevor's audience was the only way to disarm him.

"You always knew how to make a dramatic exit," Trevor called out after Zac as he walked back into the resort. Zac didn't glance back.

Kory was relieved to see that the show was apparently over. Trevor retreated from the tables as if to demonstrate that his swishing exit could be even more dramatic than Zac's. He left Kory and the group of men there in virtual silence as he joined his awaiting fan club at the tiki bars and dance floor.

Kory stared at his plate and made a concerted effort to push the remaining food around. Fortunately, every other man at the dinner seemed to be doing the same thing. No one wanted to address whatever had just happened. And what the hell did just happen? Kory thought.

Whatever confused thoughts ran through all their heads, it wasn't long before the momentum of the tropical night took over. Curious questions were whispered. Shoulders were shrugged. Multiple answer of "I don't know," "Don't ask me," and "This is going to be one hell of a trip" were offered up with absolutely no resolution. No one dared ask Kory. It was probably the look of sheer bewilderment on his face that let them know he had no answers to offer.

As the last scraps of food were pushed aside and the picnic tables were carried away, conversation and cocktails resumed their flow. Music started. Lights went down and strobe lights came on. Confrontation forgotten, dinner easily turned to disco as the men stepped from the beach to the dance floor beyond the pool. The other resort guests, men from beyond its bamboo gates and Trevor's troupe of gyrators quickly transformed the evening into a full-fledged nightclub.

Kory stood with the other members of his motley travel group along the edge of the pool and dance floor as they assimilated into the scene. Everyone already seemed to know everyone else. The Steve-Rick-Chris-Andy crowd from Djorvzac Travel was there. Jeff and Jon headed up the city boys with names like 'Topher, Rory and Armin. Kory knew most of them. He had introduced some of them in person or secretly online. But for the most part, they had taken care of introductions themselves. Kory had set up this trip and chosen its travelers carefully, creating the custom E-male portal to offer these men the activities and interaction they needed to make the most of this trip. And that's just what they were doing.

"This is one wild and crazy trip!" Jeff said.

"Is that a good thing?" Kory asked too seriously.

"Of course it is," Jon clarified in a rare burst of speech. He was a shorter, quieter handsome brunette. Just the kind of man Jeff needed to balance him out. That's why Kory had chosen him. "We're having a great time."

"As long as Zac doesn't bring the wrath of Queen Baytown upon us," Jeff said, looking toward the front of the dance floor where Trevor and his boys reigned supreme. "What's that all about? And how the hell do you know him?"

"I don't know him. I just ran into him today in town," Kory insisted. "I don't know what's going on. But he certainly is intimidating."

"Oh, you should be intimidated," Steve, one of the travel agents, chimed in. "These boys take their circuit parties very, very seriously. And whoever this Trevor is, he seems to take it way beyond serious."

"You get between them and the spotlight and you could lose a limb," another travel guy added.

"They do look pretty dangerous," Armin the waiter said,

looking toward the stage-like risers where Trevor and his backup dancers twisted and thrust in shirtless, muscled abandon.

"Oh, this is nothing," travel Chris said. "This is just rehearsal for Beach Ball."

"Yeah they're just doing their stretches up there now," Andy added. "Any minute now their preseason starts."

"Their what?" Rory asked.

"The nightly box dance-off."

"You've got to be kidding," 'Topher scoffed. "Box dancing is a sport now?"

"It's a vicious competition," Rick corrected. "Trust us; we've been booking circuit party trips for years. It's not about dancing. It's about competing for the center of the circuit's attention. Seems the best way to do that is to shake your hips in a pair of tiny underwear."

"Unbelievable," Kory said.

"Don't worry," Steve told him. "Just stay out of their way. You don't have to box dance."

"I hope not. I step on my own feet whenever I try to dance at all," Kory said. "All I need is a box to fall off." Kory laughed at himself, and the others all joined in.

"You'd be stepping on their toes if you even tried," Andy said. "As long as we all stay down here on the dance floor, we should be out of harm's way. Let's dance, you guys."

Some of the men paired up and hit the floor. Others hung in groups and bounced to the beat. Kory stood back and watched his work unfold. Whatever discomfort Trevor had created was slowly dissipating as these men let the tropical rhythm of night take over.

Despite the drama, Kory had to admit that things were going well. The men were all having fun. Zac was deliciously uncomfortable. And the new beachwear had gone a long way to making Kory feel more at ease, both in terms of temperature and local fashion mores. The vacationers were complimenting Kory's trip as much as his outfit. What more could a gay boy ask for?

But something just felt wrong about this situation. Seeing Zac shocked and then horrified was not as thrilling as it should have been. Watching him walk away stabbed at Kory, no matter how he thought he wanted to revel in Zac's defeat. This tenuous victory only made Kory worry more that everything could fall apart. Trevor was trouble with a capital "TR." And however he knew Zac, whatever past they shared—Kory was not about to let this stone-age rivalry interfere with the success of the trip. It would be just like Zac to throw some scandalous wrench into Kory's plan and bring the whole thing crashing down around them. If Trevor and his topless posse managed to intimidate the travelers or somehow ruin Beach Ball for all these men, the initial success of Kory's trip would be erased from their minds.

As if on cue, the music got louder, the spotlights swept over the crowd, and the box dancing began in earnest. Glistening men in impossibly small swimsuits or underwear or shorts all writhed at the front of the dance floor. There were several levels of risers and boxes there that led to the highest, center box. Without any formal direction or prompting, the men cycled through the multilevel course, moving fluidly from lower platforms to higher perches, seeking that central peak in the spotlight as the crowd cheered them on.

The applause seemed to dictate the dance as much as the beat. A muscleman would linger at the apex, swinging his hips and flexing his abs as the audience whistled and clapped. Then the cheers and attention would shift to another shiny torso, and that man's ascent would culminate as the first dancer stepped down in rank. Man after man, they climbed and fell, each taking his turn at the top before admitting he didn't belong there.

Kory noticed Trevor swaying at the sidelines. He was practically licking his chops in expectation, just waiting to go in for the kill. All these other dancers were his sheep. He was about to pounce. But then the smooth progression of tan flesh was interrupted. From the look on Trevor's face, this was not part of the plan. A new dancer entered the fray. He didn't look like the others, and he didn't follow their drone-like dance.

Most of the dancers were much alike—buffed tan muscles without a strand of body hair; bleach-blond crew cuts and spiky do's; sexy sneers that could easily be mistaken for half-lidded disinterest.

This man was different. He had olive skin that wasn't burnt or bronzed. Its glow was natural, but paled pleasantly compared to burnished lacquer on these boys. His torso was outlined perfectly with dark hair—fanning across his wide pecs, bisecting his stomach, spreading out along each defined abdominal muscle.

He was wearing square-cut purple trunks that framed his hips and broad thighs—not to mention cupping the significant bubble of his bulge. Most dramatically, his face was hidden completely by a multicolored feather mask that started at his upper lip and reached upward above the top of his head with bright plumage.

He entered the dance floor with a flourish. He spun to the beat. He leapt from risers to boxes with no regard to the assembly-line efficiency of the other dancers' progression. He bent and swayed as if a wave were passing through every muscle of that thick manly torso. And he ran his own hands along his body in a way that made each man in the room understand what it must be like to touch him.

Near the top of the box-dance ascent, he paused. He raised one muscled arm straight up, turning his face into the bulge of that bicep—as if he weren't watching what he was doing to himself—and ran his other hand down his torso. His fingers started at his collarbone, the edge where muscle and fur began. The motion was so confident and unhurried that it seemed he let gravity rule its course. His hand fell in slow motion—across his chest, one finger grazing a nipple, his thumb catching the flat crevice of his navel, each finger strumming strands of hair and washboard abs like a master guitarist—until his hand caught on the waistband of his tight shorts. He hooked his thumb there, tugging the band just low enough to reveal the v of his oblique muscle and the point of his hipbone. Then his entire body exploded into dance.

Cheers roared through the crowd till it seemed he was dancing to their beat alone. He bounded onto the top box without hesitation, without challenge, and he spun with his hand on his own waist—the perfect dance partner for everyone watching. They all loved him, but no one knew who this mystery dancer was. The others dancers stopped to stare. Trevor's mouth came unhinged in disbelief. Every member of the travel party hooted and hollered. But Kory knew. He looked around at his companions and marveled that they couldn't see past the disguise.

But had any of them ever seen this man with his shirt off? Had any of them ever touched that body as he now touched himself? And would anyone else here ever suspect that such a sensual and senseless act could be performed by a man like Zac Djorvzac?

Kory pushed through the crowd. He heard the song come to an end. He watched the man step and sway and sink into the depths of cheering onlookers. But as soon as the music ended, it was over. He had disappeared as quickly as he had danced into the night. If Kory hadn't known better, he would have stopped to look for a glass slipper. By the time Kory had fought the crowd, turned down a dance and a free drink, he arrived in the resort lobby moments too late. Trevor had beat him to it.

"I didn't know you'd stopped waxing," Trevor said bitterly to Zac, stopping him dead in his tracks. Zac stood there in the empty corridor, steps from the door that would have led to his escape toward his cabin. His feathered mask was in his hand. Sweat ran down his furred chest. There was no disguise to obscure his look of disgust.

"I didn't, Trevor," Zac said without humor. "Some of us just grow up."

"Yes, that was very grown up," Trevor hissed. "I don't give a shit if you are a bear now. But like you said, just remember these are not the good old days."

"Good or not, I haven't lost everything from the old days. Just in case," Zac said. "And I haven't forgotten a thing. I'm not that out of practice that you can walk all over me, Trevor. You don't own this town. And you don't own me."

"That's yet to be seen, Z." Trevor snapped. "You were my biggest disappointment. You were the one who just walked out of here, walked away from me and everything I had to offer. Your chance is over. Don't think you can pull this at Beach Ball. I've won that box dancing contest every year since you left the circuit. Don't think you can just come back and pick up where you left off without paying your dues."

"I have absolutely no intention of picking any of that up ever again."

"Then you should have known better than to show your face around here again," Trevor said ominously. "Even if you're not actually showing your face."

Kory stood in the lobby, unseen by the two men whose locked eyes prevented them from seeing anything but their rivalry. What the hell was Zac up to? Was he trying to make things worse? Was he trying to ruin everything Kory had worked for?

Whatever was going on, it was clear to Kory that there was more to Zac than his gruff businessman façade. Whatever had happened back in suburbia on Zac's office floor, whatever had convinced him to come on this trip in the first place, whatever had caused him to pull tonight's outrageous stunt—there was something unpredictable, spontaneous and possibly very dangerous about Zac Djorvzac. It was something Kory couldn't ignore, even if he had wanted to. So he stepped from the shadows, confronting the men just as Trevor turned to leave.

"Oh, yes, the consultant," Trevor said menacingly to Kory's face. "This is turning out to be one very interesting partnership, isn't it? Welcome to the real world, little Kory. You're not on the internet anymore." And then Trevor sashayed away, leaving the two men there in awkward silence.

Kory took one step toward Zac, to show him he was serious, to show him he wasn't afraid, and quite possible to get a close-up view of the sweat drying on that torso. "We've got some talking to do partner," Kory said calmly. "This safari just got a hell of a lot wilder. But at least your outfit is an improvement."

Kory looked Zac up and down, smiled despite his panic, and walked back into the night.

CHAPTER 7

delish: What a first night!
freEasy: Did you see the look on Zac's face
vaca4me: I've never seen him that pissed off.
  not even at work.
trvlr44: and that's saying something.
beachboy: Who was that Trevor guy?
clthswhore: And Kory knew him too???
lushlife: Very suspicious.
delish: What are they up to?
DoneThat: Enough with the conspiracy theory... how
  about that box dancer?
beachboy: Wow!!! Hot!!!
newbie: I thought the other guys were pretty sexy.
  But that man can move!
DoneThat: I'll be watching for him tonight.

"I'm calling a business meeting," Zac said as soon as Kory peeked his mussed head around the edge of the door.

"At dawn?" Kory asked sleepily, rubbing his eyes and hiding his body behind the door. Zac could see one naked shoulder, smooth and pale, stretching all the way to the point of Kory's collarbone where the rough-hewn slab of the door abruptly cut the view short. "Has the sun even come up?"

In answer, Zac simply pointed to the deep orange orb that was just bobbing above the horizon of palm trees.

"Well, I see you found your shirt," Kory said, waking up little by little as he stared out at Zac and the tropical morning, "and your pants."

Zac wasn't going to allow himself to be fazed by Kory's sleepy quips. He was wearing a fitted navy polo shirt and knee-length seersucker shorts. "I thought it was more appropriate for a business meeting. Perhaps you'd like to find yours."

He waited while Kory bumped around sluggishly in his cabin. Zac resisted the urge to peek through the cracked door to see exactly what was taking Kory so long to get dressed. Or to see what it looked like to watch him get dressed. When Kory finally appeared in the small garden he was wearing long cargo shorts cinched around his narrow waist with a studded belt and a sleeveless black tee shirt. Zac could see the hint of tawny down peeking from under those pale arms.

"You can't take the city completely out of the city boy," Kory said when he caught Zac sizing up his ensemble and the rest of him. "So where's the conference room for this meeting?"

"Follow me."

Kory remained fairly quiet and cooperative as he tromped after Zac along the roads and paths and twisted trails. He had only insisted on stopping once on the edge of town for a cup of black coffee. But now that they were deeper in the moist forest, the foliage was getting denser and the incline was getting steeper, and Zac could hear Kory back there huffing, obviously more out of frustration than exertion.

Zac was acutely aware of two things. One, he was divulging a lot of information to Kory simply by leading him along these hidden pathways. And two, Zac knew his ass was on display in the sung, light-blue stripes of the seersucker pattern, directly in front of Kory's face as they trudged uphill.

"The view is not getting any better," Kory said suddenly. It caught Zac completely off-guard, but he just kept forging ahead. "I can't see ten feet through this swamp."

"Technically it's a rain forest."

"So is this a science field trip or a business meeting?" Kory asked. "Forgive me if I'm a little confused."

"We're almost there."

Zac wasn't going to waste his time explaining now. He knew there was plenty more explaining to do soon. He hadn't slept all night. Instead, he had worried. But at least he had figured some things out. And he knew that telling Kory was the only responsible thing to do. After all, if Zac's theory was right, Kory was just as involved in this as Zac himself was.

Besides, who else could he tell? Kory was the only one who might believe what was going on. He was the only one who might just understand. Kory was the only one who had recognized Zac shirtless last night. He was the only one left in Zac's life who might be able to envision his past or guess what Trevor was capable of.

Suddenly, they emerged from the gray bark and tangled vines onto the exposed ridge Zac knew was hidden up here. It was a crack in the shadowed forest. The wide ledge had solid green above and below. It was a bare shelf that brought the pair out of darkness and into a bright morning vista. The entire city and sea was spread out before their secret perch. Green, blue and glitter. And there they were, hidden on a smile etched in a hillside.

"Wow," Kory said before he could pretend to be unimpressed.

"Welcome to your conference room, Mr. Miles."

"I don't know whether I should ask why we're here or how you knew this was here," Kory said suspiciously. He looked over at Zac, momentarily ignoring the breathtaking expanse beneath them. They both had a sheen of sweat drying on their foreheads, and Kory's blonde bangs clung to his brow, making his serious expression appear softer here in this slice of morning.

"I think I can answer both questions at once," Zac said. He let the breeze blow against his skin and wash away the humidity of the forest that lingered only steps away. He held Kory's gaze and thought about how much he was about to give away. Zac hadn't seen this magnificent view for a decade, but that wasn't what was demanding his attention right now. "Trevor."

Kory was confused and exhausted and amazed all at once. Somehow Zac had dragged him all the way up here on only one cup of coffee to tell him about something, or someone, he already knew about. Clearly, there was something else Kory did not know. So he said nothing, and waited for some real answers. Seeing a flat spot on a sun-bleached boulder, he sat looking at the emerald and sapphire before him. This view, not the hike, was why Kory was out of breath, speechless. The very last thing he expected was to be confronted by the sight of a world he had never seen before.

Kory had been convinced that Baytown was a flashy and trashy strip of humidity, overpriced clothes and nightclubs. He thought the entire city had been hacked out of a swamp and fabricated to attract drugged-out gay men to an over-commercialized circuit party with corporate sponsors. It made brilliant business sense, but it didn't make Kory want to be in Baytown for any reason other than business.

He had not expected to be on the side of a tropical mountain with Zac Djorvzac looking down at colors he never even knew existed. Kory had hated Baytown from the moment he'd stepped off that plane. Just as he had hated Zac Djorvzac the moment he'd met him in his office. Why did everything look so different now?

"Trevor is the reason we're here in Baytown," Zac said. "And by the way, where you're sitting used to be my spot." He sat definitively on a rough patch of the boulder near Kory.

Kory looked skeptically over at him. Zac was all clean-cut suburbanite. The perfectly parted black hair. The ironed collar of his shirt. The tan diamond-shaped muscles of his forearms and calves poking out of his clothes. What did he know about Trevor or Baytown? And why were they halfway up a mountain together?

"As I said, partner," Kory repeated, staring straight out into the view of a beautiful Baytown beneath him, "you have a lot of explaining to do."

"Well, I didn't bring you up here for the hike alone," Zac said. He turned toward Kory and waited till his gaze forced the other man to turn away from the panorama of Baytown and beyond. When Kory's golden eyes locked with his own, Zac told him what he had convinced himself of throughout the long night before. "Trevor brought us here. You, me, E-male, Djorvzac Travel. He manipulated this entire thing."

"That doesn't really make any sense at all," Kory said. "I planned this trip, remember? So how about we start with why you were dancing in purple underwear last night."

Kory kept staring at Zac. He didn't know why he was here, why he was sitting inches from this man on a boulder early in the morning. He certainly didn't know what Zac's conspiracy theory was supposed to mean. But he was worried that this was all a trick to sabotage what he and E-male had created.

"It was a bit impulsive," Zac said. "I admit that."

"You, impulsive?" Kory scoffed. But as soon as the words were out of his mouth, he had a sudden flash back to Zac's office—that impulsive moment when Zac had grabbed him and kissed him, and then everything that had followed. Kory actually did know firsthand that Zac could have such impulsive moments and then retreat just as quickly to his guarded businessman demeanor. What was hiding beneath that?

"You don't know everything about me, Kory," Zac said simply. The statement was not defensive or angry. It was the exact opposite, almost an admission or an invitation to find out more.

"Apparently," Kory admitted, a flush rising to his cheeks. It must have been the tropical heat or the morning sun. He hoped Zac couldn't tell what he was really thinking about, or thinking those same thoughts himself. "That obviously wasn't your first time on a box. But what caused last night's particular impulse?"

"I couldn't let Trevor get the best of me again," Zac said. "He is too used to winning. And he'd already attacked me in front of you and the entire group. The damage was done."

"So dancing half naked was supposed to lessen that

damage?" Kory asked.

"It was supposed to damage Trevor right back. Nothing hurts him more than getting knocked off his dancing pedestal," Zac said bitterly. "Besides, no one was going to recognize me...except you. And I didn't actually think you would."

"I've seen your impulsive side before," Kory said before he could stop himself.

The two stared straight ahead now. They couldn't bring themselves to look each other in the eye as they danced closer and closer to the truth. They looked forward as if they were admitting their sins in a confessional to someone they couldn't see. But no partition separated the two men as they sat side by side, mere inches between them, watching Baytown wake up hundreds of feet below.

"Yes, well, perhaps it wasn't the best solution," Zac admitted. "But at the time, I just wanted to get revenge. I didn't realize until later, that revenge is exactly what this entire thing is about."

"You're not making any more sense, Zac," Kory said. "I don't understand what you think Trevor has to do with all this. It seems to me that you're just causing more trouble for this trip by challenging him."

"Trevor is the reason for this trip," Zac insisted. "It's the only thing that makes any sense. I didn't realize it until I calmed down and had time to put the pieces together. I know it sounds crazy, but you don't know Trevor."

"Yes, it is crazy, Zac," Kory said. "And, no, I do not know Trevor. Just how do you know him? And how do you know he has anything to do with all this?"

Kory didn't have to turn his head away from the view to detect the awkward moment. Zac had already said too much to turn back. But he hadn't said nearly enough to explain his irrational paranoid theory. Kory could sense that he was about to get a glimpse under that businessman shell of Zac's. Here in this secret place, he might just discover a few of Zac Djorvzac's secrets.

"It's been a long time," Zac said finally. "I thought it was all behind me. I thought coming here after all these years would be different, just bad memories. But Trevor will never change. He'll never be any different. I came here when I was younger," Zac continued. "And I loved Baytown—the party, the dancing, the whole tropical fantasy of it all. And it was fun, too much fun. But Trevor could never have too much. And eventually, he was just too much to take. When it was time to move on, time to leave, Trevor wouldn't. He couldn't. And he could never get over the fact that I left Baytown. That I left him."

"So after years and years, you run into him again back in your old haunt," Kory said, slowly processing the information he'd been given. He never would have pegged Zac as a young and wild Baytown boy, but it wasn't the most shocking revelation in the world. Time passes and people change. It still didn't explain all this. "What's so crazy about that? He sees you again. He's still pissed off. And he makes some bitchy comments. It sounds like pretty typical gay drama to me. I know it's against your triple-D rules, but it doesn't mean there's anything more to it. It's certainly not worth ruining this trip over."

"If Trevor has his way, he'll ruin a lot more than this trip," Zac insisted.

"Zac, honestly, you know this trip means a lot to me," Kory admitted. "The only thing that's going to ruin it is if you let some age-old grudge spiral out of control and turn into some ugly bitch-fest. So you have some skeletons in your closet—or out of the closet, as the case may be. Just leave them there. It's not a conspiracy theory."

"Kory, how did you choose Baytown for this vacation?"

"What do you mean? It's the only place to be this time of year. Beach Ball and everything," Kory said unconvincingly, sweeping his hand out across the view to indicate all that Baytown had to offer.

"You didn't know that," Zac said, pointing out the obvious. He looked Kory up and down in his summer-fied city attire. "Who told you about it?"

"E-male," Kory admitted. "I chatted with the guys on there who knew about that kind of thing."

"Exactly," Zac said as if his entire theory had just been proven.

me all what?" Kory asked, still angered and on

"Wait," Kory started, snapping his head suddenly toward Zac. "You don't think I'm part of your crazy theory, do you? That I conspired with Trevor somehow to bring you back here? That I'm some double agent? Because..."

"Kory, no," Zac interrupted. "Listen, if I didn't trust you, I wouldn't have brought you here and told you all this."

"Told me all what?" Kory asked, still angered and on edge. "That Trevor is some evil mastermind? You haven't explained a thing."

"Kory, I've got to trust you because your business is involved too," Zac said. "I know E-male is important to you or you wouldn't have done all this. I've seen E-male work. I've seen how passionate you are about it. But do you think no one else could use it against you? We've both seen what it can do."

"Just because someone on E-male mentioned Baytown to me?" Kory asked in disbelief. "I may not have known about it, but it's not like it's a big secret. Just look at this place."

"You've got to trust me too, Kory," Zac insisted. "Because I know Trevor. And because my business is involved, too. I did not send you that original offer, Kory. Honestly. I think Trevor did."

"Why?" Kory could not think of anything else to say. Zac's sudden paranoia caught Kory off-guard more than the view before him. It surprised him nearly as much as realizing Zac had a past, that there was more to him than that gruff business boss he had encountered that first day. More than the one-dimensional man Kory had assumed had made that offer, changed his mind, backed out, and then reconsidered. Since arranging this trip and convincing Zac to give it a try—no matter how begrudgingly—Kory hadn't given one more moment's thought to where that original offer from Djorvzac Travel might have really come from.

"Because playing games with other people's lives is what Trevor does," Zac answered. "You've just had a taste of it. In all these years, Trevor hasn't been able to find enough ways to waste his trust fund building himself up and knocking everyone else down."

"So you think he made me a business offer in your name,

then convinced me to bring you to Baytown, all so he could ruin your life years after you left?"

"Exactly," Zac said as if it all made perfect sense. "For starters at least. He could also ruin my company, corrupt my employees, try to buy out E-male from under you or just destroy both our reputations beyond repair."

"You've got to be kidding!" Kory almost laughed. But it wasn't funny at all. Just absolutely preposterous. "That is too elaborate and ridiculous to fathom."

"And that's exactly why he'd love it," Zac insisted. "What a fun game for a spoiled little rich boy. You would not believe how bored he can get. Especially when the rich kid isn't even a kid anymore."

"But it doesn't make any sense," Kory said. "It's just too complicated to be true."

"I know it seems that way," Zac said. "And that's what kept me up all night long. But it's like a jigsaw puzzle. Don't look at each complicated little piece and doubt they all fit together. Look at the end result—the big picture. Then deconstruct it. Work backwards.

"As soon as we got to Baytown, Trevor shows up out of the blue to humiliate me in front of everyone; he says he's heard of E-male and expresses interest in acquiring an internet company; he threatens me that he's going to destroy me all over again; he even managed to run into you earlier in the day. It's all too perfect not to fit together."

"It could all be one big coincidence," Kory offered.

"Like falling in love?" Zac countered. Suddenly the forest around them seemed quite still and silent. The city far below didn't make a single sound that reached them on their mountain. "Isn't that how you described E-male to my employees? Two people just happen to bump into each other who are completely compatible. Everything fits. It could happen, maybe. But E-male finds them for each other. What if Trevor used E-male to do the opposite?"

"What in the world do you mean?"

"He discovers E-male as an anonymous way to make

contact, get inside my company and get me back to Baytown," Zac explained. "He knows I wouldn't be able to overlook a good business opportunity, even if I hadn't made the deal myself. And he knows you wouldn't suspect an internal sabotage from your own web site. He got E-male to match up our companies, match up this trip with this location. Essentially, match me back up with Trevor. It's a match made in Hell."

"I never would have done that," Kory said "That's not what E-male is for."

"But you didn't know," Zac pointed out. "E-male just did its job. It matched Trevor up with exactly what he wanted. But that's the one part I can't figure out. There's one missing piece to this puzzle."

"And what is that?" Kory asked weakly. It was as if these dizzying heights had gone to his head. But it was the theories and absurdities swirling around him that made him faint. Kory had to admit that Zac had piqued his curiosity. It's not that Kory bought this conspiracy theory completely. It was just that Zac was so logical about each and every detail. If he was an absolute lunatic, he was a very, very logical one. And Kory wondered if he was crazy himself, because he was almost starting to believe Zac's reasoning.

"If E-male was working as well as it seemed, if it was so successful at matching people up that it could even match my past with Trevor's present, why would you agree to a complete change in your business model?" Zac asked. "Why would E-male want to partner with Djorvzac Travel if it was so successful as a dating site? How did Trevor convince you to get into the travel business?"

"He didn't," Kory said, looking away nervously as if a tiny glint of sunlight reflecting off something far below had suddenly caught his attention. It could have been a car windshield moving along the main drag or a disco ball being strung up for parties to come. Or it could have been Kory's internal panic and desire for any kind of distraction. But he didn't have any excuse or any escape. He was momentarily stranded way up here with Zac Djorvzac and his odd version of the truth. And somehow,

Kory didn't really mind. Zac's paranoid theories and past indiscretions somehow made Kory feel more at ease. His openness and admissions made Kory understand that there was a real man under the business suit. And it made Kory realize that he wasn't the only one with secrets and fears. "Trevor didn't have to. E-male is successful, a bit too successful too fast. And not everyone knew I was actually the owner. OK, no one knew. I mean, what would they think when they found out a waiter was in charge of their love lives?"

"So we both have secrets. I guess I never thought about it like that," Zac said. "But all your friends are here now. They know."

"You can thank Jeff," Kory laughed. "He worked his magic. He told them about the trip and the boys and by the time he mentioned that E-male and I had helped make it possible, they would have gone on this trip with Ann Coulter. But that's a handful of other waiters who already know me. Jeff can't convince thousands of E-male members across the country to hand over their personal lives and data to a 32-year-old diner employee. I can't give everyone a vacation to convince them of E-male's validity."

"It worked with me," Zac said, laughing.

"And all this time I thought you just liked me," Kory joked. But then he blushed and retreated to his business confession for cover. "I needed to have the legitimacy of a larger company behind me. I needed to get away from it all for a while. So I put out some feelers, just to see if there was any interest from other companies. The offer from Djorvzac—or whoever—was in the right place at the right time."

"What a coincidence," Zac said sarcastically. "Which is exactly my point. It's too much of a coincidence. Because if coincidences like these happened, who would need E-male?"

Zac left a dramatic pause hanging in the moist mountain air between them. Kory was close enough to see the fresh shave along his jaw. He could see the determined sparkle in Zac's green eyes, almost the exact color of the forest stretched around them. And for some reason, despite all his better judgment and business sense, Kory wanted to believe him. He wanted this wild theory and that wild look in Zac's gaze to be real.

"So what do we do?" Kory asked.

"First, we get back to town before anyone misses us. If we're ever going to figure this out, figure out what Trevor is trying to do—we can't let him know we suspect a thing. We've got to be smarter."

"E-male can do that," Kory said, his own technological conspiracies beginning to form in his mind, as he followed Zac back into the forest's shadows and twisted pathways.

"And this old boy has a few tricks left in his bag, too," Zac added from over his shoulder.

"So I noticed," Kory said. As soon as the innuendo left his lips, he clamped them shut. He was going to have to get a tan to cover this new tendency toward blushing. And he was going to have to stop walking so closely behind Zac's tight shorts.

"But we have to be careful, Kory," Zac said. "Trevor has the money and destructive personality it takes to be a lifelong club boy. I've never seen him lose. Not even after I left and I thought I'd gotten away. He wouldn't lose me either."

"Drama, drama, drama," Kory said as he picked his footing carefully along the root-clogged path. "That's a check for drama. And after last night's performance, dancing—check. The rules seem to be changing."

"Well, maybe if we'd stuck to the rules, we wouldn't be here," Zac said. "But sometimes I guess you have to break the rules."

"I guess," Kory agreed. "And now that your ex is back to haunt you, that's dating—check. All three Ds, Mr. Djorvzac."

"Well, not quite," Zac countered. "Ex is a strong word. It was more like we were all on one big date with the party. This whole world is my ex."

"So Trevor was never your boyfriend?" Kory asked. He tried to sound only mildly interested, just making small talk as they descended slowly back into the fantasyland that was Baytown. He didn't want to admit it, not even to himself, but the thought of Zac dating that slick, middle-aged brat made Kory squirm. Seeing how unarmed Zac could be in the man's threatening presence was bad enough. But the idea of them dating, being romantic, intimate—it went against every notion of romance Kory had. He reasoned it must be his innate Cupid, his E-male persona, cringing at a bad match. That must have been it.

"If we used that word, I never heard it over the loud music," Zac responded. "Nothing back then was that clearly defined."

"Well, I certainly never would have matched you two up," Kory said.

"From the expert, I'll take that as a compliment."

By the time Zac and Kory returned from their business summit on the mountain, the rest of the travel party had already been to the breakfast buffet, the beach, the shops, the poolside bar and the volleyball courts. It was early afternoon, and everyone was shaking sand out of his sandals and preparing to shift yet again from activity to debauchery.

"Where the hell have you been?" Jeff demanded when Kory showed his face back at Cabana Boy. Jeff was floating across the pool on an inflatable lounge complete with a cup holder and an umbrella-adorned frozen beverage. However, it appeared Jeff needed the umbrella more than his cocktail. His pale skin looked as if it might burst into flames in the tropical sun.

"Just taking care of business," Kory replied. "Looks like you're taking care of sun cancer and third-degree burns."

"Jon rubbed sun block all over," Jeff cooed filthily. "Thanks, honey buns."

"Hi, Jon," Kory called out. Jeff's little suburban boyfriend floated nearby on his own raft. His lean, sporty body looked tan and absolutely rugged next to Jeff's translucent torso. That didn't change the fact that Jon was about five-two and rarely spoke. He waved at Kory.

"What you looking at?" Jeff demanded in his best ghetto voice. "Get your eyes off my man and go get ready."

"Get ready for what?" Kory asked suspiciously. He didn't know what Jeff was up to, but Zac's speech had Kory peeking around every corner and questioning every motive. Even without a potential conspiracy, Jeff's ideas were usually suspect enough.

"God, don't you check your own E-male?" Jeff scoffed, flipping his blue bangs and slurping at his drink. "We're all going to AC's—The Arctic Circle with plenty of AC as I hear it."

"I have AC in my cabin."

"It's a personal invitation to the afternoon party on the strip," Jeff said haughtily. And Kory could just imagine who would issue such a "personal invitation." "You do want to be part of this trip's success don't you, Kory? Or maybe Trevor was right about online success not translating into real life."

"When did you...?" Kory stopped himself and smiled. "Maybe you'd like to float that theory by your online boyfriend. I'll see you both at AC's."

☆　☆　☆　☆

The Arctic Circle was right in the middle of the heat-soaked strip of Baytown. Beyond the ripples of sunlight reflecting off the pavement, beyond the buzzing neon and the steaming sidewalks—AC's was a blue sparkling oasis of ice.

Inside AC's no one would ever have known it was the middle of the afternoon. There were no windows. There were no bright lights. But there were countless blocks of ice lit from under by blue. Vertical slabs separated booths with wavy glimpses of faces beyond. Inclined ramps with troughs cut in them cooled liquor as it was poured from the top and traveled down frozen pathways to awaiting mouths at the other end. And most unbelievably, there were enormous cubes of ice standing throughout the cave of a place where dancers perched themselves to thrust and sway without a single slip.

If this was afternoon in the tropics, no one seemed to notice. They were all tucked in this tiny gay version of the North Pole. However, there was no Santa in sight. The men here were the same buffed, waxed, gyrating fools Trevor had swarming around him the night before.

Zac and Kory were bumbling through a crowd of Baytown

tourists, including people they already knew. In little more than 24 hours, it seemed every waiter and travel agent had given in to the rhythm of Baytown's beat. They were making out with each other and complete strangers. They were dancing with box boys and anyone else who came within close proximity.

It was like anarchy, or at least it seemed that way to Zac and Kory with their paranoia sensors on high. Everywhere they turned they saw things they didn't want to see. They heard things they didn't want to hear. And above it all, Trevor rotated his hips on the highest ice pinnacle like the king of some frozen underworld. The universe he had created spun below him in near-darkness.

"Trevor gave us tickets to an all-night club, members only," someone said. Zac and Kory couldn't tell if the comment was directed toward them or not. It seemed they picked up every bit of conversation as they stood side-by-side speechless in the crowd, their ears pricking up at the sound of Trevor's name.

"Trevor is big into the stock market and investment capital for internet start-ups," someone else said. "He thinks Kory should take E-male public. Or maybe Trevor will just invest in a bigger site and take gay online dating to the next level."

"Trevor says there's a huge travel market here. Why not get the travelers when they're traveling? Get to them before they even get home to think about the next vacation? Great job opportunities."

"Did you hear what Trevor said about them? Oh...My...God!"

There seemed to be spies and sabotage around every corner. At the very least, the men, friends and coworkers they had brought here seemed to look straight past them and headed directly toward the carrot Trevor was dangling before them. They were ripe for the picking. And if Trevor truly had sabotage on his mind, it wouldn't be difficult to enlist these men. They were relaxed—mentally and chemically—and open to suggestion. When the music kicked up another notch, everyone started to dance right on cue like good little puppets.

As the Arctic Circle thickened with more and more mesmerized patrons, Zac and Kory were forced together, just one more pair of travelers pressed between the blocks of ice. They looked at each other as everyone danced around them. There was nowhere to go, nowhere to run. They were the only people there on the icy blue floor not dancing. Instead, they were simply standing looking at each other, wondering what was going on around them.

Somehow, suddenly, they were not enemies. Their eyes met and seemed to communicate that sudden realization. They were not trying to prove one another wrong. Their only choice was to stand here together in the seething, frozen sea. It was almost good to have a new enemy. Whether or not it was true.

"I guess we have to dance," Zac said.

"I told you, I don't dance," Kory said as Zac began to sway effortlessly before him.

"Sometimes you don't have any choice," Zac said as he took Kory by the waist.

Kory stepped awkwardly from foot to foot, swinging his hands slowly in front of him as if he were going to clap them together in applause. Meanwhile, Zac didn't need to lift a foot as his body moved subtly to the beat. They looked at each other in their mismatched dance, locked in the odd business partnership that was getting odder by the moment.

Men danced above them on glowing icy pillars. Music pulsed through the cool air. And all around them, the men they thought they knew were letting loose and going wild. The rumors and random thoughts that Trevor had somehow planted in their vacation-softened minds spread amongst them like wildfire.

"Ladies and Gentlemen," a faceless voice bellowed from over the speakers, "or gentlemen and those who think they're ladies, welcome to the Arctic Circle. We're glad you're all here to freeze your balls off and get ready for Beach Ball! And now for your host, the Beach Ball ball-buster and the perennial champion of the world-renowned box-dancing contest—Trevor!"

An old-fashioned silver microphone appeared from the darkness above and descended slowly toward the highest ice tower, where the prince of cold reigned. Trevor was there in a pair of silver bikini briefs glistening and smirking with his bleached teeth aglow in the blue lights. He grabbed the mic like a small, petulant child's arm.

"Hello, my pets," he purred. "You need to dance better than that if you ever want to beat me! I just dare you to try. Now where is my spotlight? Over there, Mr. Spotlight. There's tonight's lucky couple."

The cone of cold light bobbed across the crowd until it froze Zac and Kory in its snow-white beam. They tried to keep dancing casually, moving stiffly with the crowd around them as if nothing out of the ordinary had happened.

"I've been waiting for you all day," Trevor screamed as they were caught in the searchlight. He glared down at Kory's stiff footwork and Zac's hulking sway. "This is just the kind of dancing expertise I'm looking for to really challenge me. Feel free to jump on stage at Beach Ball, boys!"

The crowd surged with laughter as the spotlight mercifully returned to the attention-hog atop the ice castle. Trevor began to thrust and buck with full abandon, and the crowd, of course, went wild. It was getting wilder every second.

"Now do you believe me?" Zac asked insistently, leaning close to Kory's ear to be heard above the crowd and ensure that no one else could hear them.

"It doesn't really matter," Kory said, barely moving on the dance floor because of the shock and embarrassment. "Now I hate him anyway."

They almost smiled at each other there in the midday darkness. Because they were scared. Or because they didn't know what to do. Or because they had almost told one another the truth that day somewhere between warm sunshine and cold glares. But it was really because they knew these half-truths were not enough to battle whatever they were up against.

It was a fact that Zac had come to Baytown when he was younger. It was true that Kory had kept his ownership of E-male a secret. But those things seemed so superficial compared to the hidden truths beneath. Nothing was as straightforward as it seemed on the surface. Simply calling Kory the owner of E-male was as much of an understatement as calling Zac a typical tourist in Baytown. The connections were much deeper. The truth was much more complicated. Maybe Zac was right. There could be a lot more at stake here than the success of a two-week vacation.

CHAPTER 8

DoneThat: Damn AC was so cool it was HOT!

punkid: Trevor is amazing!

newbie: I don't know how he does it all.

punkid: He makes me want to stay here forever.

beachboy: Yeah. But could what he says be true?

freEasy: Really makes you wonder who you can trust.

DoneThat: Def made Z&K look like dorks.

beachboy: But they WERE dancing together.

Sporty1: You call that dancing?!?

freEasy: I call it Suspicious

trvlr44: There is something fishy going on with those 2.

clthswhore: Def up 2 something. they r acting weird.

delish: Lets ask Trev about it.

DoneThat: He knows more than we do about both of them

freEasy: Yup. he told me...

<E-male is Temporarily Unavailable.
We apologize for any inconvenience>
<Goodbye>

Despite brutal hangovers, most of the group managed to get on a boat and hold down their breakfasts the next day. Everything was bright white and blue. The brilliantly clean sailboat cut through the sapphire waves like a jet stream through a clear sky.

Zac and Kory had suffered enough at AC the previous night, but they were two of only a few people on the vessel who were not physically battered from the experience. The rest of the boys had boundless energy anyway. Topher and Rory snapped towels at Gary and Andy. Armin and Rick tossed snorkels around the deck in an improvised game of hot potato. Stuart was doling out shoulder massages like free candy.

Here in the sparkling morning sunlight, wearing bathing suits and sarongs, it was difficult to tell who was a waiter, a travel agent or something else completely. In just a few days everyone had bonded over E-male, mingled in group activities and melded into one cohesive unit. There seemed to be friendships and potential relationships sprouting in every corner of the boat's deck. If Zac and Kory hadn't known better, they would have sworn everything was working out as planned.

Zac watched Kory watching everyone else. Both the boss of E-male and the boss of Djorvzac Travel were acting a bit suspiciously. They were the only ones who weren't reveling in the tropical freedom of it all. They were both observing their coworkers and fellow travelers with a watchful eye.

Zac reminded himself that he and Kory were on this vacation for very different reasons than the others. They both had a serious business interest in this expedition. They weren't here to enjoy themselves or cut loose. They were working. And Zac reasoned that the others should recognize that fact. But in every glance and comment, Zac felt the suspicion that had been raised on E-male that morning.

Kory hadn't needed to point out to Zac that the exclusive E-male vacation site had turned into a vicious portal for gossip. Zac had seen it for himself in the wee hours of the morning as rumors and speculations flew across the screen. If Kory had ever doubted that his own creation could turn against him, they had both witnessed proof to the contrary.

Worry creased across Kory's brow as the wind blew those blond bangs back and forth. Zac knew Kory was having thoughts similar to his own. Kory glanced from face to face on the boat, trying to match up online screen names and real-life people and trying to decode the whole thing like some software program—like some complicated computer virus that had turned his own site against him.

Seeing Kory so concerned and contemplative was not what Zac had wanted. But there was something about this man stripped of his sarcasm and biting wit that appealed to Zac. Kory was a real businessman concerned about his company. He was not worried about his hair or clothes or where his next bitchy comment was coming from. He was more open and exposed than he had been back on the rough carpet of Zac's office.

Kory's loose white shirt was open and blowing in the wake of the sailboat's breeze. Slim, blue boarder trunks reached toward Kory's knees. His shirt flitted like a sail, revealing glimpses of the pale, taut flesh of Kory's torso.

Kory was thin and lean. The way he grabbed at his billowing shirt self-consciously only emphasized the smooth, sleek innocence of his powdery complexion. His body had none of the pumped-up steroid ideal that paraded itself along Baytown's main drag. Zac despised the cookie-cutter, party-boy blow-up doll. Their overworked muscles looked like they'd been inflated. Even their skin looked plastic after all the waxing, plucking, tanning and whatever else went into their beauty regime.

There was nothing artificial about Kory's body. And his narrow build had none of the awkward bulk Zac felt in his own frame. Zac's wide shoulders and thick thighs made him feel like a bumbling linebacker when he swam, ran or danced. Despite Kory's discomfort on the dance floor, he looked streamlined and elegant just the way he held his body. Zac couldn't help but think how their two contrasting bodies would feel against one another—muscle and leanness, hairy and smooth. Not in the rushed heat of anger and passion they had experienced in those moments on his office floor. But slowly peeling off that shirt to hold Kory's smooth slim torso against Zac's solid chest.

The sudden shift Zac felt in his trunks brought him back to reality. He was glad he'd thrown a pair of khaki shorts over his square-cut swimsuit. Especially when he realized Kory was looking straight at him. Zac's eye had been lingering on Kory's body, not his eyes, but now those golden orbs were fixed on Zac's wondering gaze.

Zac blinked heavily as if he'd just been staring into space and Kory's young taut body had just happened to be in the way. But of all the thousand questions written across Kory's face in that moment, accusations of leering were not among them. Concern, worry, anger and fear mingled to create a weary expression that fought with Kory's boyish appearance.

Zac could relate, and that feeling of camaraderie exaggerated his guilt for letting his mind and eyes wander south of Kory's face. There were more serious issues to think about than how Kory's perfect, tan nipples would taste.

"Hey, Kory," a travel agent named Steve called out, "what's up with E-male? I haven't been able to log on to the vacation section all morning."

"Yeah," Chris chimed in. "You're not gonna leave us stranded out here, are you? How am I supposed to flirt with these guys without E-male?" He reached over and pinched a waiter's ass for emphasis, and everyone on the boat laughed except for Zac and Kory.

"Just regular maintenance," Kory answered. "A few updates is all."

"I hope so," Rory said. "We need E-male to figure out what the heck in going on in this town."

"Perhaps if you paid more attention to the actual town," Zac butted in, "and less to online gossip. That's what vacations are for."

"But that's half the fun," Gary insisted. "That's what makes this better than a regular vacation. Kory has already proven that."

"Yeah," 'Topher agreed. "There's no getting-to-know-you B.S. We already know everything about everyone here."

"That's the problem," Zac said.

"Man, you're never going to get it," Rick said. "E-male is like having a crystal ball to Baytown. It's not like vacationing here was in the old days."

Zac wasn't sure what shocked him more—the way his own employee challenged him fearlessly and called him "man" or Rick's reference to the "old days" as if he knew something about Zac's past. He only hoped the lack of respect wasn't connected to any knowledge of those days long gone by.

"Just get us back online, Kory," Stuart said. It wasn't clear whether his tone was pleading or demanding. Every comment seemed threatening now—as backhanded and potentially devastating as the chats had become on E-male.

Zac knew that taking E-male offline must have been devastating for Kory. It was an admission of defeat that must have cut to the core. E-male had made all this possible, and now because of Trevor it was working against them. Zac could see that Kory had no explanation to offer the men he was stranded on this sailboat with.

"Reef, ahoy, strike the sails and drop the anchor!" the unfortunately straight, mop-headed skipper called as he slowed the boat. He probably hadn't received as much attention as a straight sun-bleached blonde usually did from a boatload of gay men. But then again, most snorkeling expeditions probably didn't have as much gossip, flirtation and scandal to distract them from the local-boy eye-candy. However, the sudden lowering of the sails and sloshing off seawater as the boat came to a halt was a welcome change of pace and conversation for Zac and Kory.

"It might look like we're in the middle of the ocean," he said to the group who seemed to be noticing him and his improvised sailor outfit for the first time. "But there's actually a reef right under us. In some places the water is only four or five feet above the coral. Don't worry, there are clear paths marked with arrows on underwater signs and there are even plaques that will explain the fish and coral you'll see down there. It's all very safe and simple. And I'll be able to see all of you from the boat. Just strap on your gear, stick the snorkel in and breathe through your mouth."

All the men strapped on their masks and wedged their feet

into flippers. However, they seemed much more interested in the rest of their outfits as they watched one another strip down to the tiniest bathing suits imaginable. There were strings and bikinis and snug little pouches everywhere.

Zac actually felt quite conservative in the black square-cut trunks. Regardless, as he slipped off his khaki shorts and tugged off his tank, he slipped quickly over the side of the boat and into the warm, silky salt water instead of waiting at the back of the boat with the others to use the ladder. He didn't want to take any chances that someone would recognize his half-naked body as that of the mystery masked dancer from the other night.

As soon as Zac bobbed to the surface and adjusted his mask atop his head, he looked back up at the boat to see Kory standing there, fumbling with his snorkeling equipment. He had the snorkel's mouthpiece twisted so that it pointed away from his mouth and he struggled to keep his bangs out of the mask as he pulled it over his eyes. Unlike the rest of the boys on the boat, Kory had not stripped down to a shiny bit of spandex. He wore the same pale-blue board shorts that reached nearly to his knees. He had, however, removed his shirt. And Zac stared up at the lean muscle of Kory's arms and abs, flexing as he battled with the equipment. The endearing sight of his awkwardness lightened Zac's mood.

"Ith thith thing on thtraight?" Kory asked Zac through the tube of his snorkel when he managed to get it in his mouth.

"'Straight' isn't the word I'd use," Zac called up at him. "It actually gives you a lisp. But it's fine. Just jump in."

Zac watched as Kory awkwardly swung his duck-like, flippered feet over the railing of the boat. He teetered there holding the rail as Zac waved him toward the waiting water. When Kory finally did find the courage to jump the few feet, he overestimated and nearly jumped on top of Zac where he was treading water below.

Zac caught Kory by the hips as he landed just inches in front of him, keeping them both afloat. At the same time, however, the protective gesture caused them to brush against one another as Kory briefly sank into the sea and again as he bobbed back up.

For those split seconds, Zac felt Kory's torso rub against his. He felt every hair on his chest brush against that smooth skin. That brief moment when they touched was so close to fulfilling Zac's earlier guilty thoughts that he was completely caught off-guard. He just floated there with his hands on Kory's hipbones, steadying him and holding him so close that their crotches grazed as their legs moved to tread water. Kory gagged a little on a mouthful of ocean and suddenly spit out his snorkel's mouthpiece and an arch of saltwater that hit Zac square in the face.

"Oops," Kory said. "Why is it we took the hard way in?"

"I didn't need to parade around in front of my employees in a bathing suit," Zac said, finally releasing Kory's waist and letting them bob farther apart. "Besides, I didn't want anyone to recognize me."

"As the dancing queen?" Kory asked, looking him up and down as best he could through the turquoise ripples of the water. "Well, you didn't have to wear the same outfit."

"This one's black," Zac protested. "Besides, how long is it before Trevor outs me anyway?"

Right on cue, a shrill horn sounded as a large boat pulled along the other side of the anchored sailboat. All around, snorkeled heads popped up, taking a break from following underwater plaques and chasing schools of brightly colored fish to see what the commotion was about. The boat had smoky windows and shiny brass accents. There was an oversized captain's wheel and white leather swivel chairs were bolted to the deck. Everything about it screamed money and pretense. And as soon as the engines purred to a standstill, Trevor was on deck screaming out to the sea of men.

"Well, if it isn't my favorite little travel group of guppies!" he shrieked.

The men all waved from the waves and called out to Trevor as if he were a long-lost friend. They hadn't been snorkeling for more than a few minutes, but suddenly Trevor was the flashiest, most exotic specimen on the entire reef. He wore a tiny rainbow-striped bikini and a shark-tooth necklace. Quite appropriately, he looked like a brightly colored predator.

"You got to be kidding me," Kory said quietly to Zac on the other side of the sailboat.

"It seems all I have to do is say his name," Zac grumbled.

"What a coincidence," Kory growled. "Again."

"Girls, girls, girls," Trevor scolded as he leaned provocatively over the brass railing. "What are you doing out here with your asses in the air? There are much better places for such things. A fish is a fish. And the last time I checked, gay men didn't do fish. How about a barbecue instead? I have a grill and fully stocked bar on the upper deck. If you insist on fish, we'll throw on some blowfish or there's always caviar kicking around somewhere. This is one off my more modest yachts. But I'm sure I can fit all of you on here."

The men hooted and hollered. Sea life didn't stand a chance against Trevor. It may have had an irreplaceable coral reef, but it didn't have a yacht. Trevor had won again, as usual. The men were peeling off their masks and paddling toward his luxury liner as fast as they could swim.

"Tommy, I'll take them back for you," Trevor called to the dumbfounded straight skipper, tossing a tip of thickly rolled bills into the sailboat. "Now who is that hiding on the other side of the boat? That wouldn't be our fearless leaders Zac and Kory, would it?"

Zac didn't bother to respond as he and Kory watched all their coworkers and travel companions clamor onto Trevor's deck like slippery fish being spilled from a net. Trevor had certainly caught them all up in his web—whatever scheme he was weaving.

"Are you two still dancing over there?" Trevor continued. "Kory, I think you're improving. Maybe Big Z has taught you some moves, huh? He used to fancy himself quite the little dancer before he got all burly and furry. Didn't you, Z?"

"Get me out of here," Kory said under his breath to Zac as the rest of the men stood dripping next to Trevor watching the show. It must have been like watching feeding time at the shark pool.

"Your hard-ass boss used to be a lot more about 'hard' and 'ass,' boys," Trevor cooed. "Come on, Z, you can tell them all about it over BBQ—or I will have to."

"You do what you have to do, Trevor," Zac called up to him. There was no stopping him now. There was nothing Zac could do as he treaded water, moving his fins back and forth in slow motion, hanging there in the ocean as if he were floating in time. "Come on, Kory."

Kory started toward the sailboat until he noticed that Zac was headed in the opposite direction—away from both vessels. Kory didn't ask any questions. They were leaving their fate in Trevor's hands there on that yacht. Following Zac as he swam off into the sea didn't seem any riskier. In fact, it felt like the right direction.

Kory popped his snorkel in his mouth, ducked his masked head beneath the bright blue water and kicked his fins behind him. The view below was spectacular. It was a maze of white coral and tiny brightly colored fished. Everywhere he looked there were schools of blue and yellow fish darting around the reef. Here and there, as promised, there were blue and white plaques anchored on blocks of concrete. Arrows pointed along the obvious paths between coral. Line drawings and short descriptions explained the fish, coral and vegetation.

However, Zac was not following the sign-guided tour. He swam over the coral barriers and away from the arrows. Kory was just glad to have his head below water where he could no longer hear Trevor's voice or see the mutinous travelers who had hopped on his yacht as quickly as possible. Kory could hear the echo of his own breath becoming more regular through the hollow shaft of the snorkel. He seemed to float effortlessly in the warm, buoyant saltwater. Simply kicking his feet gently caused his body to glide quickly along the surface with his arms hanging at his sides. He could swim like this forever, swim away from whatever disaster they had left back there.

Below, the view got wilder. The over-traveled and manicured reef of the tourists was behind them. They swam through fields of long, undulating kelp. Hidden within these forests there were pristine patches of white dotted with gray and brown sand dollars. They came upon much larger schools of fish—yellow and blue tangs, huge rainbow-colored parrot fish, angelfish of every hue. Zac would dive down beneath the surface and Kory would follow, holding his breath and swimming through a giant cluster of fish as it scattered around them in an explosion of color.

Finally, Zac led Kory over a rocky underwater ledge and into a cove surrounded by a reef. But this reef was not like the shallow, well-worn pathways littered with manmade signs. This reef made the spot they had sailed to look like an underwater miniature golf course. Here, wild, jagged coral reached 50 feet from the ocean floor to break the waves above. Gold, brown, green and white twisted together and branched apart. Mounds of coral the size of armchairs covered the bottom in yellows and pinks. Rainbows of fish were everywhere—shaped like long tubes, shovel spades and torpedoes. As Zac and Kory followed the inside of the protective reef wall that circled the cove, a large sea turtle swam directly beneath them with lazy strokes.

Zac made his way toward shore, and Kory reluctantly followed. They splashed through the surf and ended up side by side, breathless on an abandoned beach surrounded by cliffs. Looking back out over the crystal-blue waves, Kory could see the exposed tips of coral ringing the bay like points on a crown. The bay almost looked ominous if he hadn't just seen the magic beneath those bony spires.

"There's no way a boat could get in here if it wanted to," Zac said, "if anyone wanted to follow us. And you have to hike here if you don't swim."

Zac lay back in the soft sand, pulling off his mask and snorkel, resting with his hands behind his head and his eyes closed. His apparent exhaustion was more from the earlier efforts of the day than from the beautiful swim. Kory hopped awkwardly on one foot as he pried off his fin and tried not to stare down at Zac's exposed body.

Water glistened on his tan skin. The bottoms of his biceps had perfect creases drawn from elbow to underarm. Each wet, dark hair was plastered to his muscles, reaching up his wide, flat stomach to spread across his thick chest. And his soaked suit was plastered to the bulge of his crotch. Sunlight danced on the droplets as Zac slowly dried in the tropical sun.

"Are you trying to make me fall in love with Baytown?" Kory asked, breaking the silence. As Zac's eyes popped open, Kory looked away from him to survey the hidden cove and untouched reef. The view was almost as good.

"I'm trying to show you the other side of Baytown, the real side," Zac answered. "There's more than one side to everything."

"So I'm discovering," Kory said without specifying whether he was talking about the town or something else. "The fake side certainly wasn't working for me."

Despite whatever was happening back on Trevor's yacht—despite the gossip and conspiracies and the rumor mill that E-male had become—Kory felt a little better on this side of Baytown, with this side of Zac Djorvzac. Not only was Zac lying before him mostly naked, he had also become increasingly exposed in every way over the past days. As Zac had slowly stripped himself of his business attire, Trevor's attacks and the increasingly convoluted situation they found themselves in had peeled away the thick layers of Zac the guarded businessman.

Kory wasn't exactly sure why Zac was doing this, why he was letting Kory in. He wasn't sure why Zac was bringing him to these secret, remote locations to reveal himself. Why wouldn't Zac just ignore the rumors, stay bottled up inside, and jump on the next plane out of Baytown to retreat to the safety of his windowless office? It was a question Kory was not going to ask, because he didn't want to know the answer. For all the drama, Kory wouldn't have traded this secret moment in the sun. And whatever it was that Zac was trying to do—for whatever reason—Kory was now determined to help him.

"And that goes for the fake side of every story as well," Kory added. "I don't know what Trevor is telling everyone, but I see what he's doing. Conspiracy or not, he's chipping away at their confidence in us. They're starting to doubt us, and trust him."

"That's exactly what he wants," Zac said, propping himself up on one elbow. "But I'm afraid it's just the beginning. It could get worse, Kory."

"Is it going to make your employees abandon you? Ruin your reputation so no one calls Djorvzac Travel anymore? Make

E-male fail?" Kory asked in rapid succession. "I don't know. It doesn't sound as crazy as it did yesterday. I guess it depends how bad things get. How many secrets are revealed. And I guess I do think it could get that bad. It all depends what Trevor knows, what he's able to find out. And I'm not willing to sit around and wait to see how bad it gets."

"What do you propose we do?" Zac asked.

"We start by telling the whole truth," Kory said, sitting down cross-legged in the soft white sand next to Zac. "I have something I have to tell you, Zac."

"Wait." Zac held up a hand to silence Kory. His hand almost brushed Kory's knee where he sat, and Zac had a strong desire to place his hand there reassuringly. Because whatever Kory was about to say, whatever he was on the verge of admitting, Zac couldn't let him speak a word without telling his own truth. He couldn't let Kory make promises, commitments or declarations to a man he only half knew. "I do know what Trevor knows. Everything. Because as ugly as it sounds, his side of my story is not fake. You have to know that, Kory. You have to know my whole story."

So there on that deserted beach, where no one but the wind and the sea and the full sun above could hear him, Zac told his tale to this man. He told Kory the story he had run from, the story he had kept to himself for a decade.

"Because there are secrets that could destroy me," Zac began, "that almost did once long ago. I didn't tell you everything. You think people would abandon E-male just because it's owned by a waiter? I've got a lot more to be ashamed of than my previous employment. And that was nothing to be proud of either. I was a shot boy. Body shots, just like Trevor said—a test tube of Sex on the Beach, the long end in my mouth pouring it into someone else's; a shot glass of tequila poured down my chest so someone could lap it up.

"I did it for the dance. Free clubs. Free parties. Trevor was my idol. And I was his protégé. Dancing anywhere there was a tip or a box or the faintest hint of background music. I'd dance for anything. And I'd do anything to dance.

"But I couldn't dance my way out. No matter how many sit-ups. No matter how lean and mean. I was stuck up there on that box. And when you dance in place for hours on end, you're not going anywhere.

"When I got too good or just got too much attention, Trevor couldn't stand it. I'd get too many tips or too much applause, and he'd go ballistic. Trevor had to win. He'd steal men from me. Send men to me, if he thought it would keep me from becoming competition. Drinks, drugs, whatever it took.

"The things I did—the things Trevor did to me. The truth is I don't even know how bad it got, what I did exactly. But I'm sure Trevor does. There could be photos, videos, God knows what. I wouldn't put anything past him. One day it just ended.

"I woke up one morning covered in dried crystalline sweat with an aching head and a dry mouth, in a puddle of puke in a motel room with three men I never remembered meeting. It was the day of Beach Ball and the box-dancing contest.

"To make matter worse, I still showed up that night. I tried to win the contest. And I passed out halfway through. Collapsed right there on stage.

"The next morning, I came here. I hiked over those hills, dehydrated and miserable. I punished myself. I sat here and watched the sun rise. And I swore that I would never see it set here again."

When Zac stopped talking, they were left with that unique tropical silence. It was a backdrop of whispers with no distinct sound—waves on sand, wind through palm fronds, it all blended into a sort of warm static. Kory hadn't moved during Zac's entire speech.

"Is that supposed to change anything?" Kory asked him. "Make me not want to help you? Just because Trevor sabotaged you?"

"Because I sabotaged myself," Zac said. "He just helped as much as he could. I was the one who left me broke and broken. So I took the only experience I had—traveling and partying. I took a job at a discount travel call center, and I booked every gay traveler who called that place. That's how Djorvzac Travel really came to be. There was nothing ingenious about it. Just desperation and denial."

"Djorvzac desperation and denial. It that's where the triple-D rules came from?" Kory asked. They laughed together briefly in the warm, quiet, secret place. The sound seemed to stretch down the long white beach and bounce off the black cliffs.

"In a way, it really is," Zac answered seriously. "God, how long have I been hiding behind all that?"

"Well, I didn't know you way back then, Zac," Kory said. "And the man I met a few weeks ago is not the man I'm sitting with right now, here on this beach. People make mistakes. People change. And I don't know that I've ever seen anyone change as much and as fast as you have. Your past doesn't change a thing about how I feel or what I have to tell you."

"OK," Zac said gratefully. His simple statement was almost an agreement, as if he were giving in to Kory's view of his past. Zac closed his eyes again briefly. He had never looked back on those events as generously as Kory just had. And he had never told another person. He had certainly never expected anyone to understand. Zac reached over, and this time he did put his hand on Kory's knee. "Thank you."

"Thank you for telling me," Kory said. "But what I have to tell you isn't ten years in the past. What I have to confess is right now."

Zac just nodded his head and opened his eyes. After delving into his dark past, "right now" sounded better than ever. He almost looked forward to what Kory had to tell him, to bring him back to the present and move forward together. This moment in the sun was the closest thing to intimacy that Zac could remember. And he wondered, beyond reason, if what Kory had to tell him would confirm that feeling.

"I am E-male," Kory said.

He told Zac everything. How he had stumbled upon his matchmaking ability. How it had spiraled out of control. And how, once he had started, Kory couldn't stop his online snooping, lying and manipulation—no matter how wrong he knew it was or how quickly it was tearing his own life apart. "I know I'm a fraud and a cheat," Kory admitted. "And now you know why I was really so desperate to run away from it all."

"Oh," Zac said inelegantly. He didn't know what exactly he had expected to hear, but high-tech trickery was not it. Zac had known that Kory was the man behind E-male's curtain, but he was still surprised to find out exactly what he was doing back there. Zac realized that sometime during the confession he had taken his hand off Kory's knee.

"See," Kory said. "You may think you're hiding behind your triple-D rules. But I'm hiding behind a computer screen of lies. You've rebuilt your life. I'm digging myself deeper and deeper every day."

"No. I just thought..." Zac started. "I never would have guessed. You're much more of a romantic than I ever expected."

Zac looked up at Kory, and he sat up next to him in the sand so they would be face to face. The man's serious gold eyes and the way his blond hair had dried in thick salty strands across his brow made him look absolutely dramatic in the bright light of this stranded beach.

Zac realized that he was stranded with Kory in more ways than one. And that was suddenly just fine. Because now Zac knew that underneath all that sarcasm and bitchery, Kory just wanted everyone to live happily ever after. Zac could relate.

"Well, I may be a criminal romantic," Kory said. "But I think my crimes might just be the answer."

"Really?" Zac asked with more interest than disapproval.

"I have a plan," Kory said. "But it's not nice."

"I think we've been nice for long enough."

"When was that?"

"Just tell me the plan."

Kory reached into the deep right pocket of his long board shorts. For a split second Zac thought he was probing for that mysterious condom like the one he had produced weeks earlier from the depths of his jeans. But when Kory's hand emerged he was holding a sealed plastic bag full of what looked like large white confetti. Zac wouldn't allow himself to be disappointed.

"You've been robbing the fortune-cookie factory again," Zac

guessed.

"It might tell our future," Kory said. "And this is just the start. This is what I came up with last night after I shut down Baytown's E-male."

"Do I even want to know?" Zac asked him. He locked his green eyes with Kory's golden ones there alone on a beach big enough to host a football game even though they were the only participants, sitting mere inches apart. "OK, I do. Tell me what the hell you're talking about."

"You were right," Kory said. "No matter how I had personally misused E-male, I still wasn't aware of what it could do. With just a few of Trevor's rumors, it turned against me. The way people were using it. The things they were saying. E-male wasn't making them fall in love anymore. It's making them fall out of love with us."

"So what are you going to do to rekindle the romance?" Zac asked.

"I'm going to take back E-male," Kory said. "I've been manipulating the system all along. I've matched men up all over the country. And I still am, late at night, right here from Baytown. If I can use E-male to make them fall in love, I can use it to make them believe us, and not Trevor."

"And where do the fortune cookies come into all this?" Zac asked, pointing to the plastic baggy full of paper strips.

"The exclusive vacation site on E-male has gotten too exclusive," Kory said. "Too small. Too incestuous. Too many rumors. So I'm going to open it up. These 'fortunes' are E-male passcodes for the rest of Baytown."

"All of Baytown on E-male?"

"Only the ones we choose," Kory pointed out. "Give our boys more variety and more distractions. And give me more to work with. But unlike the passcode I gave you and the rest of our travelers, these are all unique, all trackable."

"You're going to spy on all off Baytown?"

"I'm going to have control of all of Baytown," Kory said, looking Zac straight in the eye. "My secret can be our secret weapon. And I have a special code just for Trevor. We're going to sabotage the saboteur."

"You're going to invite Trevor onto E-male?" Zac asked in absolute disbelief.

"If he wants to use it against me, if he wants to spread rumors," Kory said, "Then let him do it right under my nose where I can see him and counteract him. Keep your friends close and your enemies closer. I'll be able to keep an eye on all of them. And they won't even know."

Zac let Kory's plan sink in for a moment. He looked up and down the beach, removing his gaze from Kory's eyes so he could concentrate and process the information overload Kory had just provided. Kory was sneakier than Zac had thought. If Kory could fool an entire dating site into taking his love advice, he just might be able to sway popular opinion in Baytown. At the very least, he could attempt to perform some damage control.

Zac also realized that even with Kory's clever computer skills, he was in as much danger as Zac when it came to protecting his business. This trip wasn't just some random experiment. The success of this partnership was vital to proving E-male's true value and moving away from the self-destructive business model that had overtaken Kory's life. If this vacation failed, if their reputations were destroyed, if Trevor managed to reveal and exploit their secrets—both Kory and Zac could lose the businesses that were the sole focuses of their lives.

Kory had just made it clear that he was not giving up that fight easily. And Zac had to admire the way Kory strategized and schemed to save it all. If his plan worked, Kory wouldn't just be saving E-male, he'd be saving Zac too.

"And I'm going to enter that box-dancing contest," Zac declared.

"What?" Kory practically gasped. His eyebrows shot up into crazy angles of confusion, fighting with the line of his bangs. Kory had seen some crazy metamorphoses over the past few days when it came to Zac Djorvzac. He had seen him transform from asshole businessman to topless dancer to wounded ex-party boy. Kory had seen sides of Zac and Baytown that he was certain Zac had never shared with another human being. But after all that change and confession, Kory couldn't comprehend Zac's latest revelation. "What are you talking about?"

"I don't need to be put out to pasture quite yet," Zac said. "I can still run with the big boys, neck in neck. I am sick and tired of Trevor winning. I have to do this. Besides, E-male can only do so much. I will distract him while you work your E-magic. And I will show my employees that I'm not that drugged-out shot boy Trevor has been telling them about. I may not be the straight-laced boss they're used to, but I am not the washed up loser Trevor claims. I can go out there and dance for myself. I can get up there and show everyone what it really means for Zac Djorvzac to dance on a box."

Kory didn't know what to say. Somehow, Zac managed to catch Kory by surprise every single day. With forests and beaches and hidden reefs. With confessions and kindness and wild proclamations. And Kory realized there were very few things he wanted more than to see Zac dancing and winning.

"OK," Kory said. "Sounds like we have a new business deal."

Kory reached over and took Zac's hand to shake it. He thought it would be a humorous gesture. But somehow, there on that deserted beach with nothing but waves and sand and coral to bear witness, the act seemed incredibly tender. He saw every muscle in Zac's forearm and bicep and shoulder ripple with the shake. He saw that furry pec bob with the movement. Kory looked Zac in the eye and felt suddenly shy all alone with him.

"It's a deal," Zac said, returning the shake with a solid grip. "Now that we know everything about each other, I guess we can really work together."

"Yes," Kory hesitated. He let go of Zac's hand awkwardly. "There's just one thing. I'm really sorry about what happened in your office. That was totally unprofessional of me."

It was completely ridiculous. But it was something he just had to get off his chest. Kory had felt guilty enough about that crazy lustful moment of impulse and revenge when he'd hated Zac. But now that he was beginning to trust him, to confide in him, to actually like him—he couldn't let it be an unspoken obstacle to the crazy plan they were hatching.

"Oh, well, there are more important things to figure out now. We just didn't know who the real enemy was then," Zac stammered. "I only have one question—the condom?"

"Oh, right," Kory stammered back at him. "That must have made me look very...prepared. It was the 'just-in-case' condom I promote on E-male. It's written on the bottom of every page. 'Be a carrier—of a condom not a disease.' So whether I need it or not, I practice what I preach. Always in my front pocket."

"Like fortune cookies?" Zac asked.

"I intended to hand those out after the snorkeling trip," Kory clarified. "The condom's in the other pocket. But don't worry, I promise not to let it happen again."

"Of course," Zac said. "Strictly business."

"Absolutely."

Kory reached over and shook Zac's hand again. This time he felt less self-conscious. As if they truly were sealing a business deal, as if physical contact was necessary at this point here next to one another on the sand. But as Zac shook his hand, the grip was tighter, more complete. And he didn't let go.

Instead, Zac pulled Kory near. Kory felt the soft sand shift beneath him as his body moved within it, and he felt the sudden contrast of Zac's body against him—hard muscle and soft hair. A split second later he felt Zac's lips.

And Kory kissed him back. He wrapped his arms around Zac's broad shoulders and let his mouth melt into that kiss. And then it was broken. Suddenly Zac's mouth was at Kory's collarbone, his sternum, his nipple. Zac kissed down the indentation that bisected Kory's thin, pale stomach until his lips caught on the waistband on Kory's shorts.

And then Zac ripped the Velcro fly apart. Kory was already hard. He could feel himself throbbing against Zac's own hardness from one simple kiss. He didn't have to look down to confirm what was happening, but he did. Kory watched as Zac slowly but insistently took the head of Kory's cock into his mouth.

Kory was startled by the sudden warm wetness and his own sharp intake of breath. He felt Zac's lips and tongue slide slowly down his shaft until the pressure of Zac's nose and the steam of his breath were buried in Kory's tawny pubes. He couldn't keep the gasping noise from escaping his own lips as he looked up to the brilliant turquoise sky above their secret beach.

So many thoughts ran through Kory's head in that moment that they seemed to bump into each other before he could grasp them: the sunlight, the sky, the sound of waves, the impossibility of this place and scene, and the storm of passion and sensation that coursed through him. It blurred together in a bright flash of ecstasy. It was all too much and too perfect at once—paralyzing him.

And then he was free of it all. That feeling he had experienced in Zac's office overtook him. It was a feeling that was stronger than reason or facts or the details of scenery. It mobilized and empowered him. But this time—as he reached for Zac's body hungrily—there was no anger or rage. This was definitely not a hate-fuck.

Kory twisted his body without allowing his erection to break the seal of Zac's lips or the rhythm of his mouth around it. In fact, Kory thrust his hips slightly as he turned his body on the sand. He pushed himself deeper into Zac's mouth as the man swallowed him greedily. Kory grabbed Zac's hips. He positioned himself so that his own face was now at the level of Zac's crotch.

Kory could clearly see the perfect outline of Zac's own erection in those tight black trunks. He could see the thick shaft and the solid bulb of his cock-head poking past the black band at his waist. And he wasted no more time.

He kissed the tip of Zac's erection, tasting salt and heat and the pulse of blood beneath. He forced his mouth down, pushing aside the snug fabric with his face and hooking his thumbs under the elastic to find the concave muscles along Zac's hips. Kory peeled away the cool, wet blackness of the suit and slid that thick hard piece of Zac fully into his face.

And as they both swallowed one another completely, their torsos pressed fully together—chests against stomachs, bottoms of ribcages kissing. They fit perfectly with that smooth paleness against muscle and fur. Their skin radiated the sun's heat between them—reflecting back the magic of the day into the darkness pressed between bodies.

Kory worked his mouth back and forth, from the fat head to the broad shaft, feeling the scratch of the hair there just as he felt the simultaneous scratch of Zac's stubble against his own scrotum. They worked together as if to music. Swallowing at the same time. Or taking turns so that one could catch his breath as the other plunged, so they could focus on one another, enjoy one another, and ignore the beautiful world around them. They worked faster and frantically, panting around each other's cocks, sucking and thrusting and grasping at thighs.

And they held each other as they sucked, wrapping their arms around hips, waists and buttocks. They were locked in one long embrace, completely connected. And when they came, it was not a climax. It was a long slow moment of pouring into each other, like a current passing between them. Like the tides washing over the reef out there. Like the natural course of things. A flow that would repeat itself.

"When I said I wouldn't let it happen again," Kory finally said as they tugged on sandy suits, "I guess I meant after this time."

"Of course," Zac answered as if it were really all business. "Besides, that wasn't sex."

"No, not exactly," Kory agreed.

"Fine," Zac said, wiping grains of sand from his knees. "Then we can move ahead as planned."

"Exactly as planned," Kory agreed, as he had a bit of trouble realigning the Velcro fly of his shorts.

"They're going down," Zac said forcefully.

"So to speak," Kory blurted out before he could help himself.

And they both laughed without looking at each other, where no one else could hear them. Where even the cliffs were too far away to answer them with an echo.

"Let's just stay and watch the sun set," Zac said.

And all Kory said was, "Absolutely."

So they did, side by side, silently, almost touching.

CHAPTER 9

<E-MALE IS BACK ONLINE>
<new & improved>
<new features>
<new boys!!!>

"Here you go. Welcome to E-male."
"E-male secret code just for you."
"It's like shopping online for men."

Kory, Jeff and Jon ran through the humid strip of Baytown like fairies sprinkling pixie dust. However, their dust consisted of strips of paper with E-male passcodes on them.

They popped into the bars. They cruised the streets. They intercepted men halfway through dance moves, shopping sprees and drinks. They spread their Baytown fairy magic seemingly at random. No one would have ever guessed that there was an exact, computerized science to the spell they were casting.

Kory had explained it immediately after breakfast, right after he had handed all the Djorvzac travelers their new personalized passcodes. Actually, he'd grabbed Jeff by the scruff of the neck and explained it very, very clearly.

"Now you're actually going to help me, you little traitor," Kory had sneered into Jeff's pierced ear as he dragged him to the other side of Cabana Boy's pool.

"What? We thought you'd drowned," Jeff jokingly protested. "No reason we shouldn't enjoy a free yacht ride."

"Thanks for the concern."

"Nothing a little mouth-to-mouth wouldn't cure, huh?" Jeff winked and nudged, and Kory elbowed him right in the gut.

He hoped that he had knocked enough wind out of Jeff that he wouldn't notice the sudden flush pass over Kory's face or the new tan that had been there before it. Tans didn't come from a computer screen, no matter how late Kory had stayed in front of it last night. He did not need to explain to Jeff why he was suddenly sun-kissed, and had no tan line to show for it.

"Now listen..." Kory started.

He explained that muscle boys got codes starting with the number one. Twinky little slips of things got codes with twos. Anyone displaying any kind of bitchy attitude automatically got a three code. There were codes for lechers, sweet old men, nasty little queens, leather daddies and everyone in between.

The tracking system sounded much more benign than it truly was. And Jeff didn't need to know anymore than he already did. However, Kory had mapped out specific demographics so that the E-male pool would be deep and diverse. He needed a cast of characters to work with, and he needed help assembling them all.

That is how he found himself running with Jeff and Jon through the main streets of Baytown, along the beaches and through dark cruise bars. The couple was almost cute again as Kory watched them tap muscley biceps and hand passcodes to flirty little waifs. The sun had bleached Jeff's blue bangs a greenish yellow. And Jon's short, sporty brand of outdoorsyness had a certain boyish charm with his newly sunburned nose.

All Kory had had to do was take them out of Trevor's clutches—distract them from the gossip and treachery with a little bit of fun. Just a small dose of drama.

Dancing. Dating. Drama. Kory believed that was just what the doctor ordered for everyone here. No matter what the old Zac claimed, those were not always poisonous things. And since Zac was now taking care of the "dancing" part, Kory could only assume they were on the same page—at least when it came to breaking the triple-D bra rules as much as they could possibly be broken.

Because dancing, dating and drama were precisely what Kory was planning to give to all to Baytown. And he planned to leave his and Zac's own drama where it belonged—hidden and secret on their deserted beach. As hot and passionate as it had been, Kory knew it had just been their mutual frustration with Trevor and the raw honesty of their secret lives that made them cling to one another like that. No matter how it had felt, no matter how Kory himself felt when he thought of Zac's body and mouth and arms—he knew he had to leave it behind. This was business—not exactly business as usual—but business nonetheless.

So Kory focused on the bright day and the crowded beach ahead—so unlike the one he had shared with Zac yesterday. He handed a couple of slips to some muscle boys working out along the beach. Their skin was an unhealthy mahogany, as if they had sunburns beneath their tans and just kept bench-pressing there in full sunlight and tiny tank tops.

"Here you go, fellas," Kory said. "Free passes to E-male online dating. A new exclusive section just for Baytown visitors."

"Hey, I think I've heard of that," one grunted happily.

"Online dating," another added between sets, "that's gotta be better than the real thing."

"Inline skating?" asked another.

"Online dating," Kory corrected. "It's called E-male—as in male, not female."

"Oh, yeah, I get it," The skating guy said. "If it's exclusive, I'm all for it."

Most people didn't need a hard sell or any explanation at all. They had either heard of E-male or they were dying to try this newfangled way of meeting men. Even current E-male members were dying to get behind the velvet rope of the new exclusive Baytown section. Kory's little fortune cookie slips were an immediate sensation along the strip. He may as well have created a new party drug. People tried it immediately. And they were addicted.

     PecsnAbs: Hey, Baytown boys!
  dancedancedance: here we are!
      Thhrust: welcome to the hottest chat on the beach
      sexUall: anyone want to get naked? on the nude
          beach ... or at my place?

   <NUDE BEACH: click here to create a group outing>

   MkeMynaDbl: what's up 2nite?
  dancedancedance: dancin' till dawn. what else?
      Thhrust: now we're talking. whos got
          the hottest moves?
   MkeMynaDbl: who's got the hottest shotboys???
  dancedancedance: Trevor of course!
      talk2me: and did you hear the shot boy scandal?

  <HOTTEST DANCE SPOTS: click here to see the top 5>

    <PVT CHAT—Dancing—click here to meet
      your dance partner>

      Partee: What about this new site/features/etc?
    beachboy: Sweet. So much more to do...
     freEasy: So many mor boyz!
    beachboy: Hurray for K! Kory rocks!
     vaca4me: What about Kory and Zac??
   clthswhore: They have been spending lots
          of time together.
     vaca4me: Whats up with that?

    <NEW MATCHES—Alert—
You're a match with: Howbout2night. Click to chat>

<SURVEY—What to do tomorrow?
—click here to take survey & make plans>

Everyone willingly logged on, handed over their personal information to Kory and created names that kept them anonymous to everyone else. But on Kory's computer, he could see the special tracking numbers of their passcodes. He could identify them by type, location or name. He could see them checking out each other's stats, their private chats, flirtatious e-mails, and the things they said "aloud" in the public room.

If anything or anyone got out of hand, E-male's new "suggestions" could pop up at any time. "Suggestion" was E-male's way of saying that Kory was "interrupting." If Kory had been the gracious host at a large online party before, casually nudging guests in the right direct, now he was the pushy socialite who butted into conversations, changed topics and threw people together in such an enthusiastic and fun-loving way that no one noticed just how obnoxious and distracting he was.

Kory didn't even have to be there for it to work. The surveys, recommendations and conversation-starters were so haphazard, that any random distraction could pop up at the mention of any preprogrammed keyword or name—box dance; shot boy; Kory, Zac, or Trevor.

If anyone started gossiping or spreading rumors, E-male would suddenly ask about favorite bars or suggest a private chat for people into parasailing. It didn't have to make sense. People would click on any link E-male suggested. They would chat with anyone it recommended. And no one could resist multiple-choice questions and the resulting bar charts that just spit back the preference of juice flavors at the local smoothie bar, or whatever.

Despite the clever, distracting bells and whistles Kory had tacked on to the E-male functionality—Kory's matching skills were still what validated the entire system. No matter how out-of-the blue some of the new "enhancements" seemed, people trusted them because when E-male paired them up, Kory's intuition was still spot-on. With this many excited vacationers typing away frantically, he wasn't always as precise. A member may not get matched with the love of his life the first time he logged on, but he'd get introduced to someone he found physically ideal, mentally compatible, or just a heck of a lot of fun for a date if nothing more.

Despite Zac's earlier accusations, E-male was definitely something better for people to look at online than pornography. If they wanted scandal, sex and romance—they didn't need to look at porn, cruise bars or listen to Trevor. They didn't need to stand there with mouths agape each and every night waiting for him to climb onto a box and grace them with his gyrating presence. They did not need to dance in his shadow any longer.

And Kory had plans for Trevor, too. He had exact codes for all Trevor's "back-up dancers" and hangers-on—all those who gathered around Trevor like flies around something very rotten. And Kory had special passcodes for the people who planned and manned Beach Ball—deejays, bouncers, bartenders and road crews. Everyone who had anything to do with Trevor's life.

Kory planned to cover Trevor's world better than if he had planted bugs and cameras. This was more insidious. This wasn't just observing—it was manipulating.

☆　☆　☆　☆

"The one with three sixes is for Trevor," Kory said to Zac as they walked along the Baytown strip at dusk. Everything was purple and orange. The colors seemed to be trying to compete with the neon and flash of the street.

"Isn't that a bit obvious?" Zac asked. "Three sixes?"

"It starts with six, ends with six and there's one right in the middle," Kory said as he showed Zac the strip of paper with '6246716' printed on it. "Just so I can't miss him."

Zac was doing his part by passing out the remainder of the E-male passcodes like flyers as they walked down the street. He had to hand it to Kory. The bag was almost empty now. And the E-male chat room was constantly abuzz.

"I've never met a person who can miss Trevor," Zac said. "I doubt he even needs a code to be identifiable."

"Speak of the devil," Kory said, nodding down the block toward the square where he'd first encountered Trevor. Trevor lounged there shirtless, leaning against one of the concrete blocks as boys danced around him. The tropical orange sunset reflected eerily off his orange spray-on tan.

"I still can't believe you're inviting him into E-male," Zac muttered as they approached, repeating the disbelief he'd already expressed several times.

"If your theory is right, he's already been on E-male," Kory pointed out. "He just doesn't have keys to the secret room our vacationers do. He won't be able to resist. And I'll be able to see every move he makes."

"He does love to show off his moves," Zac said.

Kory walked straight into the square of cement and dancers. It was the kind of place where boys would be skateboarding in a normal city. But Baytown was not a normal city. And the boys here were seeking very different thrills. Trevor, the biggest kid of them all, perked up when he spotted his latest victims approaching.

"If it isn't my favorite couple," he called out, placing his hands on his hips and flexing his abs. "Here to practice your dancing, Kory?"

"I haven't quit my day job yet," Kory replied, "which is what I'm here to talk to you about."

"Ready to sell your little start-up already?" Trevor asked.

"Why don't you take it for a test drive first," Kory offered, handing Trevor the special number as if the paper strip had been selected at random from the bag. "See what all the boys in Baytown are talking about."

"I already know that," Trevor replied cattily. "They're talking about me, and whatever I tell them to talk about." But he took the slip of paper anyway, feigning indifference as he tucked it into the slim little pocket of his shorts.

"So we've heard," Zac said accusingly. He was not about to let Trevor intimidate him anymore. He knew Trevor had been talking, and Kory had confirmed as much on E-male.

"I only speak the truth," Trevor cooed innocently. "They boys deserve to know that."

"Well, if you're so determined to relive the good old days and tell everyone about them, I might as well show them what you're talking about," Zac said. He paused to enjoy the uncomfortable flicker that passed through Trevor's too-blue eyes. "Because I prefer to live in the present."

"Whatever do you mean, Z?" Trevor batted his eye, and Zac wondered briefly if he was wearing mascara.

"I'm entering the box-dancing contest," Zac said simply, staring right into Trevor as all the batting and coyness suddenly ceased. His eyes were as cold and icy-blue as a menthol cough drop, as cold as what Zac knew was really deep inside.

"You want to self-destruct? That's fine by me," Trevor practically spat. His bleached-white teeth glowed like fangs. "You're just making it easier for me. I warned you."

"I'm not a 20-year-old kid anymore," Zac said. "You can't threaten me. You can't do a thing to me."

"You're doing to yourself, sweetheart," Trevor said, regaining a small amount of composure. "I'm just enjoying the train wreck. How about we make a wager so this whole disaster is a little more interesting?"

"What do you have in mind?" Zac asked. He couldn't wait to hear what cockamamie scheme Trevor's twisted mind had fabricated over the past few moments. Zac knew he had caught Trevor off-guard, and he knew the dancing queen was just reeling. But whatever Trevor's proposition was, Zac had absolutely no intention of accepting. If Trevor had come up with it, it was not a good idea.

"E-male," Trevor said. He patted the place where the passcode sat in his pocket. "If I win, you sell it to me. I'll take it off Kory's little hands for fair market value."

"Absolutely not," Zac said. "No deal. This is between you and me, Trevor. Kory has nothing to do with it. What do you have to lose?"

"I have everything on the line," Trevor screamed at him. "This is my life. Look around you. This is me. If you think you can waltz in here again and take it away from me, you'd better have some skin in this game. I want your reputation on the line too. Both of you. I want your little secret weapon, your 'business partnership,' your traveling matchmaking machine."

The entire city street seemed to screech to a standstill when Trevor raised his voice. The muscle boys paused in their dance moves and pedestrians gawked as if there had been a car crash. To Zac, the outburst seemed like little more than a ridiculous tantrum. Trevor was like a child making an outlandish demand. There was no way Zac would ever agree to complicate this situation further by giving Trevor more leverage. Their businesses were in enough danger as it was. And although Trevor may have the power to threaten their very livelihoods, he could not prevent Zac from entering that contest on his own terms.

"You want E-male?" Kory asked. Zac was as shocked as all the onlookers when Kory stepped forward and placed himself between Zac and Trevor, inserting himself in the middle of their confrontation. Kory placed his thin frame between the two larger men, but somehow he seemed to fill that space confidently. And there was something in his voice that wasn't surprise or outrage. It was an idea forming. "Fine. It's a deal. If you win, I'll sell you E-male. But if Zac wins, you leave us and our companies alone."

"That's all you want?" Trevor asked and laughed. "How about a convertible or something?"

"Kory, you don't want to do this," Zac interrupted. "Really, this isn't your battle to fight."

"It is now," Kory said. "We're in this together."

"Are you sure?" Zac asked. But he could tell from Kory's determined look that he was. Kory stood there between them, with all Baytown's eyes focused on him, and he had the steadfast presence of a man twice his size. Zac recognized that look from the unwavering city boy who had shown up in his office just weeks before. But now there was something stronger, more mature, more moving about Kory's stance. And seeing Kory before him now made something in Zac's chest catch, like the moment in a song when the music's crescendo would just grab him.

"You really are so romantic," Trevor giggled. "You two

can have your fun. But in the end, I'm going to have the little internet company I always wanted."

"We'll see about that," Kory said as he turned and walked away, pulling Zac after him. "And you'd better dance your ass off, boy."

☆   ☆   ☆   ☆

With so many members all thrown into the same chat room, the E-male party was chaotic. And that's exactly what Kory wanted. He didn't want his usually tidy soirée with people organized into friendly groups by likes and location. He didn't want them to be able to carry on a coherent conversation that could just spiral into gossip and anonymous accusations as the initial travel group had.

He wanted them to be overwhelmed and amazed by the many, many men at the party. So many men, so little time. And although they had a hard time remembering who they had talked to as they moved on to the next and awaited E-male's suggestions—Kory knew exactly who was who and what was what. It was an intricately stitched patchwork, and Kory had sewn it himself.

He knew which muscle boys were into twinks. Which dancers were into accountants. Who worked for Beach Ball and who had all the control. Who was a top, a bottom or dog-collar fetishist. And when that special number with three sixes flashed red onto his computer screen, Kory knew very well who it was.

When Trevor did finally enter the room, Kory steered him into conversations where he couldn't do much damage. He would find out Trevor's plans and location and next move. Kory was amused that Trevor didn't admit to the room who he was. But Kory didn't need his admission to know exactly what he was up to.

> bXXXdncr: So this is where all the boys are.
> Flirty: where else? E-male is the new hotspot.
> bXXXdncr: Hot? I don't see any dancing boyz
> beachboy: plenty of time for that later.

grrreg: this is more entertaining.

bXXXdncr: Speaking of—did you hear Zac is entering the box contest?

trvlr44: Zac the travel guy??? U gotta b kidding/

vaca4me: What is that all about?

bXXXdncr: I could tell you all about it... I myself am quite the boxdancer.

whoare: is that where the name came from? lol.

bXXXdncr: don't start with me. I know everything about Btown. And Zac.

Flirty: Do tell.

trvlr44: Give us the dirt.

vaca4me: I knew there was something going on.

bXXXdncr: Oh, the stories I could tell!

whoare: bring it on

<ATTN: bXXXdncr—personal invitation to
The Port Hole. Dinner tonight.>

<ATTN: Flirty —personal invitation to
The Port Hole. Dinner tonight.>

<ATTN: trvlr44—personal invitation to
The Port Hole. Dinner tonight.>

"Oh, you won't need reservations on a Thursday here," the man at the restaurant said to Kory over the phone. "It's dead till the weekend."

"I wouldn't count on that," Kory said with a smile that the man on the other end may have actually been able to hear. "Could you just put me down for seven? Thanks."

The Port Hole may well have been the cheesiest restaurant in Baytown. It had actual portholes for windows, thick nautical ropes draped between tables, and fishing nets stretched across the ceiling rafters. There was an anchor in the front and a giant plaster clamshell by the restroom.

It served over-cooked seafood and cold baked potatoes. Straight day-trippers and buses full of senior citizens clogged its driftwood-gray booths on the weekends. Despite being located in Baytown, it didn't have a lot of gay diners. And it had never had this many gay men stuffed into its dingy interior. Suddenly, on a weeknight, the place was brimming with muscles and Miss Thangs.

Kory and E-male had suggested this particular locale to every couple going on a date tonight. He had thrown it into chats about what to do this evening. He had recommended it as the new, hip, underground hotspot in surveys and top-ten lists. E-male claimed it was the place for singles and chowhounds and party boys. There was not a person who had logged on to E-male's Baytown site without hearing about the Port Hole.

Zac and Kory sat across from each other at a tiny booth that seemed to have a gangplank for its tabletop. They were tucked into a corner near a papier-mâché mermaid, but the rest of the restaurant was jam-packed.

"I no longer doubt what E-male can do," Zac said. And Kory saw the corner of Zac's mouth lift. Kory realized that Zac's smiling-without-smiling routine had actually been replaced with full-fledged genuine smiles. No matter how recently Zac had shaved, there was always a bluish-black shadow there, and it framed his full lips and green eyes to make his new smile seem absolutely enormous.

"I can't believe I'm probably giving all these men food poisoning," Kory responded. "But I thought Trevor might like to see what E-male can really do. He's not the only one who can control Baytown."

And as if on cue, Trevor—also known as bXXXdncr—walked into the Port Hole. He looked around at the crazy scene. There were at least 100 of Baytown's finest crammed into this trashy tourist trap. Everywhere he looked, people were paired up with dates. Boys were initiating an impromptu game of football using the baskets of buttered rolls. Someone was stuffing the jukebox with quarters and pumping whatever music he could find into the nautical eatery. And people were taking to the sticky floor as if it were a high-class nightclub. For once, Trevor's dramatic entrance was lost amid other people's own dramas.

"Can you believe E-male predicted how hot this place would be?" someone called out.

"It's the best," another added. "I'm taking all its recommendations from now on."

"Let's dance, boys!"

Trevor slid into a barstool shaped like a pirate's barrel of rum and bellied up to the "grog bar." Around him, people danced, kissed, ordered fish fingers, and did exactly what Kory had told them to do. No one seemed to notice Trevor at all.

Chapter 10

bXXXdncr: one week till Beach Ball!!!
Circuitboy69: what are you planning to do there
bXXXdncr: Win. what else?
lushlife: should be some pretty hot dancerz
bXXXdncr: That's me
Partee: who are you?
bXXXdncr: wouldn't you like to know... and you will
when I take the trophy

<SURVEY—Who will win Beach Ball?
—click here to vote now>
___ Bobby
___ Pedr
___ Trevor
___ Zac
___ Other

"Time for rehearsal," Zac said.

"Are you just going to make a habit out of showing up at my cabin door every morning at dawn?" Kory asked. As usual, he was sleepy, disheveled and looked surprised to see Zac silhouetted against the glistening dew in the tropical morning sun.

Somehow Zac looked forward to these glimpses of vulnerability. From mountainsides to desolate beaches, it was almost as if he searched out those places where Kory's boyish face would take on that bewildered look of confusion and honesty. One place Zac could be certain to find that moment of clarity was here at the threshold of Kory's cabin.

"The sun has been up for hours," Zac said. "And so have I. I need your help for the Beach Ball contest."

"My help?" Kory said, almost opening his eyes fully. "What do I know about dancing? Do you need your toes stomped on or something?"

"I'm just asking you to help now," Zac insisted. "I helped pass out all your fortune-cookie thingies, didn't I?"

Somehow that logic was enough to drag Kory, blonde and tousle-headed, from his bed to the backstage area of Cabana Boy's entertainment complex. On the outside, Cabana Boy was all slick disco bars and upscale seaside resort. Behind the scenes, it had every imaginable prop crammed between spare lighting systems, piles of dusty velvet curtains, and folding tables and chairs. There was one long, thin window that ran along the top of a wall that allowed a glimpse of reality—a six-inch slice of real palm trees, sky, sea and sunshine. Like a grumpy child on a school morning in his sweatpants and faded rock-and-roll tee-shirt, Kory stared in confusion at the cardboard palm trees with crepe-paper fronds.

"So are we putting on a show?" Kory asked as he took in his surreal surroundings.

"You could say that," Zac answered. He could see the sarcastic sensibility seeping back into Kory's expression as he slowly came fully awake. Zac felt a small tinge of regret, but he realized that he needed this side of Kory too; he realized that he actually like it almost as much. Zac handed Kory the large cup of black coffee he'd stashed here earlier. "I've been thinking about our plan."

There were two spare disco balls rolled together against the wall like a pair of glitter-encrusted testicles. Kory gave them a nudge with his sneakered foot, and they jostled against one another in the corner.

"Well, I've been implementing my part of the plan all night," Kory said, sipping his hot coffee gratefully. "I've reprogrammed all of Baytown."

"So I saw. I hope the management of the Port Hole gives you a cut of the profits."

"Oh, that was nothing," Kory said modestly. "Just a little demonstration for Trevor and the boys. Online is where all the magic is happening."

"I'll have to check it out," Zac said. "I've been thinking about my part of this plan, too."

Kory had been shut away in his luxury cabin with the bamboo shades drawn. He could have been anywhere. He could have been back at his apartment in the city, hidden in the dark to shield the truth of his glowing computer screen from the outside world. And Zac had been doing pretty much the same—going over dance moves, squeezing in sets of sit-ups and thinking about what strategy would really make a difference in this lopsided contest. So as a tropical paradise blew gently in the breeze around them, both Zac and Kory had sat alone in near darkness planning their individual parts in this scheme.

Zac, for one, realized being alone was not the answer. The only times he and Kory had succeeded during these few crazy weeks was when they stole away to confer in secret, when they bonded, told the truth and put their heads together to figure it all out. Zac had built his life and business all by himself. And he now realized that it took more than that. His life would require more than just him.

"I was thinking," Zac said. He put a foot up on a pile of canvas that could have been old sails or the discarded backdrop to some stage's set. "What's the one thing that's going to push them over the edge? These Beach Ball boys and judges and the whole town? Talent alone can't do it. Trevor has attitude, history, mystique. Just being better isn't good enough. To win, you have to be more fabulous..."

"Zac Djorvzac, did you just use the word 'fabulous?'" Kory asked, suddenly awake and completely in shock. "Someone's going to start thinking you're gay."

"You don't think these will convince them?" Zac asked, as he held up the short, shiny spandex trunks he intended to wear for the Beach Ball box-dancing contest.

"Is that pink?" Kory gasped.

"It is very pink," Zac conceded. "And so is this."

Zac held another pair of shorts up in his left hand that perfectly matched the pair he already held in his right. The shorts were identical, but smaller. Zac stood there in the dim, dusty light of backstage with his offering held before him and watched Kory's eyes narrow into suspicious slits.

"Is that your spare pair?"

"I don't think these are my size," Zac answered without lowering the pink suits a single inch.

"Oh no!" Kory said. He took a step back and sloshed a steamy dollop of coffee onto the plywood floor.

But Zac didn't flinch. He waited until Kory looked back up from the messy starburst of caffeine. Zac's eyes held a steady path to the man across the room. That path led between two matching pairs of pink square-cut briefs—one Zac's size and one Kory's.

"You are the secret move, Kory," Zac said without looking away. "You and me, on stage together. That's the one thing Trevor isn't suspecting. The one thing he can't dance away from. He can't beat us if we're together, Kory."

"But I can't dance," Kory reminded him.

"I can," Zac said. "And I can teach you how."

Before Kory could answer, Zac tossed the smaller pink shorts at him. Despite himself, Kory reached up to catch them one-handed while balancing his coffee cup with the other hand. Suddenly music filled the prop-graveyard. Zac had flipped the stereo switch, and electric dance music broke the silence. Its steady beat made dust motes bounce.

"Dance with me."

That was all Zac said. He tossed his own pink pair aside, and they landed on a painted Styrofoam boulder. He reached out his hand. And he waited as the music blared around them in that isolated morning.

Finally, Kory set down his coffee. He dropped those pink pants. And he shrugged as he approached Zac. Then he took Zac's hand. And the music took them. Zac pulled Kory to him and held him there, letting him feel the music around them, between them, within them. They barely moved as the rhythm coursed through them. They swayed. Their hips were pendulums. Their feet were the loose broken hands on a clock. And their bodies ticked away each second of that song in unison as if it would never end. As if they had all the time in the world.

<NEW CHAT—Beach Ball Contest—
click here to get all the latest!>

ballboy: 6 days to Beach Ball!!!!!!
dancedancedance: is Zac really entering the contest??
JdgeMeNot: I've seen his name on the official list.
ballboy: I know. I've worked Beach Ball
for 4 years. It's legit.
MkeMynaDbl: the travel guy??
vaca4me: the travel OWNER!
trvlr44: the BOSS
dancedancedance: Hell I'd pay to see that
curiUS: what the hell you think he looks
without the shirt n tie?
vaca4me: I didn't know it came off. lol.
JdgeMeNot: well, I heard he used to be quite the
dancer... and hot.
curiUS: when was that? 1970?
ballboy: I'm all for it. give Trev a run for his $.
the more the merrier.
MkeMynaDbl: the "Mary-er" you mean.

trvlr44: LOL

The list of potential Beach Ball champs was growing and growing. Kory had allowed nomination, speculation and voting. He was sure some of these box boys were just pumping up their own odds. But fair or not, E-male allowed a healthy competitive conversation to form around the typical monopoly of Trevor.

Kory d just needed to steer the gossip in the right direction. For the first time, these men were able to question why Trevor dominated the contest. They were able to talk about it anonymously with others and consider other options without fear of retribution. And Kory was able to enter Zac into the contest conversation on E-male just as Zac had entered himself in real life at the Beach Ball registration booth.

However, the one thing Kory did not enter into chat—the one entry that did not get added to the ever-growing list of contestants—was his own name. Zac had insisted that Kory's participation was a secret. It was meant to be that grand-finale move no one was expecting—it was the back flip, the lift, the death-defying spiraling jump. But a stealth dance move was not why Kory was keeping it a secret.

Kory had no idea why he had allowed Zac to talk him into this. In fact, Zac had done very little talking at all. And obviously Kory had done absolutely no thinking. At the time, tucked away in the hidden interior of Cabana Boy, Kory's mind must have been filled with nothing but music. Whatever other confusing thoughts and emotions danced in his head must have been drowned out. Especially his commonsense.

He had heard the beat. He had seen Zac's outstretched hand. And he had felt that intense green gaze pulling him with a tidal force. Everything seemed to draw him to Zac. And so Kory had moved. He had fallen into position against Zac's frame, and he had let the music move him.

Now, however, all those thoughts that had failed him came flooding back to their rational, logical place in his brain. Kory could not dance. He hated being the center of attention. He had never been on stage, but he was sure he had stage fright. In fact, he was afraid just thinking about it. And he had never, ever worn shorts that small—not on the beach, not even under his clothes.

Dancing. On stage. In public. In underwear.

What the hell had he been thinking... or not thinking, as the case may be? Somehow Zac Djorvzac had a way of getting Kory deeper and deeper into trouble, getting deeper and deeper under his skin, and taking him farther and farther away from his comfort zone. How exactly was it that Kory had ended up entering a box-dancing contest with a man he never really had a business deal with but had hate-fucked and gone on vacation with and declared war against an old enemy with and somehow kept finding himself face to face with in desolate locales? Kory had never met anyone who had infuriated and intrigued him as much as Zac Djorvzac.

He had entered into yet another deal without knowing what he was doing. But a deal was a deal. And Kory knew that somewhere deep down there was a reason he had agreed to all this. But if there was some reason, the very last thing he wanted to do was go looking for it and have to confront it when he found it.

Kory's head was spinning, but his dance moves were not. He had all he could do to focus on the computer screen in front of him. And he was supposed to be meeting Zac to work on that dance-move problem right now.

He had a company or two to save. He had a web site to control. He had a town to manipulate. And he was late to a dance rehearsal he didn't want to attend.

It was a saltwater pond. Hidden among mounds of sea-foam-colored bushes and brambles, it was like a perfect puddle. The reflections of clouds sailed across its warm surface in silence.

This is where Kory and Zac were to meet. Of course. It had to be a place that was secret and desolate. A place where no one would stumble across them. A place that Kory would fall in love with as soon as Zac showed it to him.

And like all the others—rain forests and coral reefs and backstages and even the promise of the top of a box in nightclub—it reflected Kory and Zac as clearly as the mirror of a waveless pond reflected clouds. Because all these hidden places were just real-life versions of E-male and Djorvzac Travel. They were isolated and secluded. They were places where Kory and Zac could self-quarantine themselves away from the infectious dangers of the rest of the world.

Kory's secret place was online, hidden behind the screen of E-male. Zac had sequestered himself away in that tiny dark office, behind his desk and the success he had built.

They had been hiding behind the fantasies of others—dream vacations and that elusive fairy-tale prince. They had been fulfilling everyone else while denying themselves. Certainly, Zac and Kory had more in common than it first appeared. At this point they didn't have to admit it to one another. They knew. Somehow Kory knew that Zac ran a travel company but never took a vacation for himself. And Zac could sense that despite E-male and those cupid-like instincts, Kory never went on a date.

They had never admitted those specifics to one another. But they didn't have to. They each recognized in the other a kindred workaholic—a unique brand of success that allowed them to ignore their own realities beyond their companies.

Kory was E-male in so many ways. But in the same vein, Zac was Djorvzac Travel. Exposing their weaknesses—their true selves—could potentially rip the hearts from those companies.

But it wasn't just two companies that were at stake if Trevor's lies and truths and revelations worked their evil. It was two men. Because without E-male and Djorvzac Travel, Kory and Zac didn't know who they were. They would have nowhere left to hide.

"I wasn't sure you were going to show up," Zac said as Kory fought his way through the brush.

Zac had his bare feet dangling in the pond, threatening its reflections with his ripples, as he sat back in his green shorts to lounge on the flawless white ring of sand that encircled the water. He looked up at Kory, who had sweat clinging to his forehead and a heart-shaped leaf stuck there.

"A deal is a deal, right?" Kory asked unconvincingly. "But is this really the most convenient place to hold a dance rehearsal?"

"I thought you might like it," Zac offered.

"That's beside the point."

The quick, defensive comment only convinced Zac that Kory loved the location that much more. Zac had known he would. There were no crashing waves or sweeping views. The pond was tucked away like a secret gem in Baytown's back pocket. They could see nothing but the still water and brush and sky. And no one could see them. Here, it was just the pond and them.

"Let's get started," Zac said. "You might want to take the rock-star jeans off."

"They're shorts," Kory insisted.

"Cutting a pair of black jeans at the knee does not make them shorts," Zac pointed out.

"Fine, Ms. Fashionista," Kory snapped as he unbuttoned his jeans and slid them off. "You're getting gayer by the minute."

Beneath the dark denim Kory was wearing a pair of yellow running shorts. They weren't quite skintight, square-cut spandex. But they were several inches above his knee, and they were a start in the right direction. Zac looked on approvingly at the awkward strip show as he stood and brushed grains of sand from his own green swimsuit.

"So, shall we dance?" Zac asked.

"I think you're forgetting that I don't know how." Kory looked awkward and boyish there in his bright-yellow shorts with sunshine in his hair. He looked like he wanted to disappear. It was as if this truly were his first dance.

"I think you do know how," Zac said. "When you don't pay attention. When you stop thinking about it. When you just move."

"You make it sound so simple," Kory said, tugging at his tee-shirt.

"It can be," Zac insisted as he stepped closer to Kory. He meant to comfort him, but there was something unsettling about approaching Kory all alone on a beach wearing nothing but a pair of green shorts. Zac remembered quite well what had happened in that private cove and the vow they had made to remain strictly business. So he turned back toward the pond and gestured a bit too quickly—a clumsy dance move in and of itself. "It can be natural, like the tide. Just flow with it."

"Is that why we're here?" Kory asked. "In your little tidal pool?"

"Well, actually it's a saltwater pond," Zac corrected. "At high tide a stream at the far end rises from the ocean to refresh it. It's not really a tide. It's more subtle."

"You want me to be subtle?"

"Little hope of that," Zac scoffed. But before Kory could disagree, Zac added, "I want you to get in the water."

"You must be kidding."

Zac didn't hear Kory's protest. Zac splashed into the pond before he could answer. The vee of his naked back seemed to bubble with muscle. His thick arms and legs thrashed akimbo at odd angles into the water with no care for form or grace. But when he settled, waist-deep, he appeared absolutely poised, with droplets of saltwater scattered across his chest hair like diamonds. He beckoned to Kory with a sly glance of his green eyes and a nod of his head.

"I thought I was going to learn dancing?" Kory said. "I already know how to swim."

"Then we're halfway there."

"I wasn't aware that this was a water-ballet contest," Kory joked, but Zac knew he was just procrastinating. He could see Kory playing with the hem of his shirt and shifting from foot to foot with his knees too close together.

"Just get in the water," Zac insisted. "And lose the shirt. You're going to have to get used to being a little more exposed."

Zac's voice caught a little as he mentioned exposure, hinted at nakedness, but Kory didn't seem to notice. He did as he was told and rolled his tee-shirt up over his slim body. The yellow shorts made his newly tanned skin glow and the sun-bleached strands of his shaggy hair stand out. Zac realized that despite Kory's complaints and city-boy stubbornness, Baytown's tropical climate suited him. It warmed him, made him just a few degrees closer to perfect. Zac suddenly remembered exactly how that skin tasted, as if his tongue was on Kory's nipple at that moment.

"I'm in," Kory said in that awkward wading moment between thigh and scrotum when the waterline rose higher and higher. It obliterated his bright shorts, almost as if it were undressing him. And he stood there, near naked in the water.

"Now just move," Zac said, banishing the fantasy and snapping back to the task at hand and away from his inch by inch assessment of Kory's torso. "Your hips, your hands, your feet. Every move should be natural and fluid, like you're in water. You're not hopping from foot to foot or flailing your hands around if you're in the water. Every move is slowed down, made smoother. Bring your hands from underwater to over your head. They pop out of the water dramatically. Turn around, and it's smooth. You can stop on a dime without being jarring. You don't want to bounce to the beat like so many of those box boys up there who look like they're boxing. You want to flow."

Zac started to move, to show Kory how to. He swayed his hips. He spun to churn the water. The ripples of Zac's movements radiated from the center of his dance to the edge of the pond. The reflection of sky shimmered. However, Kory just stood there with a look of disbelief on his face.

"Are you kidding me?" Kory said, stopping Zac's swimming dance.

"It's easy, Kory," Zac insisted, restarting his bob and sway. "Try it."

"When are you going to lift me over your head?" Kory asked.

"Huh?"

"Zac, give me a break. This is a joke, right?" Kory asked, but he wasn't laughing. "Seriously, this is way too Dirty Dancing for me."

"What are you talking about?" Zac asked right back. The confusion on his face was as genuine as Kory's expression. Zac had no idea what Kory was referring to. "What's dirty about this?"

"Dirty Dancing. 'The best place to practice lifts is in the water.' Patrick Swayze? Jennifer Grey? 'I Had the Time of My Life?'" Kory stared wide-eyed and blank-faced. "The movie!"

"I guess I didn't see that one," Zac said. He didn't really see what the big deal was. He'd never been much of a moviegoer. It went along with his aversion to the internet, entertainment and any technology that didn't aid in booking travel.

"You've...never...seen... Dirty Dancing!?" Kory was in absolute shock. No intimate detail Zac had admitted to him up to this point had horrified him so deeply. "My God! And you call yourself gay!?"

"Well, not very often."

Kory slapped at the pond's surface and splashed water onto Zac. Streams ran down his torso, matting the black chest hair to his skin. Zac didn't even hesitate. He pushed both hands into the water and sent a small tidal wave straight into Kory's face. Kory pounced, and Zac almost caught him. The two men fell into the water, disappearing beneath the surface briefly before reemerging in a tangle of arms and a froth of saltwater. There were grunts and unintelligible sounds when they came up for air or tried to reposition their attacks on one another.

Before either of them tired of the game or the exertion, the tussle came to an abrupt end. The feeling of arms around each other, the flex of struggling muscles, the rub of wet hair, skin and fingers—it all suddenly became awkward. The reality of touching was too much. Electric. And they both knew how the physical contact would end if they didn't put a stop to it soon enough.

In an unspoken mutual truce, Zac and Kory stood face to face, panting, soaking wet. Kory's bangs were plastered to his forehead, nearly obscuring his golden eyes. Water ran down the smooth perfect line of his stomach. Zac looked like the hair had been painted onto this tan chest and stomach by some artist whose medium was muscle.

"I think that was the most graceful I've ever seen you," Zac said, absolutely dripping. "Now let's dance,"

"Yeah? Well, you're no Patrick Swayze."

"I don't know who this Swayze guy is, but it sounds like he stole my idea for training dancers," Zac pointed out. "If it's good enough for your famous gay movie, maybe you should give it a try."

Zac grabbed Kory by the waist, pulling him toward him as if he were going to kiss him. There was a moment when they both saw doubt reflected in the other's eyes about what was going to happen in the slow-motion second as their bodies came together. But when they met, Zac just held still for a moment. Then he started dancing them around the pond, moving together as if they were the tide itself.

> *MissTree*: what the hell am I going to wear
> to Beach Ball
> *freEasy*: Less is More!
> *2much*: Tell me about it. Only 5 days to starve
> down to dancing weight
> *raVer*: I'm not wearing much more
> than a glowstick
> *freEasy*: Sounds like we should get to know
> each other
> *bXXXdncr*: Sounds like you should all get
> to know me. I AM Beach Ball
>
> <SURVEY—What to Wear?—click here
> to plan your outfit for Beach Ball>
>
> *bXXXdncr*: I'll be the one in blu...
> *bXXXdncr*: Anyone there?

When Kory wasn't dancing, he was E-maling. He imagined Zac was somewhere doing pushups or shopping for more revealing dancewear. And he knew the rest of the travel group was out there having a blast. He could see them on E-male, making plans, friends and the acquaintance of hot dates. They were taking full advantage of all that Baytown and E-male had to offer. Between volleyball, kayaking, bar-hopping, the beach and the boys, they were all having one hell of a vacation, and it wasn't even the main event yet. All day long, they gossiped on E-male about what had happened the night before, and what might happen in the thrilling days ahead leading up to Beach Ball.

Kory was glad everyone else was having a good time. He felt like he was working two jobs around the clock. He still had to put in time to make sure E-male members around the country were getting their money's worth. He had to watch the Baytown site like a hawk to steer conversation in the right direction and make sure Trevor was behaving himself. On top of everything else, Zac's dance school was just as hard as Kory had thought it would be. His ability to detect a beat was coming along little by little, but his hamstrings felt tied in knots and the muscles of his ass cheeks felt like jelly. Kory couldn't imagine what good a sense of rhythm would do him if he couldn't even move. All the squatting, spinning and stopping on a dime that Zac insisted on practicing was one hell of a workout.

Right now, however, it was Kory's back that ached. He had been sitting at his computer for hours. The boys were gearing up for Beach Ball and so was Kory. He wanted to make sure they were primed for the event. And he wanted to make sure that Trevor didn't do any last-minute damage. In fact, Kory wanted to make sure that he managed to do a little damage to Trevor.

So when Trevor entered a chat room, Kory would divert the conversation away from him. He would distract the members from whatever it was that Trevor wanted to talk about—which was often some salacious rumor about Zac or, more typically, himself. And when Trevor wasn't present, Kory took advantage of that situation as well. Kory knew he could entertain and distract E-male members easily. But he wanted to control the flow of conversation, activities and public opinion, too.

<Why exactly do you think Trevor wins every dance contest?>

<Guess Trevor's real age...>

<Who is the next Trevor?>

Kory got members to gossip about the original gossip-maker. He asked questions and started conversations that made people doubt Trevor, his intentions and his all-powerful reign over Baytown. People speculated that Trevor bought the contest every year. They had a running list of the plastic surgery they believed he'd had. They analyzed his dance moves as if they were the tactics of an enemy militia. And there was a vicious, but plausible, rumor that Trevor had gray pubes.

There was no more interesting topic in Trevor's town than Trevor himself. And that included the rumors he had started about Zac and Kory.

>   *grrreg*: is that stuffy travel owner really dancing at beach ball
>   *JdgeMeNot*: that's what the list says
>   *vaca4me*: midlife crisis?
>   *delish*: gotta be
>   *talk2me*: trying to be the young slut Trev told us about
>   *clthswhore*: I can't imagine him young or slutty
>   *ballboy*: that will make BB that much more fun
>   *JdgeMeNot*: train wreck!
>   *beachboy*: And where the hell is Kory?
>   *grrreg*: who?
>   *lushlife*: Kory.... the e-male owner
>   *vaca4me*: sun poisoning ? mental breakdown ?
>   *beachboy*: did he go back to the city?
>   *lushlife*: with his tail btwn his legs?
>   *ballboy*: id like to get between his legs
>   *talk2me*: Trev says he's with Zac
>   *lushlife*: impossible!
>   *Sporty1*: They HATE each other.
>   *vaca4me*: yeah. nothin in common.

Kory shut his laptop. The entire room of his Cabana Boy cabin plunged into darkness. Once again, he had flirted, made dates and had a great time—just not for himself. Always a bridesmaid, never a bride.

He crawled into the white, cloudlike linens of his luxurious bed. He would catch a few hours of sleep before he had to do it all over again. Wake up and suffer whatever dance practice Zac had dreamed up.

Zac Djorvzac. That thought was keeping his exhausted mind from sleep. How had Kory's destiny become entangled with his? How had he ended up here? Doing this? There were too many questions to answer. This is just the way it was. He had to work. He had to dance. He had to endure all of this before he could get out. He was too tired to doubt the crazy decisions he had made. He was in too deep. He was too lost to question the twisted paths he had chosen. And as his eyelids slid reluctantly over his golden irises, he was too raw and worn and close to the truth to keep the image of Zac Djorvzac from hanging before him like something he was looking forward to.

☆　☆　☆　☆

This time it was the sea. Out where the waves broke and the sun rose. But the tide was low, and the boulders were set far back from the water at the base of a cliff. They were dollops of lava that were too heavy to be swallowed by the sea. Every day, every ebb and flow of the tide, they resisted the salty lick of the ocean's tongue.

"This is your box," Zac called to Kory, pointing to one of the giant rocks tanning itself on the beach.

Zac hauled himself up on the other sphere and balanced on top of its bumpy black surface. Kory was beyond questioning Zac's crazy requests. He clamored sleepily up the hillside and hopped onto the rough-hewn globe Zac had pointed out. Kory teetered a bit atop his boulder on its rounded, uneven apex.

"If you can balance up here, you can dance anywhere," Zac reassured him.

"Need I mention Dirty Dancing again?" Kory asked, restoring his equilibrium by widening his stance and digging the balls of his feet into the curved, pockmarked stone.

"They danced on a box?" Zac asked.

"It was a log," Kory explained.

"Huh," Zac remarked, although he couldn't begin to see what was relevant or interesting about these supposed cinematic similarities. This was real life, not the wide screen. "Well, dancing on a box or platform or stage is not as easy as it looks. There's limited space. You have to know where your edges are. And with the lights and crowds, it's easy to get vertigo."

"Great. You're really helping my stage fright," Kory said sarcastically.

Zac ignored the comment. He pulled a tiny remote control from the pocket of his shorts and pointed it at the small portable stereo he'd propped on top of his backpack. He pressed a button and suddenly the entire beach was filled with an electronic backbeat.

"OK," Zac said as he climbed back onto his geological dancing box, "time to lose the shorts."

"You've got to be kidding."

"You are wearing underwear aren't you, Kory?" Zac asked playfully.

"Of course I am," Kory snapped. "But 'under' is exactly where they belong."

"You've got to get used to being more exposed. And dancing freely in a much smaller outfit. Plus, there isn't even anyone here."

"Except you."

"And it's nothing I haven't seen before," Zac said, biting his tongue as the final syllable escaped his mouth too soon. "I mean, I'm all the way over here on my own rock. So... Look, I'll go first."

Zac pulled of his suit with his dark eyebrows raised and an intentional look of "see, no big deal" spread across his face. Underneath he was wearing high-cut black bikini briefs. The waistband narrowed to almost nothing at his hips, the v-shaped back exposed the bottom cleft of his ass muscles, and the front pouch held his package aloft between his muscular thighs. He wasn't trying to be slutty. They were just the only pair of underwear that would fit underneath his snug bathing suit. Normally, he wouldn't have worn any underwear at all. So he thought he'd planned ahead modestly for today's dance practice.

"There. See? No big deal," Zac said to Kory. Over on his rock, it was clear that Kory was trying his hardest not to see at all. He looked at the sky, the ocean, the dirt under his fingernail. "Come on. Your turn, Kory."

Unhappily, like a child trying on dress clothes or dramatically choking down Brussels sprouts, Kory pulled off his running shorts and tossed them to the sand. Paralyzed by shyness, he didn't even allow himself to look down at his own state of undress. He looked vaguely somewhere over Zac's left shoulder. Zac couldn't help but smile when he noticed that Kory was wearing briefs styled like sporty kids-wear. The only thing that kept them from being tighty whities was the fact that they were yellow with red piping. And the only thing that kept them from appearing childlike was the man-size bulge at front. Along the elastic waistband, there appeared to be a row of red fire trucks.

"Man, you're on fire!" Zac joked.

"Don't say another word," Kory ordered, finally looking Zac in the eye again. "Let's just dance."

Kory found the beat before Zac even instructed him to. He bobbed and twisted on top of his boulder, following the rise and fall of the music. So Zac joined in. He fell into rhythm beside Kory, dance partners separated by air and sand and whatever other invisible, unspoken things were keeping them apart. Without words, Zac showed Kory how to lift one foot from the stone surface while retaining his balance and beat. Zac turned. He hoped. And he watched Kory follow suit.

The music melded into a new song, transitioning seamlessly the way intermixed dance beats change moods so fluidly. The percussion got deeper and faster, booming through the stone at their feet. Electronic blips peppered the air between sunrays. And Kory and Zac flowed right along with it all. They dipped their hips and rolled their shoulders. They raised hands above their heads, maintaining eye contact and reflecting each other's moves like a man dancing in a funhouse mirror. Although their bodies followed each other in time, their appearances contrasted the identical dances.

Slim versus rugged. Smooth versus hairy. Light versus dark.

Kory and Zac complemented their dance with opposite looks. They moved on their separate pillars like yin and yang, kept apart by a boundary that was hardly discernable but undeniably there. There was a line that kept them divided, but it didn't stop the perception that at any moment they could spill into each other.

They reached out toward one another, and their arms created a bridge between them, spanning the distance that had existed between these giant rocks for thousands of years. It was as if the force of their attraction could draw tons of stone together. Their hands could barely touch. They locked their fingers at the top row of knuckles. And they felt the beat of the dance pass through each other's bodies.

Suddenly Kory's eyes went wide. There was a speck on the horizon. Someone was coming along the beach. Kory jumped down from his boulder in absolute fright. But since Kory's fingers were entwined with Zac's, he came along for the plunge too. The boulders were a good ten-feet tall, but the sand below and their practiced dancer's poise somehow allowed them both to land on their feet, side by side, still holding hands.

"Well, at least your balance is improving," Zac said, laughing as soon as he saw that no legs had been broken. "Your stage fright though, we're going to have to work on."

They huddled there in the shadow between the boulders. Kory shrank back into the crevice, as if the little old man down the beach was going to turn his attention and poor eyesight away from hunting seashells to look at Kory's little-boy briefs.

"You really are getting very good," Zac said. He let go of Kory and sat in the cool shadow of rock, leaning back against the monolith. He waited for Kory to relax, to sit down, to take a moment and wonder exactly what Zac thought he was getting very good at.

Zac flipped off the dance music as he waited. He was sure the little old man was as deaf as he was nearsighted, but he figured the silence would make Kory more comfortable. Finally Kory settled into the shadow of his own boulder. He still looked apprehensively up and down the beach and placed his hands in his lap modestly. But Zac could see the sharp angle of hip bone above that fire-truck waistband. He could see how the blonde down of Kory's calves grew tawnier and thicker as it climbed his inner thigh to disappear beneath his briefs; how it poked out again briefly to trace a thin line to his navel. This sun-kissed, mostly naked man was not the same pale, skinny city boy who had barged into Zac's office and demanded some forged business partnership. Kory was the man who was saving Zac's ass. Guarding his secrets. Putting everything on the line for no reason at all.

Zac realized that he had never given his trust to anyone as he had to Kory. And it had happened without his knowledge, without a conscious decision. Secret by secret, day by day, he had slowly found himself here with Kory in this situation—whatever that was. And as odd as the lack of control and understanding was, it just felt right. They were the center of things—with everything spinning crazily around them like unnamed planets.

But Zac also knew that no matter how good that confusion felt, he couldn't allow it to interfere with their plan. A deal was a deal. So he would have to be content sitting here, inches apart, and not reaching out for Kory. Now when Zac danced with Kory, he would also have to dance against his own desires in constant, exquisite pain.

"Your dancing is great," Zac said. "I knew you could be a real dancer. You just needed to forget about everyone else and trust yourself."

"It doesn't really matter if I can't do it in front of anyone but you," Kory said, finally giving up his surveillance of the tiny dot in the distance that could have possibly spotted him dancing in his underwear. "But thanks."

"A lot has happened over the last few days," Zac ventured. "The last few weeks. A lot has changed."

"Tell me about it," Kory said. "You certainly aren't the Zac Djorvzac I met back at the office."

"I never was," Zac said absently.

"And what's that supposed to mean?"

"Well, do you want the literal or figurative answer?" Zac

asked, but Kory just stared at him skeptically as if he had all the answers he could handle. Somehow Zac felt compelled to tell him anyway. "Zac Djorvzac is whatever I built up and hid behind all those years. The party. The agency. The desk in my windowless office. That wasn't me you met. That was someone hiding from the real me."

"Deep," Kory said, but there was less joking in his tone than Zac would have expected. Perhaps less than Kory himself had intended. But Kory's biting sarcasm was just one more thing that had changed over this relatively short period of time. Kory recognized the truth in what Zac said, and he had offered his own truths too. For two men with so many secrets, so many lies, truth was becoming their code, the language they only spoke to one another.

"Besides," Zac added. "It's not my real name."

"What?" Kory jumped as if Zac had pulled a knife. "Are you a psychopath? Witness protection?"

"Calm down," Zac said, placing a steadying hand on Kory's knee. "'Zac' is just a nickname. From 'Djorvzac,' which is impossible enough to pronounce. Adding 'Czcibor' to it would be a killer."

"Chest is bore?" Kory asked quizzically.

"Czcibor. It's my real first name," Zac admitted. "It means 'battle of honor.'"

"How fitting," Kory said. "But seriously, are you from some foreign mafia? Who gives a name like that to a kid?"

"It's some ancient family name," Zac explained. "My parents thought it would be unique."

"Well, they were certainly successful there."

"I guess they were." And Zac laughed. "But 'Zac Djorvzac'? My parents may have given me a first name just as hideous as my last, but they never would have named me something that rhymed."

"Why not?" Kory asked. "My parents named me Kory with a K"

"Yeah, but that's kind of cute," Zac said. "Cute with a K, of course."

Kory slapped at him. And looked him straight in the eye.

"You have no idea how cute," Kory said. "You want a name secret to beat yours? I'm named Kory with a K because my parents are named Karl and Krista...with Ks."

"KKK?" Zac asked through his laughter. "That is a lot worse than triple D."

"Enough, Czcibor."

For a moment, they just laughed there together in that cool pool of shadow, hidden from all that sunshine by the ancient boulder gods whose heads they'd just danced upon. And they didn't need to kiss. They sat so close. Their words were so intimate. That's what Zac told himself. This was enough. This was more than he'd ever had. Two elbows in the sand, propping up heads that were very near. There was no need to take this too far. Their truths were like kisses.

"How many more secrets are we going to tell each other?" Zac asked. But he didn't really want an answer. He wanted the surprise of it. And Kory seemed to know this, because he didn't even attempt to respond.

Zac suddenly realized that his hand was still on Kory's knee. He realized that neither of them had moved it, to shift positions so that their contact was broken. Slowly, almost without thinking, almost as if he were watching someone else do it, Zac ran his thumb back and forth slowly through the bleached-white fuzz on Kory's kneecap.

It wasn't that Kory stiffened. It wasn't that he recoiled. It was more like he caught himself relaxing, like he had started to nod off when he promised himself he wouldn't. He snapped his head and gathered his thoughts. Awkwardly, he stood and brushed sand from places where they was no sand.

"Sorry," he stammered. "I just can't stay out here all day. E-male, you know. So much to do. Only a few days until Beach Ball."

"Tomorrow?" Zac asked, keeping any trace of disappointment from creeping into his voice.

"Beach Ball?!" Kory choked out. "Beach Ball isn't tomorrow!"

"No," Zac said quietly. "Dancing. Tomorrow?"

"Oh, yes, dancing," Kory said. "Tomorrow. I'll see you tomorrow."

He grabbed his shorts from a sunny spot in the sand and jogged away. Zac watched the yellow butt of Kory's fire-truck underpants bob away from him. And he just lay there in the shade, which somehow, alone, just felt like hiding.

Czcibor. Zac hadn't told anyone but his accountant that name in over a decade. Battle of honor. And now here he was, with Kory, locked in their own battle of honor. Against Trevor and their companies and the entire rumor mill of Baytown. Who knew if they would win? Zac wasn't even sure what they were fighting for anymore. He wasn't sure if he and Kory were on the same side or fighting the same battle. They might think they were, but what would winning mean to either of them? The same thing? Anything at all? What did "winning" even mean?

And despite all that, was there anything, any secret, he would not tell Kory Miles? As soon as the thought crossed Zac's mind there in the cold sand, he knew that there was one thing. It was the secret he held about Kory Miles. The secret that Zac would not even whisper to himself.

bXXXdncr: 4 days till Beach Ball & Z Djrvzac thinks he can change history??

bXXXdncr: Take a look at his past. He was the biggest whore in Baytown

<SURVEY—Baytown Whores—click here to take survey >

bXXXdncr: It wasn't just shots he was giving in that club

<SURVEY—Favorite Drinks—click here to see the top 5 >

bXXXdncr: the real reason he left town was bc he ran out of men

bXXXdncr: or his reputation made the men run away
from him

<SURVEY—Men's Running—click here to start a group activity>

Kory was exhausted halfway through the afternoon. He reasoned it must be heat or dehydration or stress. He had run all the way back from the beach. And he couldn't tell if he was running toward something or away from it. He knew E-male desperately needed tending. However, he also knew how it had felt to sit there on the beach, alone yet again, with Zac.

Kory could have just as easily been running toward his responsibility as he could have been running away from his feelings. He couldn't tell what was or was not happening. He didn't know if he was happy or not. But when he slammed the bamboo door behind him, sat in his dark room and opened his laptop, he knew exactly how he felt. And it was distinctly not happy.

The wedge of high-tech light spread through the room like a rising electrical moon. And when that screen was at full, Kory saw just how bad things could be when they were exposed out in the light. Kory hadn't been there to keep Trevor out of chats about the box-dancing odds. He hadn't been able to keep the criticism, speculation and other contestants' opinions from Trevor's prying eyes. And the protective features that he had built into E-male had simply failed.

Reviewing the records of the many chats he had missed earlier, Kory could see that E-male's attempts to counteract Trevor's attacks had not worked. Maybe Trevor had figured it out. Maybe Kory just wasn't that good at programming. Or maybe there was just no way to stop the flow of gossip and E-male's downward spiral.

Kory reviewed the evil snippets of conversations that Trevor had started. In bits and pieces, Trevor had dropped every sinister rumor into the conversion. He had planted seeds of doubt, scandal and conspiracy. Predictably, the entire Baytown chat room had eaten up the salacious stories. They couldn't get enough.

Whether they believed it all or not, they couldn't wait to see Zac's comeback performance at Beach Ball. They may have even been looking forward to his defeat and humiliation at the hands of Trevor. They just wanted a dramatic disaster.

> *bXXXdncr*: How does some washed up slut think he
> can challenge Trevor?
> *bXXXdncr*: A bloated businessman is no match for
> the real king of Beach Ball

Whether or not they were now rooting for Trevor again, he had diverted their attention from questioning his perennial championship. He'd managed to drag Zac's name through the mud. And he'd managed to get a few anonymous plugs in for himself amid the barbs and slander—dragging the spotlight back onto his own box.

But what bothered Kory was not that Trevor was getting his way again, or even that he had used E-male to get it. It wasn't that more rumors were out there in the open, poisoning the pool of public opinion against Zac, the box-dancing contest and the entire E-male/Djorvzac Travel experiment. Suddenly all those worries that had consumed them and hatched this crazy plan didn't matter at all.

More than anything, what worried Kory was that there might be truth in there, on his screen, somewhere. He already knew that many of the damaging revelations Trevor had made about Zac were, in fact, true. Zac himself had told Kory.

But Kory worried that there was a deeper truth between those lines of chat. Somewhere between Trevor's vicious jabs, the shock of the chat-room audience, and the obvious delight they all took in the contrast between Zac the washed-up go-go boy and Zac the tyrant boss. Kory felt absolutely sick that there was something more true. Not just facts and dates and regrettable acts. Not that Trevor had infected all of E-male and even Kory with his seeds of doubt. But a truth that Kory could feel in his gut. One that challenged the truth in his heart.

Because suddenly everything felt different. And everything made sense. Kory knew why these past several days of dancing had gotten more and more tense. He knew why he flinched at every touch of Zac's skin. The brush of his hand or his stubbled cheek. Kory felt as if he were locking up, losing what little rhythm he had gained. There was something wrong with the entire situation. And now it was staring him straight in the face. It was Zac Djorvzac.

Zac was no different than he had been before. If Kory forced himself to consider everything carefully, unsentimentally, he could see that. Drugged-out club boy or stick-in-the-ass boss—Zac was doing whatever it took to put himself first without thinking of anyone else.

He was trying to use his power and knowledge and persuasion to make Kory do what he wanted. Was it really any different than how he bossed his employees around and orchestrated every move of his travel empire? How he switched roles from club kid to businessman when it suited him? How he had used up Baytown until he had squeezed all the fun out of it and was left with nothing but dried vomit and regrets?

It may have been a drastic conclusion to draw, but it all suddenly clicked when Kory saw the truth about Zac in the plain light of his computer screen where all of Baytown could point out its absurdity. A man who would do things like that. A man who would then go on to found a travel agency run like a dictatorship. How could Kory have believed that there was any other man beneath that? His confusing emotions were just obscuring these obvious truths. And it became suddenly clear that these emotions were a fabrication of Zac Djorvzac, too. No wonder they made absolutely no sense.

Why else would Kory feel this way? Why else would it seem that Zac had evolved so dramatically over just the past week? How could things change so quickly and completely, as if Kory were tumbling out of control?

Zac hadn't changed at all in the last decade—let alone the last week. He had simply morphed to survive. And now he had simply shifted his form again to appease Kory, to tell him what he needed to hear. It wasn't that Zac had lied exactly. It was just his nature—the proof of which Kory could now see right in front of him on screen—whatever quality that had passed for charm ten years ago or business suavity ten days ago. Basically, whatever it took to get what Zac wanted.

And what Zac wanted in this case was to fulfill his self-centered fantasy about winning and validating and reclaiming a past that was long gone. What was in it for Kory? What possible benefit could he get from dancing in this circus? The entire plan was as ridiculous and doomed as the confusing, uncomfortable intimacy that had been developing during this entire "rehearsal" process.

Zac was just using Kory for his own means. And Kory didn't feel like being used. He felt a cold sickness inside when they danced or locked eyes mid-move. What was this intensifying feeling? And why did it anger him so to think that this was all a game, a mere manipulation so Zac could get his way?

It didn't really matter what Zac was trying to do. Kory would not allow his feelings to be manipulated. Kory was much more used to being the one in control, pulling the strings to make others dance. He was the manipulator. With a few key strokes, he could change opinions, spark romance or destroy a reputation.

So Kory pulled up a chair and tucked into E-male for the night. Ensuring his own success, not Zac's, was why he was here in the first place. It was why he had met Zac Djorvzac. Why he had ended up in Baytown. And it was why he had to do what he was doing now. It was time for Kory to take back control.

The Pump had hubcaps instead of disco balls. There were unusually tall parking meters on boxes for pole-dancing. And the jukebox was fashioned as a gas pump. The old club wasn't quite what it used to be. But that only made it all the more perfect for Zac's afternoon dance practice. The owner had assured him that no one came in till well after dark. In the ebb and flow that was the popularity of bars in Baytown, what had been the hottest spot in town back in Zac's day was now a local watering hole for middle-aged businessmen and drag queens with sloppy eye shadow. But as Zac knew all too well, tides changed quickly around here.

Zac was on stage preparing for Kory's arrival. He was busying himself so he wouldn't think too much or notice how late Kory was. Zac pulled back a dusty black velvet curtain and swept away last New Year's faded confetti. He moved some old orange crates, and he cleared the stage as best he could.

Despite the distractions, Zac was buzzing with nervous energy. Beach Ball was only three days away. But more exciting than that looming finale to the trip, this whole crazy scheme was working better than Zac had imagined. Kory could really dance. He was one of the best Zac had ever seen. When the music came on, something came alive between them, or they allowed it to come alive there between the rhythmic beats.

Zac never would have guessed that his past could come back to haunt him in such a positive way. He had spent the previous decade running away from it. He had focused on the travel agency as if he could continuously travel forward, building enough momentum to outpace his history. But in doing so he actually had gone nowhere. He had built rules and walls around himself as drab as those back in his office, countless roadblocks between him and a real future.

But Kory Miles had brought that all crashing down. He had dragged Zac back to face his own dark ages. And he had helped Zac see that his knowledge of Baytown was not all a bad memory. There were magical moments and places here. And Zac's internal rhythm—that somehow had not suffocated over the years—was what had finally allowed him to feel as if he were dancing with someone for the first time ever. That very past may be what would save their companies—what would end up saving them. But until Kory came along, Zac hadn't even known he needed to be saved.

Zac did want to save his agency. He did want to protect E-male. But more than anything, it was the fact that Kory had put himself on the line for Zac. He had stood up to Trevor and taken control. He had walked into the tropics in a pair of black jeans and taken over. Kory Miles had taken all of Baytown by storm. And Zac was shaken by the aftermath.

Stunned and vulnerable, Zac felt stronger than ever. He was going to face Trevor's threats head-on. Because he was not that scared, confused boy who had followed in Trevor's glittering footsteps down a very dark path. But he also was not that walled-up man who had forbidden Dancing, Dating and Drama in the workplace and in his own life. Now he was going to show everyone that no matter what truth was in those rumors, he could stand up to them, own them, and dance his way past them—with Kory at his side.

Kory stormed into Pump with very little sense of rhythm and with a very big scowl on his face.

"Let's get this over with," he said to Zac without looking him in the eye.

"OK." Zac popped a CD into the stereo and cranked the volume. He knew Kory was exhausted. He knew Kory had been working overtime to make E-male work as hard as it could for them. So he wasn't going to let Kory's tardiness or even his cute little pout disrupt the rehearsal.

Things had been going so well. Zac had even worked out a few new moves and steps. It was harder than it seemed to prevent two people box-dancing from looking like they were doing the tango. They were dancing that fine line between strip joint and ballroom.

Kory reluctantly came on stage when Zac beckoned. He dragged his feet, kept his eyes turned away and made no effort to remove his shorts and tee-shirt. That was fine. Zac had at least gotten him on stage. They could keep their clothes on today.

"OK, now step toward me and turn, like this," Zac instructed. He fell in time to the music and waited. But when Kory stepped, he completely missed the beat. Zac put a hand to Kory's waist and tried to guide him back into the rhythm. Kory was so far out of tune that Zac's helping hand caused him to stumble slightly into the wall of Zac's chest. Zac steadied him there, practically holding him. It was all he could do not to pull Kory fully into his embrace.

"What's wrong?" Zac asked.

"Nothing," Kory snapped. But even as he said it, he pulled away from Zac's touch. And the music blared on.

"It's just that," Zac began, "that you don't seem to be enjoying yourself. You're just not dancing as well as you have been these past few days."

"Oh, now you're telling me the truth." Kory walked to the other side of the stage, crossing his arms and keeping his back to Zac.

"Why would I lie to you?" Zac asked. "Kory, you're the only one I've ever told the complete truth to."

But Zac's comment didn't soften Kory's disposition. In fact, Kory's spine stiffened. And he didn't offer a single word in response. So Zac knew exactly what this was about.

"You can see for yourself," he called out to Kory. "Everything I told you is what Trevor is telling everyone else right now. Yes, I saw it on E-male too."

Zac had seen it. He'd been watching for Trevor online just like Kory. But somehow Zac didn't think it mattered anymore. He had sat alone in the dark, too. He had imagined Kory sitting in the next cabin over, working behind E-male to protect him, to protect them both.

When Zac had seen all of his secrets and fears on screen, he felt an odd relief. He had known it was coming back to haunt him. And this time he was ready. At least he had thought he was. He couldn't believe that Trevor had finally gotten to Kory, too. Infected him like all the others. Zac had wanted so badly to believe that Kory was immune.

"Kory, what am I supposed to do about it?" Zac asked to Kory's back. "This is all I can do. You can see I don't have any other choice. You can see what I'm up against. What we're up against."

"We're not up against anything," Kory said bitterly, finally spinning around to look straight at Zac from across the stage. With the music pouring from the speakers and the dramatic words being flung across the expanse of the stage, the scene could have been a great theatrical tragedy, or something much sadder. "You just want to win."

"Well, we're never going to win this way," Zac said simply.

"Fine. Good," Kory spat at him. "Maybe we shouldn't. Maybe we should lose."

Suddenly the song came to a stop. And the silence was like another person in the room. Because despite the glare that cut across the stage like a knife, there was definitely something standing between Zac and Kory now.

"What are you talking about, Kory? What's wrong with winning?"

"I'm saving your ass online every day, and now you want me to save it by shaking mine up there next to yours?" Kory's question did not want an answer. His face was red and breathless and full of anger. "All I wanted was for this trip to work. But you and Trevor have made that pretty difficult."

"I warned you about Trevor," Zac said softly. "I'm doing everything I can for us."

"This isn't about you and me. This is about you and him. So why don't I just sell the damn thing to Trevor if he wants it? Getting rid of E-male would solve all my problems." Kory had not lowered his voice since the music stopped. He looked lost and scared. And he looked beyond any place where Zac could reach him. His golden eyes were red-rimmed, and his bangs clung to the sweaty grease of his forehead. "Why am I out here dancing in a pair of underwear with you every day?

"That's a good question, Kory," Zac pointed out. But his voice was weaker than his argument. "Maybe you should take a good hard look at that."

It didn't appear that Kory was prepared to take a look at anything. He certainly wasn't coming to whatever erroneous conclusions Zac was beginning to draw for them earlier. Kory's mind was obviously made up, and his face was set like the eternally disappointed countenance of a gargoyle.

Zac felt as if something solid had fallen out from beneath him. Like in a dream, on the edge of sleep, as if he'd been holding on to that gargoyle's clawfoot on a ledge and he'd lost his grip. He'd just been dreaming that he was falling. But the reality of it all was no less of a crash. Because there was no greater disappointment—no greater fall—than when something had been built up with hopes and emotions and expectations, only to fall so much farther to the depths of the truth.

Kory didn't want to win? Kory didn't want to help him? Kory didn't even want his own business to succeed? Zac had failed before in life. But he could never remember a single time when he hadn't wanted to win.

"What kind of businessman would want to throw away his company?" Zac asked.

"And what the hell do you want to win?" Kory challenged. He took a step toward Zac, advancing across the stage without really bringing them any closer. "Do you want to go back to your musty little office and rot? Is that winning?"

"It's something," Zac answered. "And it's more than that. It isn't quitting."

"It isn't more than that," Kory insisted, as if whatever Zac was implying was absurd, as if these past weeks hadn't even happened. "You can't change the past, Zac. And you can't use me to try and do it."

"Use you?" Zac was horrified and insulted. "This has always been about both of us, working together."

"No, Zac. This is your grudge match that is somehow affecting me." Kory explained. "We can't win. We can't have it both ways. Winning would just mean you get your meaningless moment of pride. But I'm right back where I started, stuck with E-male and no way out. Losing isn't really losing for me. Selling E-male is what I wanted before I ever met you. I'd walk away from Baytown with money in my pocket and forget all this ever happened. Because it never should have."

"You want to lose?" Zac asked. None of this made any sense. This didn't sound like the Kory he thought he knew. The man standing across the stage from him now sounded like a crazed version of the slick city kid who had walked into his office full of demands and declarations.

"I want what I've wanted all along," Kory said. "Somehow I forgot that. Somehow you distracted me or convinced me that I needed more. But I don't. I'm not just one more person in your life who you can take advantage of, boss around and get what you want from. I can't believe it took me this long to see it. I can't believe I've spent almost a week pretending you were Patrick Swayze."

"Well, I guess 'Nobody puts Baby in a corner,'" Zac said,

quoting what was perhaps the most famous horrible line in cinematic history.

"You watched Dirty Dancing?" Kory asked, suddenly caught off-guard.

And the entire situation could have been funny. It could have been the punch line to the joke Kory had been making all week. They could have laughed at the image of Zac sitting alone in his room watching a movie made for teenage girls. Zac wished that they could explode into laughter, dance and forget this conversation had ever happened. But he could tell from the look on Kory's confused face that there was nothing funny about it. This was no joke.

"At the time, I trusted the person who recommended it," was all Zac said.

"Well, I do feel like I'm in a corner," Kory said. "Backed right up against two walls—E-male and this contest walling me in. And you're standing right in front of me, preventing me from going anywhere."

"I'm not standing in your way Kory." Zac said. "I'm standing here for a reason."

"And whatever that reason is, it's not mine," Kory said. "It's your reason, Zac."

Zac opened his mouth to explain, to articulate the reason that he felt so strongly. He wanted to close the distance between them, fill it full of reasons why. But what was that reason? Was it revenge for Zac's past? Was it success for this trip? Salvation for E-male? Or was it something more? Something that was an unspoken result of all those other insignificant reasons, of everything they had done since meeting each other? Because Zac didn't actually care if they won or lost. There was only one thing he cared about. And now, he couldn't say it.

"If you're not standing in my way, Zac, then I can walk out of this corner," Kory said, taking a step toward the stage's edge. "I can leave you alone with your contest and your grudge."

"You want me to lose?" Zac asked, grasping at words and logic to keep Kory standing there until this was right again. "Alone? Throw the contest?"

"Do whatever you want. Just do it without me. This is your battle, Zac," Kory said definitively. "Win if you want to. If it matters that much. It won't change a thing. For me or for you. Anyway, you have a better chance without me."

And Kory walked away. He jumped from the stage and walked out of the club. He may as well have jumped off a cliff. Zac could feel him falling away.

"I don't want a chance without you," Zac said.

But Kory didn't hear him. He was too far gone and too entangled in the voices inside his own head. Zac just heard himself there on that empty stage, but even he himself wasn't sure what he meant.

CHAPTER 11

<Join the Trevor fan club—click here>

<Vote for Trevor now—click here>

PecsnAbs: is he going to do it again this year?
MissTree: Trev has never failed us before
Partee: 2 days til we find out!
raVer: who could outdance him???
bXXXdncr: No One!
JdgeMeNot: sounds like u know what yr talking about. U should talk to me.
bXXXdncr: And who the hell are you?
JdgeMeNot: I know who u are. and you should def know who i m.

<PVT CHAT—bXXXdncr you have a private invitation to chat with JdgeMeNot>

Kory watched the private window open as a sidebar to the main chat room. There were dozens of these little private nooks at any given time. Any member could initiate a private chat with any other member. If that member accepted, then a new box would open up. The E-male members could only see the chat windows they were personally involved in. Kory, however, could see layers and layer of these windows. He could peek into any one he wanted, to see their intimate chatter, flirtations and secrets. He could use this view to match up men, test compatibility or weed out bad apples.

This time, he was solely focused on the window containing bXXXdncr and JdgeMeNot. Kory knew very well who they were. The first was highlighted in red on his screen—the one and only owner of a passcode with three sixes. The second had a combo code. His passcode began with a five, which meant he was a dirty old man. But the last three digits of his code identified him as a senior official of Beach Ball.

Kory knew exactly who he was. He was a potbellied pompous ass with a greasy gray comb-over. He had been involved with Beach Ball since before the dawn of time, and somehow he thought that entitled him to pinch the ass of every boy who walked by. He was important in his own mind, and apparently at Beach Ball. And now he wanted to chat with Trevor.

<Welcome to PVT CHAT>

<bXXXdncr and JdgeMeNot>

    bXXXdncr: Who are you?
JdgeMeNot: calm down trevor
    bXXXdncr: So you do know who I am. Interesting.
JdgeMeNot: i've been waiting a long time to
               finally meet u.
    bXXXdncr: The pleasure is all mine. I'm sure.
JdgeMeNot: u have no idea how pleasurable.
    bXXXdncr: Do tell.

JdgeMeNot:	i think we could increase each other's pleasure quite a lot
bXXXdncr:	How so?
JdgeMeNot:	i'd hate to see you lose that contest
bXXXdncr:	That makes two of us..
JdgeMeNot:	u don't have to
bXXXdncr:	mmm... tell me more.
JdgeMeNot:	do u know who judges the box dance?
bXXXdncr:	Hmm... There was never any question who was going to win.
JdgeMeNot:	well i guess there will be this year.
bXXXdncr:	So who judges?
JdgeMeNot:	me
bXXXdncr:	Really? That does sound pleasurable
JdgeMeNot:	but i thought mayb u could help me judge this year.
bXXXdncr:	There's an open position?
JdgeMeNot:	very open
bXXXdncr:	How much?
JdgeMeNot:	i wasn't talking about money
bXXXdncr:	ok

Kory could have stopped it. He could have kept Trevor from entering these contest conversations as he had in the beginning. He could have stopped promoting this topic and the subject of Trevor. He could have kept these two men from ever meeting on E-male. He could have terminated their chat session as soon as it started or undone the deal as soon as it happened. He could have stopped them from setting up a rendezvous or sealing the deal. But he didn't.

Kory had allowed each and every step toward this conclusion to take place. He had even helped it along. Some deeper part of himself wanted to see it all play out. He wanted Trevor to sell himself, his reputation and his body. He wanted Trevor to wear the uncomfortable crown of hollow victory. And he wanted to lose that bet and finally be rid of E-male's burden.

If Trevor cheated. If Zac lost. E-male would be gone. And so would this horrible sense of power. Kory wanted to make a tidy profit by selling E-male and relinquishing the control that let him do evil things like this.

Because that feeling of delight in his chest when he matched two compatible men had gone dark. That power he had used for good had now been misused too many times by himself and everyone else. And this new dark feeling of supremacy did not feel bad. It felt strong and protective. Because he could see the future and twist it to his will. Because it was not always under his control. And because, for some reason, Kory also wanted to see Zac lose.

In its own twisted way, this was the perfect solution. Kory would be getting secret revenge on both Trevor and Zac. Trevor would have to sell out to get his way, and he'd know that he'd needed E-male to do it. And Zac would not get his way this time. He'd know once and for all that he couldn't control everyone and everything. He could not use Kory and his emotions to play his games.

And best of all, Kory would be selling E-male. He would be able to forget about all this and return to real life. Because he would be severing that visceral tie between the dark inner part of himself and the real Kory—as if he could cut an umbilical cord between the flesh-and-blood Kory and the virtual Kory that was E-male.

☆　☆　☆　☆

"What the hell are you doing, Kory?" Jeff asked as he stepped onto the patio surrounding Cabana Boy's pool.

Kory was on a raft in the middle of the pool, wearing a straw hat, enormous sunglasses and sipping a double piña colada with a hundred-proof rum floater.

"I am on vacation," Kory snapped with a bit of a slur. "Everyone else seems to be having a good time. So leave me the fuck alone!"

"It's 8:00 in the morning," Jeff pointed out.

"So why are you bothering me?"

Jeff grabbed a pool net with a long handle and used it to pull Kory's raft to the edge of the pool.

"Dude, watch out for my drink!" Kory screeched, paddling furiously with his free hand against Jeff's net.

"Is that breakfast?" Jeff asked as he grabbed the inflated edges of the raft and anchored Kory's vessel poolside.

"It's dessert," Kory said, annoyed. "I've been up for hours."

"Apparently," Jeff said, flipping his bluish bangs out of his eyes as he struggled to keep Kory from floating away. "Aren't you supposed to be taking care of E-male?"

"Oh, I took care of it all right," Kory said, waving his drink in the air. "Haven't you joined the Trevor fan club yet?"

"What are you talking about?" Jeff asked. "Last I heard, we weren't allowed to play with him and his yacht anymore."

"Never mind," Kory slurred.

"You're talking nonsense," Jeff said, pulling Kory's limp body off the raft and onto the concrete. "I think it's beddy-bye time."

"You're spilling my drink!"

"I think you'll be fine without it."

Jeff got Kory to his feet and dragged him away from the pool, past the tiki bar and through the tropical gardens to his cabin. Jeff plopped Kory's carcass down on the luxurious plush comforter. Then he called room service.

"Yes, one large pot of coffee. Thank you."

"I've got work to do," Kory insisted as he lurched from the bed and grabbed at his computer. "E-male."

"I thought you said you took care of that?" Jeff asked him.

"I need to," Kory started, but never finished. He didn't know what he needed to do. Or what he would be able to do at this point. He just had the nagging feeling that something was left undone. Unfinished.

"Look, buddy," Jeff said, "I think you've been working a little too hard. You need to relax."

"But Beach Ball," Kory protested, and all those b's blurred together without forming a coherent sentence.

"Here's an idea," Jeff said. "If you want to play with E-male, Mr. Matchmaker, sit down right here and find yourself a date."

"What?"

Jeff sat Kory in his chair and scooted it toward the table. He opened the laptop and made Kory focus on the screen. "Just pretend you're someone else."

"What're you talking 'bout?"

"Look, I think you've had enough stress and overtime and handing out passcodes to the populace," Jeff explained. "You've got two days left. Just enjoy it. For once, Kory, why don't you use E-male for yourself? Just find some nice Baytown boy and have a date, go to dinner, fuck his brains out, whatever."

"Whatever," Kory said, but it wasn't clear if he was parroting the statement, agreeing or disagreeing.

"Seriously, Kory," Jeff said. "This is just a vacation. After Beach Ball, we all get on a plane and this all disappears. Do something for yourself for a change."

The pot of coffee arrived. And Jeff departed. He left Kory there slumped in front of his computer screen as usual.

☆　☆　☆　☆

Zac was less than 20 feet away. He sat in his own cabin that morning, across the garden from Kory's, questioning how these final two days could possible pass. He hadn't slept enough to matter. And now he was sitting, staring at E-male and wondering if Kory was doing the same thing. Zac had done this before, peeked in at Kory's online world to see what Baytown was doing and what Kory was doing to change it all. But this time was different.

Before, when Zac had seen rumors, speculation, or just spirited flirtations—he had assumed Kory was taking care of it. Zac thought that it was all part of Kory's plan or that he would fix it if it wasn't. Now Zac wasn't so sure. He wasn't sure Kory had been there to protect them all along. And he certainly couldn't count on Kory being there now that Trevor had finally gotten to him. So Zac stared at all those names and notes, and he didn't know if Kory was even watching E-male at all.

Was this all it was—silly names and senseless banter on a computer screen? This was what had brought him here to Baytown after all these years? This is what had spread the rumors and hatred? This is what had ultimately turned Kory against him?

It seemed ridiculous. But, then again, Zac didn't understand these things. He didn't know how this virtual, online make-believe world worked. But one thing was for sure—it had certainly worked against him in the real world. He wondered if he should finally find out.

Zac pulled a crumpled shred of paper out of his wallet. He hadn't exactly known why he'd been saving it. By all rational estimations it was, literally, a piece of trash. It was one the leftover E-male passcodes from that day they had handed them out like candy along Baytown's streets and beaches. The code started with the number 1, which meant that it was a generic code to identify "muscle boys." Zac wasn't on steroids, but he did work out. He figured he fit the bill close enough, and with this spare code no one—specifically Kory—would ever know who he was.

What harm could it do just to slip into the conversation and see what happened? Zac needed any distraction he could find. And it was absolutely infuriating watching all this chatter, knowing that Kory was no longer there to get his back. Besides, Zac had no intention of leaving his room or facing the rumors of Baytown until he had to. So he figured he may as well face them here on E-male, where they all started.

Zac typed in the passcode and followed the instructions for creating a screen name. He stuck a Z in the middle of his online pseudonym. But other than that hint, he left all the other personal information blank. And as easy as that, he was no longer an observer. He was inside the Baytown chat room. It was as if he had slipped on the mask of his new screen name and entered the masquerade ball.

> *PecsnAbs*: if Trev is right Beach Ball should be an xtra blast
> *Partee*: and a complete trainwreck if zac steps on stage
> *Thhrust*: can't wait
> *freEasy*: anyone looking for a date?

> *sexUall*: I'm lookin for a couple
> *freEasy*: LOL
> *PecsnAbs*: B.B. will def be the hilite of this trip
> *danZer*: Is Beach Ball the only thing you people can talk about on here?
> *raVer*: It's in 2 days buddy. what else shld we talk about?
> *danZer*: There's a lot more to Baytown than partying
> *ballboy*: like what?
> *danZer*: You're in the most beautiful place on earth. Why hide in clubs?
> *MissTree*: what else is there?
> *danZer*: Sunrise, sunset, and everything in between.
> *beachboy*: hey, I appreciate natural beauty. I go to the beach for the boys
> *danZer*: Are there any boys who go there for the beach?

☆　☆　☆　☆

A nap in a puddle of his own drool and an entire pot of over-priced, lukewarm, room-service coffee had done wonders for Kory's mood. He was now slightly less belligerent and groggy. But regardless of his state of consciousness, E-male kept chugging along at full steam right there in front of him. Kory looked at the rows and rows of chat in E-male's exclusive Baytown room. He watched as each new entry bumped the column up, line by line. It was this living thing that he had thought he could control. But even as he was completely zonked out, it pulsed on.

As if to prove Kory's lack of godlike power and omniscience, E-male greeted his sleepy, glazed eyes with a chat conversation that Kory never could have fabricated. No amount of spying and manipulation on Kory's part could have diverted the Baytown boys' conversations away from Beach Ball at this late date. But that diversion was exactly what Kory saw on the screen in front of him.

Suddenly there was talk of sunsets and beaches. There was someone who dared ask why Beach Ball was such a big deal. There was truly a human challenge to the club mentality, one that Kory and E-male hadn't had to force on the room.

If this new guy had joined E-male earlier, Kory wouldn't have had to create all the complicated—and ultimately useless—programming to safeguard his site. Whoever danZer was, he was fighting the good fight. And he was completely different than anyone Kory had ever seen on E-male.

> *MissTree*: What do you mean there's a river in Baytown?
> *danZer*: A beautiful river. There's even a waterfall at the base of the mountain.
> *ballboy*: there r mountains???
> *danZer*: with great hiking.
> *bXXXdncr*: how about box dancing?
> *Partee*: now that's what I'm talking about!
> *danZer*: climbing a box really isn't the same as a mountain.
> *bXXXdncr*: right. it's better.
> *Thhrust*: damn right
> *danZer*: You can't be serious.
> *bXXXdncr*: just wait till Beach Ball contest. You'll see. I'll show you serious.
> *danZer*: does that contest even matter?
> *bXXXdncr*: It's about the only thing that does!

As usual, when Trevor entered a room, everything started to spin into chaos. This unique glimpse of something real—of someone real—was quickly being obscured by Trevor's larger-than-life persona. Kory felt as if this small window was closing before his eyes. He had seen something he had never seen on E-male before—a man he himself was interested in.

In that moment, before it was too late, before he had a second to doubt himself or talk himself out of it, Kory did something insane. He had lied, spied and manipulated E-male from the day he had created it. But he had never done anything this crazy.

<PVT CHAT—danZer you have
a private invitation to chat with Krazy >

<Welcome to PVT CHAT>

<danZer and Krazy>

Krazy: I'd love to see that river.
danZer: That makes two of us. Only two of us, I guess.
Krazy: 2 is a start. It's not a bad number
danZer: it takes two to tango for example.
Krazy: I'm not much of a dancer.
danZer: So I won't see you at Beach Ball.
Krazy: No chance! Lol.
danZer: What's Lol?
Krazy: "Laugh out Loud." New to the internet?
danZer: It shows? "lol" I had this code crumpled in my pocket for a while.
Krazy: Well, I'm new to town. And to chatting online.
danZer: I know my way around pretty well. Maybe we should chat offline.
Krazy: Where?
danZer: How about the river?

It was as if Kory's fingers typed the words before he could think them. He didn't know what he was doing. And he didn't know this man. His profile and personal information was all blank when Kory snooped. All Kory knew was that the passcode identified him as a muscle boy, and he seemed to be a Baytown local. Kory didn't stop to think that a river may not be the best place for a first date. He didn't stop to think about much of anything other than, a sensitive, muscle-boy nature lover! Perfect!

Kory wondered if he had handed this man that code himself. He wondered if he had seen him around town, on the beach, at a restaurant. He flipped the Rolodex cards of his memory for a face that might fit the bill. And he came up empty. For the first time, he felt that anxious excitement he had given every other member of E-male when setting up a date. Would Mr. Realife live up to Mr. Online?

> *Krazy*: I'd love to. Where is this river?

☆ ☆ ☆ ☆

Zac hadn't planned on leaving his room until Beach Ball. And in all honesty, he wasn't looking forward to that event either. But he hadn't expected to stumble on a single person in this town, let alone on E-male, who felt the way he did about all this craziness. Someone who would talk about something other than circuit parties, something that actually interested both of them. Something real.

He and Krazy chatted throughout the afternoon. They E-maled each other on and off into the night. They talked about loving Baytown but not the hype, the scene or the monarchy of pretense that ruled the club-land. They talked easily, as if they already knew each other well, without the overblown flirtation and sexual innuendo that buzzed through E-male.

So despite his best intentions to fume and stew and be a recluse, Zac found himself welcoming this amicable distraction. He wasn't looking for a date or a lover. God knew he felt too raw and bruised to consider that. But if he could share a friendly walk and conversation along the river, he couldn't see why he didn't deserve it. Just a few hours out of this entire stressful experience. Just a moment of rest before he had to put on those tight pink shorts and crawl up there on the altar of Beach Ball for all to sacrifice. Let Beach Ball bring what it may. Let everyone else go crazy and stab him in the back. Zac was going to allow himself this one thing.

> *danZer*: I'll meet you there tomorrow morning at 9.
> I'm looking forward to it.

☆ ☆ ☆ ☆

The river was cool and quiet. There was more shade and silence than Kory had expected. Trees on either bank reached across, barely touching the outstretched fingers of branches on the other side. The leaves allowed dappled sunlight through to dance on the dark water below. Somewhere downstream, the river poured into the sea dramatically, plunging into its saltiness like a lover's kiss. But here, the barely perceptible ripples only tickled Kory's ear. Moss of varying greens clung to the banks like sea foam. And Kory's footsteps were cushioned into silence as he walked upriver, against the current, toward the place danZer had described.

The first thing Kory saw was the waterfall. It wasn't hundreds of feet high or a torrential flood of mist and noise, but it took his breath away as it appeared around a bend. Water splashed white and blue, zigzagging through sharp angles of black rock where the mountain broke into flat land.

The second thing he saw was the man's broad back. It had to be danZer, and he must have been standing there looking up at the falls himself. He didn't seem to hear Kory approaching. And then Kory must have made a sound, let out a small breath. Or perhaps it was just the sense of another body approaching in a wide open space. Because suddenly the man turned around.

Zac and Kory stared straight at each other. The moment stopped completely. Even the nearby falls went silent. Countless expressions, emotions and accusations passed across their faces and flew back and forth between them. They could feel each one, understand their meaning without translating them into words. Was that surprise, hate, relief, inevitability? Or was it all of those things and more?

Kory knew there was no way Zac could have figured out who Krazy really was. And Zac was sure that danZer was just one more screen name with a muscle-boy passcode. They both knew the rules of this game too well to accuse the other of cheating. They knew they had ended up here like every other couple who met on E-male. They could not fight or lay blame. There was nothing left to say. And that silent understanding turned their shock and outrage into absolute fury. At once, they rushed toward one another, flying into each other's arms.

Their kiss was hard and fast and desperate. Their mouths fused together. Hands pulled at necks and shoulders and clothing. If that had been a hate-fuck back there on Zac's office floor, they hadn't seen anything yet. They ripped at shirts and shorts, scraped at skin. Their kisses were like animals snapping and snarling at one another. Kory bit one of Zac's large dark nipples and got a solid mouthful of fur and muscle. Zac grabbed the back of Kory's head, pulling him off and forcing his face back against Zac's own mouth. Their tongues battled, too.

Kory pushed Zac to the ground, climbing on top, straddling his wide hairy chest. He pushed the head of his erect cock between Zac's lips and thrust into the wetness of his mouth. Zac grabbed at the pale mound of Kory's ass muscles and pulled him harder and faster into his throat, as if we would swallow him whole. As if somehow they could consume one another.

And in a moment Zac rolled them over without losing his lock on Kory's cock. He sucked him deep, spat him out, and then Zac ran his tongue and stubbled chin up the smooth length of Kory's torso. He lapped and kissed and scraped at that flat stomach, the divot of Kory's navel, the heaving ripple of abs and ribs, the tan button of each pert nipple. Finally he lay fully upon Kory, naked, weighting him down into the moist moss with his heavier bulk of muscle, cock and fur.

The mist of the falls hung around them. It settled on them in a cold shiver of sweat and sex and passion. They panted into each other's mouths, exhausted and exhilarated, breathing each other in as their bodies tried to meld together.

"Where's that just-in-case condom?" Zac asked insistently into Kory's face, continuing to lap and kiss and gasp between his words.

"Here," Kory answered, reaching for his shorts blindly as his other hands grasped at Zac's back and ass and thighs.

"Get it out," Zac demanded.

Zac ripped at the wrapper with his teeth. He reached behind

him with his hand. And with a quick fluid movement and a handful of spit, he sat slowly and fully upon Kory's rock-hard cock. Kory ran his hands up and over Zac's stomach and chest, brushing the dark hair over flexed muscles as Zac rode him. Zac leaned forward, bracing himself with his hands against Kory's breastbone. He rocked his hips so that Kory slid in and out of him, and when Zac came down fully his own hard cock slapped Kory tight stomach.

Kory grabbed the muscled tops of Zac's thighs and pulled him down onto him harder. Then he reached around and took one solid buttock in each hand and thrust up into Zac until the man's mouth opened in a silent scream of ecstasy.

Kory took advantage of the frozen moment of desire and took over. He rolled Zac off him and onto all fours. He grabbed Zac's hips and spread his thighs and reentered him even deeper than before. Kory pounded his muscled ass from behind, feeling the cinching of Zac's hole and the warm depths beyond as Kory reached forward across the muscular expanse of Zac's back to grab those wide shoulders and pull him into the thrusting rhythm.

When Zac collapsed flat onto the mossy floor, Kory fell with him and onto and into him, panting against the slick hot skin of Zac's back. But Zac didn't lie there long. He rolled again, bringing them face to face, and lifted his knees and hips to let Kory enter him from yet another angle. Kory sank into that opened hole again eagerly. He lifted Zac's huge thighs and pushed them to his hairy chest. He pressed forward and slid into Zac slowly. He pressed his body closer and closer to Zac's, staring him in the eye, leaning into him and fucking him deeper until finally their gaping mouths met in a desperate kiss.

It was as if that kiss—attained over all of those bent limb, strained muscles and pulsing cocks—was the brink itself. Their lips and tongues met as Kory's last thrust buried him all the way in. Zac felt that final moment deep inside him, and he came in wild spurts between them—throbbing against Kory's stomach as the echo of that powerful orgasm pulsed around Kory's cock, and he poured himself into Zac completely.

☆ ☆ ☆ ☆

They held each other several moments too long. They both knew it and ignored the warning bells in their heads. They knew that there was always that immediate switch after orgasm, like some god had unplugged their sex. A man could only hold on like this out of pity or pretend or something else that neither of them would allow themselves to think. You don't hold on after a hate-fuck.

The sound of the waterfall crashed around them. In that horrible, bleak backlash of orgasm—as if all sex and desire and passion had poured out of him—something dark and cold seeped into Kory. He finally pulled away from Zac and went in search of his scattered clothes.

Zac lay there for another moment on the moss alone. He felt hollow, as if Kory had somehow taken more than just his penis out of Zac's body. Zac couldn't tell if this sensation was good or bad. Had he allowed himself to open up even more? Or had he given up a part of himself he couldn't get back? Was this reconciliation, forgiveness, understanding? Or was this something much less, something that had lessened them further?

As Kory buttoned his shorts, he tried to convince himself it didn't matter. None of it. Not E-male. Not Baytown. Not Zac. Why shouldn't Kory just take what he wanted from Zac at this point? It was all over. Kory wasn't going to dance with him or do business with him. But that didn't mean he couldn't have his body against him one last time. A hate-fuck to fuck all hate-fucks.

But now Kory felt that he could see this for what it truly is. It was worse than a hate-fuck. It was worse than a lie. Because if this had been hate, it wouldn't have felt like this. It wouldn't have felt like goose bumps and welled tears and a lump in his throat that reach much deeper inside him.

Zac pulled himself together. The spray of the falls chilled him now. And putting his clothes back on didn't seem to help. He desperately needed the warmth of reassurance, of knowing something for certain. He stepped up behind Kory.

"So you like the river?" he asked Kory. There was an awkward seriousness in his tone as he broke the silence.

"Yes," Kory said without turning around. He was staring up at the falls, but the tightness of his voice betrayed him. Obviously, he wasn't really thinking about natural beauty. Then suddenly Kory spun around and that tightness unraveled completely. "Stop dragging me away to beautiful places! Stop wasting my time! Distracting me!"

Kory's outburst would have sounded absurd, ridiculous. But he and Zac hadn't needed words to communicate since they'd unknowingly chatted on E-male. The fury and confusion behind Kory's words were perfectly clear.

"OK," Zac said quietly. It wasn't what he wanted to hear from Kory, but he almost understood. Kory did like the river. He liked more than that. And that was the infuriating part they didn't understand.

"It's just that I need to be in front of my computer," Kory added, unsuccessfully trying to soften his rage, "taking care of my company."

"Your company did this," Zac reminded him. "E-male matched us up."

It was true. E-male had taken on a life of its own. It was so out of control that it could even trick Kory. There was no taking care of it, no managing it. Kory had no idea how to regain control, of E-male or himself.

"I've never met anyone with whom I'm less compatible," Kory snapped.

And it was true. Neither of them could imagine why they had walked into each other's lives. They couldn't understand why they kept getting thrown together or why it was harder and harder to pull themselves apart.

"It's your system," was all Zac said.

"More like Frankenstein's monster."

"We all know how that story ends," Zac said. And this time, he was the one who walked away.

☆　☆　☆　☆

dancedancedance: tomorrow is THE day!
          Flirty: Beach Ball here I come!!!
     MkeMynaDbl: iv got my dancing shoes on
          grrreg: and nothing else?
         Thhrust: this is gonna be a party and disaster all
                  rolled into 1!
       bXXXdncr: that's if Zac dares show his face
      JdgeMeNot: You have to show a lot
                  more than face to win Beach Ball

Kory crawled into bed with the blinds drawn. He was going to shut out the tropical sun and every other element of Baytown until it was time to get on that plane and get out of there. He was going to unplug his computer and himself. But the glow of E-male pulsed through the room as if it were a drug pulsing through Kory's very veins. He couldn't sleep, and he couldn't bring himself to turn off his laptop. The hours till Beach Ball were ticking away. And Kory knew that his time with E-male was drawing to a close, too.

       bXXXdncr: Well, Zac's face alone is enough to lose
       beachboy: I thinks he's kinda hot in a stuffy
                  kinda way
       bXXXdncr: Hot my ass!
      JdgeMeNot: now that is Hot! and more than enuf to
                  win! I can vouch for that!
       bXXXdncr: Zac is an old slut. Worn out in every
                  way imaginable.
           raVer: sounds horrible. i can't wait!
       bXXXdncr: he's used and used up. sloppy whore used
                  to just give it away.
          Partee: ouch.
       bXXXdncr: Or sell it for a tip.
           Krazy: ENOUGH!
       bXXXdncr: Who the hell are you?
           Krazy: Haven't you already gotten your way?

bXXXdncr: I always do and I always will. No such thing as winning too much.

Krazy: You've already lost to Zac. He's a better man than you ever were.

bXXXdncr: Hardly. Zac is trash. The day he last left Baytown...

<ACCESS DENIED>
<bXXXdncr—your membership has expired>

danZer: Thanks, K.

Kory pulled the plug without even looking back up at his screen.

danZer: I love you

Chapter 12

ballboy: Today is Beach Ball!!!! WoooHoooo!!!!!

ballboy: Anyone there?????

Baytown was transformed—every tourist, every outfit, every patch of sand. The backside of Cabana Boy spilled out onto the beach in a massive explosion of lights, music and men. The resort was unrecognizable.

Man-made fog rose like breath from some secret internal organ, filling the circuit party to its ceiling of stars. Red shafts of light cut through the mist, pulsing like an ever-shifting system of veins and arteries. And at the very heart of Beach Ball was the music. Its beat throbbed through the dark, keeping everything moving, dancing, alive. It throbbed with its own uncontainable life.

Men danced everywhere. Twirling on the dance floors, spinning on the sand, splashing in the sea. They were a sea of their own, seething together in an endless tide that rose to engulf the entire event as far the eye could see.

There were costumes of all white. Headdresses of every color. Men in leather, lace and every imaginable material. Between the scraps of latex, metal, feathers and denim, skin was the most pervasive element. It was the outfit of choice. Bare chest, legs and buttocks glistened with sweat and glitter.

It was a party unlike any other. Most of these men had ever seen anything like it. And the returning participants were back precisely because they had never found another party to rival this debauchery on the beach. There were no nightclub walls to restrict them. There were no boundaries to where they could go or what could happen. Everything was possible. Everything was permitted.

Zac stood in the middle of it all, and he was the only one in the crowd who wished he was someplace else. He just didn't know where that place was—a private cove, a saltwater pond, the safety of his windowless office. But not here.

However, this was the one place he had to be. Zac refused to turn back now. Everyone already knew he was a contestant at Beach Ball tonight. They knew everything. And they were all looking forward to his dance or disgrace or destruction. Across the crowd, Zac could see the man who had made all of that such a hot topic.

Trevor was the epicenter of his own universe. Men rippled out from him like shockwaves. He wore an electric-blue muscle shirt and matching capri pants. He danced a bit without really trying. His electric-blue eyes shot through the crowd. He was obviously saving himself for the main event. Nonetheless, he was a man-magnet, a circuit celebrity. He was Trevor.

Zac, on the other hand, was a man alone in the mob. He hung in the shadows of pillars and the absence of spotlights. He practically disappeared there in his white tank undershirt and cutoff khakis, as if he were headed out to the garden to pull weeds. Because Zac didn't need to be seen. He had no desire to take part in all of this until he had to. Despite the rabid online media attention that Trevor and E-male had provided for Zac's box-dancing challenge, this wasn't about pleasing a crowd.

Zac needed to face things head on. Stand up to Trevor. Finish his dance this time once and for all. Win or lose, people would know who Zac was. He needed to get up there and be the real Zac, whoever that may be. Zac himself was hoping to find out.

His employees would see the truth beneath the boss, the man he had become. Those who had heard the most disgraceful details of his past would see how far he'd moved beyond all that. And finally, Zac would prove to himself that there was a reason for all this—for this long uphill journey that was his life and for the seemingly crazy events and decisions that had suddenly brought him full circle. Zac just hoped that as he was up there dancing, that reason would come to him. He wasn't feeling so reasonable right now.

Zac leaned into the dark wedge of a pillar's shadow, watching and waiting as the night unfolded around him. The crowd roiled in dance. The boys screamed above the music. And Beach Ball continued to inflate, in numbers, volume and excitement.

It was the last hurrah on the last night of vacation, but Zac didn't share the thrill. He didn't feel the culminating magic, the final gasp, the single moment that mattered. Tonight could have been very different for him. It almost had been.

But now, Zac didn't need to win. Whatever the stakes were, he had no control over that, for the sake of E-male or Trevor or anybody else. He was simply keeping his word. It was a word that was no longer as harsh and domineering as "No Dancing. No Dating. No Drama." But it was not as frivolous and demeaning as "shot boy" or some even nastier words. He simply wanted his word to tell everyone that he still took himself and all of this seriously, but not so seriously that he couldn't dance up there in a pair of pink trunks.

He focused on this one thing—all these ideas and promises and uncertainties boiled down to this one act. Just dance. Dance through it all. Don't get distracted by any other thought. Because it wasn't stage fright or performance anxiety or the threat of Trevor that twisted at Zac's gut right now. It was Kory.

Kory ran out of his cabin with one sandal on. He hadn't been able to shut the booming sound of Beach Ball out of his cabin with doors and windows and blinds and towels shoved in the cracks as if he were blocking smoke from a fire. But as he rushed into the humid night, the blaring music nearly bowled him over.

Half stumbling, Kory shoved his other sandal on and pushed through the crowd. Even back here, in the dense tangle of pathways and tropical gardens that wove their way between the cabins and the main resort, there were men everywhere. They all pushed forward, seeking out the party in back like slutty zombies trudging through the woods of some horror film. And Kory actually was scared to see what was out there.

He hadn't intended to leave his room, to speak to anyone, to be a part of the climactic night everyone else had spent the entire vacation counting down to. He had fully intended to hide inside his locked cabin as the demons raged around him. But now he was among them. He jogged past men with horns and angel wings, shoved aside leather daddies and drag queens, and hurriedly made his way toward an area that he had only previously known as a luxurious pool, beach and seaside.

When Kory emerged from the gardens onto the exposed backside of Cabana Boy, he stopped short, as if he'd found himself on a cliff's edge. It was sheer vertigo. The sea below reached all the way from its normal tide line to the very tip of Kory's sandal. And that sea frothed with music and men. Kory didn't recognize the place where he'd lived for almost two weeks. But he took a deep breath and dove in.

Cabana Boy's pool was covered with yet another stage. There were enormous pillars and platforms dwarfing the usual tiki bars and lounge chairs. It was a jungle of soaring pedestals from which any number of dancers could fall, literally and figuratively, from grace.

As Kory gazed up at these still-vacant perches above the dance floor, he saw dozens of disco balls covered in longitudinal rainbow stripes that made them look like real beach balls. They scattered wild spectrums of light throughout the dark like thrown handfuls of sequins. Several hit Kory right in the face. He flinched and grimaced, but the spot of lights skidded right across his skin to reenter the dance. The lights and fog blinded Kory. The throb of electronica deafened him. And still he searched through the impossible crowd of partygoers as dancing arms and legs shot out to impede his progress.

He'd had so much time to make things right. He could see that now. But tonight he had so little time to keep things from going wrong. He didn't know if any amount of minutes could add up to make a difference. But he was stuck in the middle of men who never wanted this night to end. That just might be enough time.

Suddenly, the box-dancing contest started organically, as if the whole thing wasn't orchestrated and manipulated and predestined. The music swelled in what could only be described as an electronic drum roll. Lighting shifted and intensified. Spotlights swept across the crowd and ocean as if searching for shipwrecks. And the entire night full of men seemed to hold its collective breath as, one by one, dancers ascended the various mini-stages.

Kory was too far away. There were too many platforms. Even if there had not been a single person dancing where there were now thousands, he could not have run to each box to check who was there. He watched as vaguely familiar muscle boys claimed the tops of elevated dancing surfaces. They were the boys Kory had seen dancing behind Trevor when he'd first arrived in Baytown. They were the boys online who had used E-male to boost and speculate on their own odds for success.

The music rose to a crescendo, and there in the middle of it all on center stage, Trevor rose with his very own spotlight. He stood for a moment glowing like neon in all his electric blue. And then he tore the skimpy tank from his booth-tanned torso and ripped the tear-away capris from his legs. Trevor stood in the middle of Beach Ball in nothing but a bright-blue thong. The crowd howled its approval.

A dancing man now perched on most every stage, platform and box. They swayed and shimmied there, buzzing with energy as the music swelled. This new city of skyscrapers was suddenly covered in King Kongs as the populace stared adoringly up at them, waiting for them to fall.

Kory looked frantically about. He could hear the music rising. He could feel the crowd inhaling. And to his left, near the beach, he saw one lone, empty cube silhouetted against the crowd and sea. Kory ran toward it. He pushed everyone out of his way as if they didn't exist. As if they were cobwebs or ghosts or something he would soon regret. And when he arrived breathless at the base of the box, he could only say one thing to change the night—to try and stop time for a moment.

"Zac!"

Somewhere in the shadow of that last box, a figure turned. With his white tank top hanging like a noose around his neck, he paused there to face Kory. It was like the music had stopped. Zac had dropped the cut-off shorts to reveal those pink square-cut briefs that had started this whole box-dancing scheme. And he had lifted his tank top to the bottom of his chin, exposing his chiseled torso and its defining covering of dark hair. But now, he looked stunned—unable to move his shirt those last few inches to complete his costume-change. When Zac didn't answer, Kory wasted no more time. He unbuttoned, unzipped and pulled down his black city-boy jeans unashamedly. He revealed his own pink square-cut briefs beneath.

"I want to win," Kory said.

"What about your plan?" Zac finally asked.

"Some things are more important," Kory said, kicking off his sandals and jeans, tugging off his shirt till he stood before Zac exposed. "There are some things worth winning, no matter what. There's one thing I won't lose."

"E-male?" Zac guessed.

"You."

Before Zac could respond or the music could speed ahead without them—before Zac had the chance or presence of mind to kiss him—Kory rushed forward, ripped the tank top fully off Zac's head and dragged him up the few steps to the top of the box.

The other contestants were already dancing away on their boxes. Across the entire expanse of Beach Ball, men gyrated to the electronic throb on tall boxes and stands that sprouted everywhere from the foggy depths of stage, stone and sand. The music pounded and the crowd roared.

There seemed to be no formal rules or process to the madness. A huge spotlight swept across the night, lighting on different dancers as they basked in the glow of the audience's attention. Like a laser-guided applause meter, the spotlight would focus longer on the dancers based on the crowd's response. From man to man, from box to box. The spot illuminated contestants randomly, lingering as the mob cheered or moving on as its affection waned.

Within moments, Trevor had grabbed the spotlight as securely as if he could hold its edges with his outstretched hands. He had center stage, commanding the main, wide platform alone as others balanced on top of narrower boxes. He raised his hands above his head, turning to lick his own bicep before spinning quickly to reveal the exposed cheeks of his ass in his thong. He shook those tan mounds to the beat, and the mob went wild. The men below seemed to have forgotten that they'd come to Beach Ball for any other reason than to see Trevor up there on his pedestal.

But then something changed. Zac and Kory started moving together in the dark—with just flecks of rainbow from the disco balls glinting across their skin. But as their bodies disrupted the pattern of light, it caught the attention of the spectators. At first it was just the motion of the latecomers up there that caught the thousands of eyes below. But soon, it was recognition that dragged the attention, and the spotlight, away from Trevor and to Zac and Kory.

Suddenly everyone realized who they were. E-male had made them famous. And Trevor had made them notorious. Gossip had put them in the spotlight, and now here they were—in a literal spotlight in the middle of Beach Ball unashamed. Whether people wanted Trevor to win or not, all at once they remembered that they were there to see more than his solo performance. They had come here expecting a showdown, a disaster, a spectacle unlike any other Beach Ball.

And when they saw that Kory had joined Zac's dance—that they had become inseparable partners once and for all—the entire congregation went absolutely crazy. Just as Zac had predicted, no one would ever have concocted this secret dance move in the craziest, wettest dream. The slutty-shot-boy-turned-tyrant-boss and the city-boy-waiter-turned-internet-entrepreneur were dancing together. They were up there on a tiny box in tiny pink shorts. And they looked more than hot. They looked in love.

Kory smiled at Zac in the bright white of the spotlight. They locked golden and green eyes, finding their footing on their miniature dance floor without ever looking down. As the beat cracked around them like an electric whip, they fell into a rhythm as smooth and mutual as they had that day in the pond, as balanced as atop two boulders, as passionate as making love by a river.

Kory wiped his blonde bangs from his eyes. Zac ran his hand up his own furry torso and reached out to caress Kory's smooth taut chest. They spun quickly together, never missing a beat, and stopped on a dime with their hands on each other's waists. They brought their hips together and held the smalls of each other's backs as they leaned away from each other over the edges of the box and ground their pelvises together. All of Beach Ball screamed in ecstasy.

Many of the other box-dancers had stopped their moves. They simply stood on their boxes transfixed. They turned toward Zac and Kory, bounced to the beat and cheered the couple on.

Trevor, however, would not give up. He danced and sweated and struggled to regain the spotlight. But every time it flitted across his stage, the cheering mob mentality dragged it back to Zac and Kory.

They held each other. They moved with the music. They were one song. And instead of some secret climactic move—some gymnastic flourish or stunt—they simply kissed.

It wasn't part of the dance. It just happened. Kory spun. Zac swayed. And his hand came to Kory's hip reflexively to stop the turn. Then Kory's hand came just as naturally to Zac's face. It was not a dance move. It was a gesture of knowing, of fitting together, of trust. And so they kissed.

It was not planned or appropriate. It was just the thing to do. Like every step that had danced them to this point—to this point in their lives and to the top of this pedestal under spiraling lights where stubble scraped lips and eyes closed. It was the right move.

They never even heard the music stop. The applause and cheers carried the final note of the song far beyond its prerecorded ending.

Silence. The music went dead.

"May I remind you all that this is a box-dancing contest," the man said into his microphone from the main stage. He had his slacks pulled up over his gut and cinched tightly with a braided belt. The lights glared off his scalp between the greasy strands of his comb-over. It was JdgeMeNot. Kory didn't know his real name. But the man stood there with the mic's cord snaking between his legs and hollered out at the suddenly silent mass of Beach Ball attendees. "This is for single, registered contestants. This is not couple's ballroom dancing. Or pornography. And those who think it is are disqualified."

Without music, the night sounded so still. A constant discontented murmur of whispers passed through the crowd like rolling thunder in the distance. But JdgeMeNot dominated the stage with Trevor standing beside him, both of them covered in sweat for different reasons.

"As official judge of Beach Beall," the man continued, "I am proud to be able to say that some people do it the right way, with class." The man reached over to wrap a welcoming arm around Trevor and placed his meaty hand squarely on Trevor's ass.

The thunder in the crowd grumbled louder as if the storm were almost there. Zac and Kory stood on their box in silence with their arms around one another. And many eyes remained on them until the man on stage spoke his final words. Then all eyes shot forward in wide disbelief.

"Trevor is this year's Beach Ball box-dancing champion!" he screamed.

He quickly placed a misshapen laurel crown on Trevor's sweaty brow, squeezed his ass once more for good measure and waddled offstage before the crowd could pounce. The music came back on with a vengeance, escalating in volume to extinguish the storm of protests and boos. The crowd was in such shock that it took several long moments for anyone to start dancing.

It was the first time a circuit party had rules, as if it had suddenly developed morals or found Jesus. As if there weren't drugs and hustlers and bookies threading through the crowd like cigarette smoke. As if everyone present wasn't going to pretend everything that occurred this night hadn't really happened—a night of reprieve, forgiveness, a confession before the sin. Convenient amnesia. A well-timed blackout.

But perhaps it was simply because they needed rules against the night's one moment that would not be forgotten. It was the single event that could not be erased from minds with alcohol or narcotics.

This was a memory. One that would live. One that would be retold. One that people not present would swear they had witnessed themselves.

"He won?" Zac asked Kory, as unbelieving as the rest of Beach Ball.

"Let him," Kory answered, nodding toward the figure of Trevor as he wove his way through the crowd and accepted false congratulations. "Look at him. This is the biggest loss he's ever had."

"That's not what matters," Zac insisted. "You can't give your business up for this."

"I'm not," Kory said, squeezing Zac tight beside him. "I'm giving it up for me. I'm giving it up for us. Because E-male needs me more than I need it. And I've finally realized what I really need."

Suddenly Trevor appeared at the base of their box. He looked small and wiry with a skullcap of too-black hair beneath his lopsided, leafy crown. But he stared up with those electric-blue eyes as if victory were truly his.

"Now don't be sore losers, boys" he called up to them. "A deal's a deal, right, Kory?"

"It's all yours, Trevor," Kory said. "If you still want it."

"I get E-male,' Trevor said. He sounded almost maniacal as he raised two hands and clenched his fists beneath his chin. As if he had finally won something for real.

The curious crowd had gathered round again, still too shell-shocked for proper dancing and still too enthralled by the couple on the box.

"And I get Kory," Zac reminded him. He reached his free hand around front to clasp the one already resting on the back of Kory's hip, encircling the man beside him.

"You never did know what was important," Trevor spat up at them, but the flecks of spittle just fell back down in his own face. "That's why you could never win."

"I just did," Zac said. And he turned to face the man beside him.

Below, Jeff and Jon and all the travel boys swarmed around the box in their finery and crazy party garb. With all the other men there, they clapped and hooted and cheered.

Zac and Kory kissed again.

"This is our encore," Zac whispered to him.

6

CHAPTER 13

trvlr44: i can't believe we're leaving today.
Sporty1: That was a night to remember
vaca4me: a vacation to remember!
beachboy: And that kiss!! did u see that kiss!!
delish: How could we forget??
lushlife: What happens now?
freEasy: Yeah, where do we go from here?

\<E-male is currently Under Construction\>

\<Important Message from E-male click here\>

The sheets glowed bright white in the early morning sun. And they wrapped around Zac and Kory's entangled bodies, highlighting the tan skin, dark hair and passionate embrace. They had just finished making love for the third time since falling into Kory's bed late last night. Slow love, face to face, with deep kisses and whispered words. Not a single hurried moment of confusion or hatred. Just moments as serene and beautiful as all the idyllic spots of Baytown combined.

Throughout the night the couple had awoken together, seemingly at the same time. They would roll together, feel each other's naked skin, or simply realize suddenly that they were holding someone in their sleep. Passion or surprise or relief constantly interrupted their slumber. That's how they were certain it wasn't a dream.

Now Kory nestled his head against the furry crevice in the middle of Zac's chest. And Zac wrapped those big arms completely around Kory's thin, tight body, drawing him as close as possible. They exhaled together.

This morning, the blinds were not drawn. Tropical morning spilled in from all angles. Brilliant green palms waved at the windows as if to say goodbye and remind the couple that they were leaving today. Dappled sunlight and shadows played over their bodies like so many hands, as if replaying the caresses that had happened in the dark.

"I love you too," Kory said out of nowhere, in response to nothing, without provocation. It was the first phrase spoken aloud since sunrise. He lifted his face slightly against the tickle of Zac's chest and watched the surprise register on his lover's face. "Yes, I saw it. Almost too late. But remember, I can see the E-male archives. Well, I could see them."

"I'm glad you saw it before it was too late," Zac said, holding him even tighter. "But I'm sorry you lost E-male. No matter what you said, I knew you didn't want to."

"But I needed to," Kory said. "And it finally helped me find something I wanted even more."

"Good answer." Zac kissed Kory's forehead, letting his dry lips linger beneath those blonde bangs.

"So I really don't need it anymore," Kory concluded. "And we didn't lose a thing. Because Trevor cheated."

"Obviously," Zac said. "But he just cheated himself in the end."

"I knew all along," Kory admitted. "I watched him set it up on E-male."

"And you entered the contest with me anyway?" Zac asked.

"Even though you knew we couldn't win."

"Of course," Kory said, snuggling into Zac. "I was competing for an even better prize."

"I have a feeling we're going to be late to the airport," Zac said, lifting Kory's face to his and kissing him deeply.

They rolled together in the bright, honest light of morning. And they told each other the complete truth with their bodies.

It was a standing ovation. Zac and Kory hurried onto the plane just as the gate door was closing, and the entire plane erupted into applause as all the passengers jumped to their feet.

As predicted, Zac and Kory had been extremely late to the airport. But it seemed the entire plane of people was waiting patiently for them. Jeff, Jon and all the Whine 'n' Dine waiters were there. Steve, Rick, Chris, Andy and all the Djorvzac Travel guys were onboard too. But even the few passengers who weren't part of the Baytown travel group were clapping away. It was clear that these men didn't need E-male to spread the news.

"So you aren't mad at me after all that?" Zac asked as he stood in the aisle and the applause died down.

"Mad?" Stuart asked. "It makes us happy for you."

"Being late to the airport makes you happy?" Kory asked. And the plane filled with laughter.

"No. Winning Beach Ball," Greg corrected.

"We didn't actually win," Zac reminded them.

"Well then just getting up there."

"Dancing with Kory."

"Falling in love."

And all the gay passengers swooned as if the in-flight movie had just played the climactic scene of one of those gay favorites that Zac had never seen.

"So all those secrets and rumors about my past," Zac said. "They didn't change your opinion of me?"

"Hell, of course they did," Gary said, "We like you better now." And a few others dared to laugh.

"We were all young once," Andy said more tactfully. "Just don't do background checks on us."

"Sorry," Zac said. "I already did. But that was the old me...or the more recently old me...whatever."

"Well, it was all worth it to see our boss in his underwear."

"You mean 'in love.' Right?"

"Right, of course."

Zac and Kory took their seats, as the cute gay flight attendants popped open champagne before the plane headed to the runway for takeoff. They all cheered as Zac and Kory toasted one another. And then they rose like bubbles into the sky.

☆ ☆ ☆ ☆

Zac and Kory walked hand in hand into the offices of Djorvzac Travel. Zac had given the rest of the agents a day off to recover from their trip, but he wanted to check in on things. Only so much had changed after all. But in the back of his mind, he also had filthy ideas of recreating the scene behind his desk with Kory.

However, all thoughts of work and fantasies of dirty sex were erased when they got into the agency. Zac's first assumption was that the place had been broken into. Chairs had been knocked over and folders were strewn about. Sheets of paper were scattered everywhere, and a trash can had been kicked clear across the main room.

"The place is in shambles," Zac said to Kory in confusion.

"Sex shambles," Kory corrected him. He was standing over by the photocopier holding a piece of crumpled paper. And Zac noticed that the copier's lid was askew. But Kory quickly hid the piece of paper behind his back as Mike and Danny suddenly emerged from the back of the office.

"Hey, boss," Mike said.

"Sorry," Danny added. "We thought everyone was still off till tomorrow."

"And I thought I'd left you two in charge," Zac said, regaining some of his tyrant bravado for this odd situation. Zac glared at the two reedy men suspiciously as Mike adjusted his trendy glasses and Danny ran fingers through his highlighted hair. "What happened?"

"Well," began Mike. "We, uh, kinda have a confession to make."

"The copier broke," Danny chimed in to amend too quickly.

"Is this your confession?" Kory asked. He knew he wouldn't be standing where he was today without these two men. He never could have convinced Zac about E-male if Mike and Danny hadn't needed their travel-agent disagreement resolved. And he never could have pulled off the Baytown trip without their travel arrangements and negotiations. But Kory just couldn't help himself.

Kory held up the piece of paper he'd been hiding behind his back. It was a crumpled sheet from the "broken" copier. But as he opened the balled paper, it became clear that it was a photocopy of someone's ass with a hand gripping each buttock.

"Is that your class ring I see there, Mike?" Zac asked.

"We were planning on cleaning up today, Zac," Mike answered without addressing the question. "Really."

"It just...broke," Danny added unnecessarily.

"Are you two dating?" Zac asked in utter disbelief. As if to answer himself, he walked toward the back wall where the "No Dancing. No Dating. No Drama." sign was posted and pointed to the applicable phrase.

"Well..."

"Um..."

"You know what this means," Zac said sternly. He reached up and pulled the sign from the wall for emphasis. For a moment, no one drew a breath. The agents' faces were as creased and crumpled as the incriminating piece of evidence in Kory's hand.

"What does this mean?" Danny asked with a squeak.

"It means, I guess I'm going to have to bend the rules," Zac said, and he tore the poster in half.

"Looks like you bent them awfully hard," Kory called out.

"You should know," Zac shot back.

Kory rushed into his arms, as if Zac had triumphed in some

final contest more difficult than any box-dancing rivalry. They kissed, and the triple-D rules fell to the floor in pieces.

Relieved and surprised, Mike and Danny exhaled so loudly that the other couple was almost jolted from their kiss. No one had known about Zac and Kory's relationship—not even Zac and Kory—till last night's Beach Ball. And Mike and Danny obviously had not yet heard the word.

"Well, we have another confession to make," Danny said bravely, interrupting Zac and Kory's kiss.

"Don't tell me you're pregnant!" Kory exclaimed.

"It's more of a technological confession," Mike added.

"I've already seen the copier," Zac said. "I don't even want to know what you did to the fax machine."

"You're not the only one who can make a match, Mr. E-Male," Danny said, ignoring Zac's remark. "But you did make it all possible."

"What are you talking about?" Kory asked seriously for the first time that day. He stepped away from Zac to move toward these two men with knowing suspicion in his golden eyes. "What did I make possible?"

"Well, we couldn't tell Zac," Danny said defensively. "Not then. You remember what he was like."

"We just thought we could let him see for himself," Mike explained. "But we had no idea he would see it quite this clearly."

"What did I see?" Zac insisted.

"E-male," Danny said with his eyes scrunched closed as if the secret word had escaped his mouth against his will.

"We met on E-male," Mike explained. "Danny and I. I mean, we didn't know. We already knew each other from work. But when we met online, when we realized..."

"It was against the rules," Kory finished for them.

"E-male matched us up," Danny said. "And it was right." He reached over and grabbed his secret boyfriend by the waist, holding him a bit stiffly there in front of their boss and their matchmaker.

"I did it again," Kory said to no one in particular.

"We just thought if we could bring E-male here," Mike said.

"Not that he would actually partner with you. But maybe he would see. Just introduce the idea of E-male."

"Maybe he would let us try E-male," Danny butted in. "Or at least understand why we tried it ourselves. I mean he'd hate it, right? That's what we thought. It was against the rules."

"But by that time, Danny and I would have already 'met' on E-male again," Mike explained. "Even if he turned you away at the door, we had an excuse to try E-male, to have even heard about it. It wouldn't be our fault."

"That's why we matched up E-male and Djorvzac Travel," Danny admitted.

"That was the plan," Mike said.

"We just didn't know how well you were going to match," Danny added. "It just kind of..."

"Yeah," Zac said in slow thoughtful agreement.

"So you sent me all those messages and paperwork?" Kory asked. "Not Zac? Not Trevor?"

"Yes," Mike said, eyes down.

"Sorry," Danny whispered.

"So you committed fraud using my company name and stationery?" Zac asked.

"Well..."

"Um..."

"Thank you," Zac said. He grabbed Kory and pulled him to him. "Oops."

"I guess we're not detectives," Kory said, cringing.

"So what are we?" Zac asked.

"Travel matchmakers?" Kory offered. "Or maybe just in love."

And both couples laughed there in the messy office. They each kissed the man that—one way or another—E-male had found for them.

☆ ☆ ☆ ☆

<Important Message from E-male click here>

>>>Get off line. Get out of the house. Take a trip. Take your life in a whole new direction. You'll know when you reach your destination. I did.<<<

<E-male is Temporarily Unavailable.
We apologize for any
inconvenience>

This wasn't their wake-up call. Kory's love letter to his members was not the death knell for E-male. They waited until E-male came back online. They logged on with just as much enthusiasm, never knowing that the site's ownership had changed. Never suspecting a thing.

But when they started noticing fewer connections, fewer matchmaking miracles, fewer men online—they figured that the message had been right. Or maybe they had just outgrown this online-dating fad. Maybe it had never been that great to begin with.

They didn't notice Kory's absence, because they'd never known he was there to begin with. They didn't know exactly what was missing, what spark was gone. And they never noticed that E-male was failing. It just did.

☆　☆　☆　☆

Trevor had basically purchased a web page with no content. He owned a list of users and profiles with no way to connect them. It was now one big crowded room with no host to keep the cacophony from drowning out the possibility of real conversation.

Essentially, it was no better than a jam-packed bar. Men could show up and push their way through the crowd; they could attempt to talk over the deafening chatter; they could approach one man out of hundreds for no reason at all and hope for a miracle.

But that miracle no longer happened. They were trying to find a needle in a haystack without the metal-detector of Kory's insight. At least in a real barroom a suitor could find solace in a cocktail after approaching yet another Mr. Wrong.

The host was gone. And the party was over.

Other sites emerged. They were powered by more money and bigger teams of web programmers. They were flashier places with matchmaking software based on logarithms instead of intuition. But the best programs were no match for Kory's instincts.

And E-male didn't have Kory anymore. So Trevor had nothing.

CHAPTER 14

"Miles & Miles Travel. How far would you go for a good time?" Jeff said as he answered the phone. He did it with as much enthusiasm as he had the first time six months earlier.

Jeff was the receptionist and office manager for the new Baytown office of Miles & Miles Travel. He had gone blonde for the beach, but he was the same old Jeff. He still hated corporate America, but he was proud to have found the most unprofessional professional job he could. He claimed his new job was the just like gossiping and flirting while waiting tables without having to touch dirty dishes or get his ass grabbed.

Jeff sat at the front of the sunny office, staring out at Baytown's main drag and the boys strolling by. Behind the reception area, there were several agents' desks where they received calls from clients or chatted with travelers face to face. Some of the agents were new hires. Others had relocated because they'd fallen in love with Baytown or someone who lived here. Behind those rows of desks were Zac and Kory's adjacent offices. They had picture windows opening into the agency and two other windows in the back wall looking out to the beach beyond.

Jeff kept insisting—to anyone who walked through the door or would listen over the phone—that punk was dead and beach boys were back. He'd even lost the eyebrow ring. Jeff also swore that Jon and the dog loved the beach even more than the suburbs. And it appeared to be true. For the dog's part, he was at least a real blonde, a golden lab that made a nice beach accessory for Jeff.

And Jon was absolutely thriving. Once they taught him to speak up and sell, he turned out to be one of their top agents. He had a way of bringing travelers out of their shells, convincing them to do things they wouldn't normally have tried. He could convince the quiet, outdoorsy guy that he could hike after a night at the clubs, and then he'd convince that guy's boyfriend that he could finally get a party-vacation out of his man. Jon had some solid experience in how an introvert could keep an extrovert happy.

While Jon lured men to Baytown, Zac and Kory did the opposite. They helped tourists get out of town. They up-sold party boys on nature excursions. They showed them the secret side of Baytown few knew existed. When travelers were sick of the scene, Zac and Kory gave them the scenic. They made them fall in love with Baytown all over again.

Then they booked them on European hikes, western ski vacations and white-water rafting trips halfway across the country. Or if they preferred the party, it was off to Sydney, London and Rio. Perhaps they'd run into Trevor there. Zac and Kory had caught wind that, like a faded rock star, he was trying to develop a following somewhere in Eastern Europe.

Wherever they went, people never wanted the vacation to end. They wanted the dream to continue. After helping them make the most of their Baytown trip, Zac and Kory would catch them at the end of their stay and book their next dream— whether it started tomorrow or next year.

And for Zac and Kory, the dream never had to end. They had moved to Baytown full time. Soon after their very unprofessional meeting with Mike and Danny back at the old agency, they had quickly realized that they couldn't go back. Too much had changed. They had changed. Even Baytown had changed, at least for them.

It was no longer the dark place of Zac's youth. And it was not the uncomfortable party town that had so intimidated a little blonde city boy almost a year ago. Baytown was the place they had fallen in love with—the place where they had fallen in love. It was home.

So Zac had handed Mike and Danny the keys and the cleaning bill. He'd told them to redecorate the hell out of the place in the process. Then he named them co-general managers of Miles & Miles Travel's northern office and headed south. Kory's handsome profit from the sale of E-male to Trevor had allowed them to open another office anywhere they wanted. So they had chosen the best location with the best view and set up shop right in the middle of Baytown's most popular street.

Kory had made the transition from internet guru to travel advisor faster than Jeff had become a perky, blonde receptionist. Just as Zac had originally taken all his gay clients at his first job at a travel agency, Kory had converted all his members from internet dating to traveling. There was no clause in Kory's contract with Trevor that said he couldn't keep a copy of the members' contact information. He just couldn't use it to start another dating site. And Kory had no intention of doing that. Besides, he figured all those old members could find true love in real time just like he had. Especially if Kory helped them.

More importantly, it was time for Kory to focus on his own life and romance. Both he and the E-male members had to get off line and get real. There was no more pretend—no make-believe to disappoint in real life. If gay men wanted a fantasy, all they had to do was book one with Miles & Miles Travel.

Now thanks to Kory, they also had a much better chance of meeting Mr. Right along the way. Because Kory had a knack for matching up desires, booking complementary trips and excursions, connecting travelers who just might connect with one another.

And finally, he didn't have to lie about it. His track record for matching men and creating romantic getaways for singles and couples alike was one of Miles & Miles Travel's main selling points. It was a new strength for their new company, and it kept the two offices more than busy.

"Well, it sounds like you should join our canyon adventure," Kory said into the phone as he consulted his computer screen. "There are a bunch of other Baytown regulars already booked. And some very cute single ones, I might add. I've actually got one in particular I'd like to introduce you to." He paused for emphasis to dangle the bait, and wait for the caller's response that he already knew was coming. "Of course," Kory said sweetly. "With your permission I'll forward your contact information to him and have him e-mail you."

With a company like this, Kory didn't miss E-male or the city. He had loved them both for the same reasons—the community, the friends, the connections he could make and share. And so his new life hadn't lost the pure essence of his past. It had just eliminated the dark parts with sunshine. Now Kory had the ever-changing Baytown community, connected to endless communities through Miles & Miles Travel. And they could jump on a plane and actually visit each other instead of chatting online.

Zac overheard his partner's romantic chatter in the office next door. And he smiled to himself. This was all a world away from the original Djorvzac Travel. As their name and catch phrase promised, this entire experience was miles and miles from where he'd started.

But the agency's new name wasn't just a gimmick. Zac had actually changed his last name. It was official. Czcibor Djorvzac was now Zac Miles. He'd never liked his given name, and no one could pronounce it anyway. So it had made good business sense. It signaled a new start for the company. When all his old customers had received the announcement, it was as if they'd gotten a wedding invitation and wanted to book their own honeymoons. It was the best PR the agency had every gotten. But more than anything, his name change was a sign of commitment to Kory that was more personal than a ring on his finger. Zac's heart melted every time he came to work and saw their shared name on the door.

The agency had really needed a new name. Because just as Kory had lost E-male, Zac had lost Djorvzac Travel, too. He may not have lost it in a bet. And he may have been wrong about the entire Trevor conspiracy theory. But the events of that fateful Baytown vacation really had made it impossible for his old business to survive.

It couldn't be the same. It didn't have the same employees. It wasn't in the same place. And it certainly didn't have the triple-D rules. Several of the employees here were local boyfriends of Djorvzac agents who had relocated. And other boyfriends and dates popped in constantly as they made their way down Baytown's strip. There was a modest amount of gay drama from time to time. But Zac didn't mind. And every Thursday after work, the entire agency went dancing.

As soon as Zac heard Kory end his call, he pressed the intercom button on his console that connected their two phones.

"Mr. Miles," Zac called out. "Could you step into my office?"

"Of course, Mr. Miles," Kory responded innocently.

"Not again," Jeff whispered and rolled his eyes toward the travel agents in the office. "At least draw the blinds this time!"

Kory grabbed the string to the blinds as he stepped into Zac's office and slammed the door behind him. He stood there coyly in his cargo shorts and tee-shirt as if he was about to take dictation.

But Kory was also the boss now. So instead he just lifted his shirt over his head and tossed it to the floor. Zac pushed back from his desk in his leather chair and corresponding beach-casual business attire.

Kory straddled his partner's knees and swayed his hips, raising his hands above his head in the perfect private lap-dance.

"Don't think you can dance without me," Zac said sternly as he stood to join Kory. "This is an equal partnership, Mr. Miles."

"Yes, sir, Mr. Miles."

Kory reached up under Zac's shirt and peeled it from his lover's body. They pressed themselves together with their arms wrapped around each other, and they moved together in perfect time. No music was required. They already had everything they needed.

For more Palari titles,
visit:

www.PalariBooks.com

Printed in the United States
140326LV00004B/17/P

9 781928 662167